The Tribe

David Reynolds-Moreton

sci-fi-cafe.com

sci-fi-cafe.com

Introduction

The Tribe, previously published as *The Inosculation Syndrome* is loosely set in the same universe as Reynold-Moreton's *Sapient Continuum* series.It doesn't matter whether you read the rest of the series before this, after or even not at all. However, the keen-eyed reader will spot threads running between these books as well as reaching out to others such as *The Single Twin.*

ONE:
Planetfall

THE SURVEY SHIP Star Search was old, very old, and as old ships go, she just about did, if you will pardon the grammar.

She was among the first of her line, and was fast approaching the point where replacement parts would soon outnumber the original fitments, with the exception of the main framework, hull plates and the drive units, and these were long past their 'best before' date.

In theory, fitting a new part should not have been a problem, although in practice the new part was rarely of the same size, and as often as not, the functions were not identical to the original and needed 'slight' modifications.

The general upshot of this over the years was that a service manual that made any sense no longer existed.

If it had not been for the loving care which the crew bestowed on the old vessel, nursing her along, she would have been posted 'missing - somewhere in space' long ago.

The five close-knit members of the team had survived eleven missions together, almost all of which were trauma free, and they had become more like brothers than highly skilled individuals from different academies.

The mission they were presently engaged in necessitated checking all the suns in sector 18R for planets which might have rare mineral ores, making sure that there was an oxygen based atmosphere on the planet for the work teams, and noting any possible dangers which might impede subsequent mining operations, should valuable ores be found.

The general modus operandi was to locate a sun, check to see if it had a planetary system that contained worlds in a temperature band that made it possible to visit, look for signs of intelligent life forms (which were very rare) and if none were present, scan the planet with the ships detectors for minerals which might be worthy of attention.

If anything of value was found, then a survey team would go down to the surface for samples, as the ship's detectors were only able to sense the presence and quantity of minerals, not the quality of the ore.

They were just finishing their work on a planet around a star, or to be more precise sun 79, when the communication unit onboard the shuttle module, affectionately known as the 'Shuttle Bucket', decided to malfunction. This meant that the crew aboard the shuttle could not contact the main ship, and vice versa.

Although this was not a total disaster, it was very inconvenient, and Kal, being one of the two electronics experts in the team, volunteered to exchange the unit for the last remaining spare when they returned to the main vessel.

There were now only two survey shuttles left in working order, and if either of them failed, then the Ship would have to return to base with the mission incomplete. It was deemed too risky to operate with one unit, in case a rescue mission had to be sent out.

Kal and his two team mates loaded in the last samples of ore, retracted the drilling rig and stowing it away in the hold of the shuttle, prepared to leave the planet to rendezvous with the mother ship.

With communications in a state of flux, the automatics were no longer receiving coherent signals from the main ship, and so the shuttle had to be flown up and docked manually.

The survey team made it back in one piece, and after a short explanation of what had happened to their communications link, copious criticism of the mining company's tight fistedness, a meal and a short rest, they began setting the co-ordinates for the long journey to the next star field system.

As the distance between star systems was considerable to say the least, some method of suspended animation for the crews was of paramount importance.

The method adopted to date worked quite well, and consisted basically of lowering the pulse rate and temperature of the body to the barest minimum when placed within the confines of a 'sleep pod', which in turn supplied an intravenous drip of nutrients, and disposed of body wastes.

When the Ship neared the chosen destination, the pods would raise the temperature, add a little adrenaline to the drip supply, and the crew would wake up feeling refreshed, and after a little exercise, ready for their next task.

The crew took it in turns to enter the pods one after another so that there would always be someone to make sure that the sleep cycle began correctly for each entrant, except for the last member, who always used the pod that all agreed was the least likely to fail. Just one of those brotherly little things one did on an ageing ship; at the very least, it increased one's chance of survival.

As it happened, it was Kal's turn to be 'last man to bed' after the vessel had been made ready for the voyage to the new system. The destination was set, the automatics keyed in, and the Star Search began accelerating on her new course to hope for riches.

Overseeing the rest of the crew into their pods, Kal remembered the faulty unit in the survey module, and decided to change it now so that they would not have to waste time at the other end of their journey.

He left the control room and headed for the stores, such as they were. Locating the last remaining communications unit, he unclipped it from its carrier, picked up a small tool kit and made his way to the survey shuttle bay.

The shuttles were dotted around the rear end of the mother ship like a series of warts, and were held in place by a group of clamps that would only release them when a certain set of conditions were met.

Closing the airlock behind him, Kal thumbed the enter button of the shuttle's hatch, waited for it to hiss open, and boarded the module. It was mandatory to close the hatch if working within the unit, and he did so, which, as it turned out was just as well.

He had removed the retaining screws and the old communications unit, and offering up the replacement. It soon became apparent that it wasn't going to fit. It needed a mere millimetre or so to be filed off one of the mounting lugs, and he didn't have a file with him.

It was at this moment in time, that the Gods looked down upon the Star Search, smiled, and threw a proverbial spanner into the metaphorical works.

During the last somewhat sparse refit of the vessel, the docking sensor on the shuttle had to be replaced, along with several other items.

It was held in place by twelve machine screws and nuts, and a tired service engineer having misplaced one of the locking washers, and not having a spare with him, gave the nut an extra hard twist with his trusty spanner, packed up his kit and went back to base for a long overdue rest.

The docking sensor was located close to the outside of the hull, and was exposed to extreme changes of temperature, depending on whether it was facing a sun or the extreme cold depths of space. It was also subject to a fair amount of vibration. In time, the nut without the locking washer worked itself loose, and fell off, landing on a ledge below the sensor unit where it lay quite happily for a time.

This would not have been a problem normally, as the other screws were quite capable of holding the unit in place, but the vagrant nut gradually worked itself along to the end of the ledge and fell onto the power relay that controlled the locking clamps of the shuttle.

Unfortunately the relay cover had not been replaced and the nut fell onto the contacts, completing the signal circuit.

The relay slammed shut, and a surge of power was sent to the docking clamps which obligingly opened, gently releasing the shuttle into space.

It was only when Kal tried to open the hatch and was greeted by a blast from the warning siren and a red light, that he realized things were not as they should have been.

This could only mean one of three things. One, the interlock system had thrown a wobbly - not very likely, as it was a simple device, and only recently replaced. Two, the main chamber in the shuttle bay had decompressed - also not likely, as no warning had been sounded. Three, the shuttle had disengaged, and was ready to go down to the planet surface, except that no planet had been selected and no one had set the release sequence.

He hurried across to the nearest viewing port, which in free fall had its own problems, and instead of the comforting view of the old ship's under belly, he was greeted by the unimpeded sight of the star field. The other ports also gave a wonderful view of the stars, but of the main vessel there was not a vestige.

At long last the impossible had happened. He was adrift from the main vessel; the communications unit was not working and even if it had been it would have made little difference, as the crew were in deep sleep and well on their way to their next destination.

As the main ship was under acceleration, it was already well beyond the reach of the shuttle which didn't have the accelerating power of the Star Search to catch up.

Kal was in deep trouble, and he knew it. There was nothing he could do to regain contact with the ship in any way; he was alone, and that was it.

By the time the Star Search had reached her new destination, he would have run out of food, water or oxygen; it didn't matter which, the result would be the same. When the crew awoke, they would have no idea of when or where Kal had gone missing, and a search would have been pointless.

Fear he was used to, but the flood of terror which coursed through him had a different flavour. He knew his situation was hopeless, as rescue was nigh on impossible. His only chance of survival was to find a nearby planet which would support life, and that was a slim chance indeed.

The shuttle had provisions for a crew of three on an extended visit planet side, and the power unit had a reserve left for at least six more flights. What he needed to do was find a sun with a suitable planet in attendance, and make landfall if the fuel held out long enough.

A chance in a million, so he set about it with as much enthusiasm as he could muster under the circumstances.

Kal knew that they were on the rim of the star field they had been exploring when they set the new course, and there were a few minor stars they had not bothered to check as their planets didn't usually have a great deal to offer in the way of rare minerals. There was just a slim chance that one of these suns might have a suitable planet on which he could survive, at least for a while.

The first thing to do was to locate a suitable sun, and that wasn't going to be easy without the main ship's sensors.

The shuttle had acquired a considerable turn of speed due to being part of the main ship when it had began accelerating towards the new star field, so he wouldn't have to waste fuel as far as travelling in a straight line was concerned. The main use of the thrusters would be to steer the module towards any sun system that looked promising.

Kal realized that he would have to lose a great deal of energy from the shuttle's trajectory when he found a suitable sun, and there may well be little to spare for using reverse thrust to slow down his forward speed.

Anyway, he would need all the fuel he could get when it came to manoeuvring the craft into position for a landing, especially as some would be used in homing in on the likely solar system using the side thrusters. But first he had to find a suitable solar system.

The main difficulty was going to be losing that forward speed when it was necessary to do so, and as that would take a lot of fuel, Kal toyed with the idea of using the other planets in the sun's system, if there were any, like a sling shot in reverse, and lose speed that way.

According to the onboard clock, it was fifteen days later when Kal noticed a medium size sun getting larger in one corner of the forward viewing window.

He did his best to work out a trajectory which would bring the shuttle into line with the sun, all the time looking out for any signs of planetary bodies orbiting around it.

Not the easiest of tasks without the main ship's detectors and computers, which did all the hard work. He was relying on light from the sun to reflect from the planets in order for them to become visible.

As he neared the sun, several bright pinpoints of light did seem to be moving a little quicker than the surrounding stars, and that could only mean one thing, he had found a system with orbiting planets.

Speeding through the outer edges of the system he realized that he was going to have to take one more chance which he had not intended to do, but as fuel was at a premium the choice was more or less made for him. He would need to go in as close to the sun as possible, and 'sling-shot' around it in order to go out to the planets again.

As far as he could tell, from this distance out, the second world in from the sun seemed to be about the right distance from it to be warmed by its solar fires.

Kal began the 'sling shot' manoeuvre, by using the side thrusters to curve the shuttle's flight path in towards the sun.

Passing by some of the planetary objects in the system, he made notes of any data he could acquire from them, so building up a picture of this system's worlds.

So far, it still looked as though his first choice for a landing was the best bet, but he couldn't be sure until he had more information on the other planets within his reach.

As the shuttle approached the sun, it began to pick up speed. This was to be expected, and the extra speed attained would be lost again when the curve around the sun was completed, and he headed out towards the planets.

Kal reasoned that by moving the shuttle in or out of its curved flight path at the right moment, he would lose some momentum, and hence the forward speed would decrease. If this was done as he swept around the other planets in the solar system, he should be able to decrease speed enough to make a landing on one of them. He had to; there was no other choice with a restricted fuel supply.

Using the side thrusters was the most economical way of utilizing the remaining fuel stock, and so far it had seemed to work. Kal completed the curve around the sun, and was now heading back into the space between the planets.

The shuttle passed much closer to his chosen world this time, and using the magnifying optics onboard the shuttle he knew his choice was the right one. There seemed to be areas of water, mountains or very high ridges, various areas of what he assumed to be coloured vegetation, and what looked like some large patches of desert as well.

It would take many 'days' of onboard time to complete his manoeuvring and swing back to his chosen world, but he had all the time he needed with plenty of food, water and oxygen. The only constraining factor was the fuel for the thrusters, and that was going down faster than he had anticipated.

While on the outward swing from the sun, he passed what he took to be a 'gas giant' planet, the gravity of which was a good deal less than he had calculated, and so the thrusters had to be brought into play a lot more than he had allowed for. More fuel gone without a loss of velocity.

Things were getting more difficult by the minute, and he had a lot more weaving among the planets to do yet before he got the shuttle's speed down to manageable proportions.

Eleven 'days' into his dance among the heavenly bodies, the shuttle's speed was reduced to what Kal thought would be acceptable for a landing.

He would not be able to descend in the usual manner, which was to chose a site, hover over it to check it out for suitability, and then go down vertically. There was not enough fuel left for the luxury of this kind of approach, so it meant a long glide in from very high up.

The main problem with a long glide in was that the shuttle was not a glider, and had no wings to give it 'lift', which would be necessary for this kind of landing.

The only way to get down in one piece was to come in at a low angle to the planet's upper atmosphere, and bounce the craft in and out of the upper air layers, so losing velocity.

This would reduce the overall speed without causing too much overheating due to friction from the thin air, and if he chose the right moment by keeping the shuttle at the correct angle, he would achieve a sort of glide, albeit a steep and speedy one.

'It's going to be like trying to fly a flat rock,' he mused.

Using the side thrusters, Kal brought the shuttle in a long low curve towards the planet beneath. The first contact with the upper atmosphere rattled his teeth a little, but he was safely strapped into his seat, and withstood the buffeting.

He had not realized that he had been holding his breath, and let it out with a whoosh as the craft bounced up into space again. The next entry was much the same and Kal noticed that with each approach, the velocity indicator was reading a little lower. Not much, but it would make all the difference to the final glide in when the time came.

The profuse sweating he experienced was not all due to fear, as the craft was heating up through atmospheric friction much more than he had anticipated. Whether he would make landfall before he was stewed in his own juices was an academic point, but still worrying none the less.

At long last the shuttle did not bounce back into space, and the long glide down to the planet's surface began. Kal had to use the thrusters every now and again, just to keep the approach angle correct, otherwise the craft would have dropped like a stone.

His ears were subjected to a cacophony of sound as the shuttle ruptured a path through the increasingly dense air on its descent towards the planet's surface.

The fuel reading was almost on zero when he broke through the cloud layer, and a vast area of blue green water was spread out beneath him, right up to the horizon.

By now the temperature inside the shuttle was like a furnace, and he was having trouble breathing as the hot air seared his lungs and stung his eyes.

As the sea rushed up to meet him, his fingers played over the controls like a well practised musician, flattening the approach angle so that the shuttle would hopefully skim across the waters like a flat stone, otherwise the impact would shatter the craft into a myriad twisted metal fragments, and him along with it.

Kal braced himself for the first contact with the planet's surface, and winced as the craft slammed down onto the sea.

The hiss of steam was accompanied by the scream of metal, as the shuttle's skin tried to adjust to the sudden change of temperature upon contact with the cold water.

After the initial impact, there was virtual silence as the shuttle bounced up into the air and began its long curving descent towards the sea again.

Each time the vessel hit the water the length of time spent in the air lessened, as did the forward speed of the craft, and Kal began to wonder if his body would be able to withstand the numbing shocks much longer.

The thunderous spray of water on the forward viewing port gradually lessened, and in the distance Kal could just make out what was probably a distant shore line.

Eventually the bouncing stopped, and the craft was just skimming across the surface of the water.

At last the heavy impacts had stopped, and Kal was only subjected to the roar of the cleaved waters and a slight shuddering as the vessel sped towards what vaguely looked like a sandy beach in the distance.

The shuttle was still travelling at high speed when it hit the beach, throwing Kal violently forward in his harness as the craft ploughed a long and deep furrow in the sand.

The shriek of the abrasive sand as it tore at the hull of the vessel hurt his ears, but at least, he had made landfall, battered and bruised, but in one piece.

The silence after the vessel had come to rest, had an almost deafening quality about it, and he shook his head to make sure that it wasn't his hearing that was at fault.

As his ears readjusted to the new environment, he was aware of faint creaks and groans as the hull tried to cope with the lower temperature, and realign its structure.

He could hardly believe his luck to have landed safely, for the odds against it were overwhelmingly stacked against him from the start.

For all Kal knew he might have landed in quicksand, and that would have put him back where he started, with no hope of escape, so a quick exit was in order.

Try as he might, the hatch would not open when he pressed the release button. Something must have been damaged on the way down or upon landing; whatever it was, the hatch would not respond.

He quickly stripped the lining panel from the inner face of the reluctant hatch, and removed the locking bars one by one. The last bar removed would allow the hatch to swing open, that's if the hinge mechanism wasn't distorted, so he was a little apprehensive about releasing it as he would then be exposed to the planet's atmosphere.

There was no way of testing the outside air from within the shuttle, as that was always done from the main ship with special detectors. He would have to breathe this alien air sometime or die, so he felt it might as well be now.

Instinctively Kal held his breath, knocked out the last locking bar, and with a faint hiss the hatch creaked open a millimetre or so. His ears 'popped' as the pressure dropped to balance with that of the outside atmosphere.

Pushing the hatch open a little, he cautiously took a breath, and found the outside air a lot more pleasant than that which he had been breathing for the last few weeks.

Kal climbed out of the hatch, and using the service handholds made his way to the top of the shuttle. From here he could see the water in the distance, and an unbelievably long furrow made by the vessel as it had came ashore.

To the landward side, there was a ridge of large pebbles which gave way to what looked like a grass covered area before merging with a band of trees in the distance. Either side of him, the beach stretched on to the horizon, and what a beach, nearly half a kilometre in width.

When he looked down, he noticed that the shuttle had sunk far deeper into the sand than the depth of the furrow it had made. Upon closer inspection it was evident that there was something moving about under the sand around the craft, and this movement combined with its own weight, was allowing the vessel to sink ever deeper.

Hastily Kal climbed down to go back into the cabin in order to gather up a few useful items should he have to leave the comparative safety of the shuttle in a hurry. It was while he was doing this, that he saw to his horror that the sand had begun flowing in through the hatchway, and was slowly spreading across the floor in a series of creeping ripples.

In sheer panic he leapt for the hatch and scrambled out. The sand outside the hatchway was in violent motion as though something was struggling to reach the surface.

That was enough for Kal, he jumped down and ran as fast as he could on the heaving sand, heading for the line of pebbles, completely forgetting his good intentions of collecting any useful items from the craft.

He reached the apparent safety of the pebble bank, and turned, badly shaken, to watch as the sand around the shuttle seemed to boil in fury at his escape.

Trembling in disbelief, he witnessed the vessel that had safely brought him so far; slowly sink out of sight, and the sand once again returning to its initial stillness.

TWO:
Wilderness

So, here he was on an alien planet, standing on a pebble bank with only the clothes he was wearing, and a small emergency food ration on his belt. No tools, no weapons; nothing but himself and his memories, and any skills he had learnt along the way.

He was alive, at any rate, but to remain in that state was going to push him to the very limits of his abilities, if the sight of the sinking shuttle was anything to go by.

There was little point in staying on the pebble bank and bemoaning his lot.

The first thing to do was to find some means of defending himself should he be attacked by any of this planet's life forms which he felt sure must exist, and the second to locate a supply of drinkable water.

Shelter would be needed, and a safe place to rest overnight, that is if this place had a night.

As his rations were limited, native food could prove to be a problem too, as he had no means of testing it for suitability, and would have to rely on his memory of the survival courses which they had all attended.

Cautiously he made his way to the upper edge of the bank, and took in the scenery. Before him lay what looked like an area of grassy vegetation, if you could stretch your imagination a little. It was only a few millimetres high, and looked as if it had been cropped by something.

That solved the doubts about animal life, but what form did it take? Usually herbivores were not aggressive, but no rule was hard and steadfast on an alien world.

A clump of rocks lay beyond the grass, with a bare soil area around them. Beyond this was what appeared to be a loose knit forest of treelike growths, varying in height from small bushes to tall solid looking trees, several metres high.

Bearing in mind what had happened on the apparently innocent looking sand, Kal hurried across the grass-like area and onto the rocks. Somehow the rocks felt safer, if they were not too different to those on his home world.

He was puzzled by the bare area around the rock pile, almost as if the vegetation didn't like being too near the rocks. It was then that he found his first piece of useful survival information.

The rocks were veined with a mineral of some kind, and Kal thought it looked a little like copper ore, but not one he could easily identify. There were pale greenish streaks at the base of the rocks as if something had been dissolved or washed out of them, and then soaked into the surrounding ground.

Maybe that was it; the local plants didn't like copper, and wouldn't or couldn't grow in its presence. Maybe other things might react to copper in the same way. That piece of information would be filed away for future use.

In an alien situation like this, all data must be evaluated for possible value, for that was the only weapon he had.

He climbed up to the top of the rock pile, considering it to be the safest place to be at the moment, and sat down. It was time for a brief résumé of the information he had gathered so far since his somewhat hurried landing.

If the planet orbited its sun with one side facing the sun all the time, then the other side would be exposed to the chill of space, losing its heat by radiation.

This would cause most of the gases in the atmosphere to condense on the cold side, and the remaining air would then travel round and also be condensed.

As there was a breathable atmosphere, the planet must be rotating about its axis, and therefore there should be day and night, or something approaching it.

The mineral stains on the rocks and surrounding ground indicated that water had probably been responsible for this, so there must be rain or precipitation of some sort.

As plants cannot grow without some moisture reaching them every now and then, it looked like rain or very dense mist, unless there was an underground source.

The cropped moss-like grass meant that there was an animal of some kind in the vicinity, and that could possibly provide protein if it wasn't poisonous.

One other thing, avoid areas of innocent looking sand, he thought, bearing in mind the sinking shuttle. Therefore other areas of bare ground should be treated with suspicion.

He had gained a lot of data from this world already, and no doubt would need to find a lot more if he was to survive for any length of time.

Kal was already feeling a lot better, and realized that water was the next item to find. Picking up a few fist sized stones from the base of the rock pile, he stuffed them into his tunic to use as missiles should the need arise.

He carefully stepped down from the rock pile, and warily made his way across the grass or 'gross' (grass-like-moss) as he now thought of it. There was no point in naming things here with the old terms he was used to, so he decided to make up appropriate names as he went along.

The start of the forest was not far away, and he reached it without incident. One thing he would have liked, was a long stave or pole with which to fend off any large animals that might decide to put him on the menu.

The first tree-like object he came to was not all that strange, except for the leaves. They were just flattened branch ends, as far as he could tell, and looked innocent enough.

Dotted about the growth were a few dark red berries, about the size of his thumbnail, and he wondered if they were edible. After he had had a general look around, Kal thought he would make a collection of all likely looking fruits, and test them out for safe eating later.

The trees and bushes were spread out on the fringes of the forest, but by the look of things, it was a little denser further in, and he would have to go very carefully if he was not to be taken by any surprises this planet had in store for him.

The gross carpeted the floor of the forest for as far as he could see, but there were a few bare patches here and there, which he avoided just to be on the safe side.

A bamboo-like structure caught his attention, and looked harmless enough. It sent shoots up to about four metres, and the main stem at the base was as thick as his wrist. If he could get one of these out from the clump, he would then have his much desired stave. Reaching into the thicket, Kal selected a shoot and tried to wrench it clear.

Although it bent, it was not going to come out easily, and despite several tries, he had to give up.

A little further in, was an apparent dead shoot, at least it was a different colour to the rest, and he thought it was worth a try. It proved to be a good choice, as, with a pistol like crack, it came away at the base, and he was now armed with his stave. Even though the shoot was not alive, it had retained a considerable degree of strength, and Kal could not break it, try as he might.

There was another clump of rocks to his left, and he went over to investigate. These obviously did not contain anything which the surrounding plant life found obnoxious, as the gross grew right up to the edge of the pile, and there was no sign of the green copper stain he had seen from the first rocks.

What passed here for a thorn thicket with a bare patch of ground all around it was just ahead of him, and he climbed a little way up the rock pile to get a better view.

Hardly had he done so, when a creature not unlike an overgrown caterpillar, but about a metre long, came into the clearing. By the way it was moving its head from side to side it was looking for something, possibly to eat.

It must have found what it wanted, for it set off in a straight line across the bare patch. It only made it about halfway.

The ground under the unfortunate creature split open, and two long tendrils complete with spikes, curled around it, the sharp points going deep into its flesh.

The tendrils continued to curl up, such that they were rolling the animal into the very centre of the thicket, and thorned branches then slowly curved around the catch, until it was only just visible.

All struggling had ceased as soon as the first tendril had made contact, so Kal surmised that the spikes must contain a very strong paralysing compound.

'That might come in useful' he thought, if he could get his hands on a couple of the spikes without becoming a meal for the thicket. He noticed that at the very base of the thorn thicket, there appeared to be a pile of white stones of varying sizes, and climbing down from the safety of the rocks he moved closer to see if he could tell what they were.

He should have known, they were the bones of creatures the thorn thicket had captured. Some had broken down into very small particles, and would in time no doubt, be absorbed by the plant, while others seemed to have only recently been added to the pile.

He thought he should be able to work out the size of the largest animal caught by the biggest bones present, and this would give him a clue as to the size of any adversary he might meet. First he needed to find a bigger bush.

It did not take him long to find a giant of a thicket, and sure enough, there were some bones there that sent cold shivers down his spine.

There were several much larger than any bone in his body, and not knowing the structure of the creature they had belonged to, his mind ran riot trying to conjure up a picture of what it might look like.

No doubt, he would see one sooner or later, and he had better be well armed when he did.

One thing Kal did see in the bone pile was what might have been the jaw of something he would rather not meet under any circumstances. It was as long as his forearm, and had a line of razor sharp teeth embedded in it.

With his pole he very carefully hooked it out from the base of the thicket. It was quite heavy, and the teeth were like nothing he had ever seen before, thin flat plates with a razor sharp edge.

Taking his find back to the rock pile, he managed to break the bone at the front of the jaw by tapping away with a pointed stone, and now had two very effective saws.

Nearby was a bamboo clump, and he wondered if his new cutting tool would be effective on the tough stems. Kal made sure he did not tread on anything nasty in his eagerness to reach the clump, and selecting a thick shoot, and tried to cut it at about waist height.

Once the 'Jaw Saw' had broken through the outside layer of the bamboo, it cut easily, and a trickle of a water-like liquid ran out. Did he dare taste it?

Remembering his survival training, he wetted his finger in the liquid, and waited a few moments. Nothing happened, so he touched his finger to his lower lip, moistening it.

If it did not sting, and his lip did not swell within a few minutes, he would put a drop under his tongue, as this was the point in the body where it would be absorbed most readily, and if poisons where present, would react, hopefully not fatally.

Kal had not realized just how thirsty he was, and was anxiously awaiting the result from the 'lip test' so that he could slake his thirst. He was fortunate, so far there had been no reaction to the fluid, and so he placed a small drop under his tongue.

Some minutes later, after noticing no ill effects, he chose a young shoot and cutting off the top, bent it down so that the clear liquid ran into his cupped hand. The temptation to drink deeply was overcome, and he took a cautious sip.

It tasted good, cool, and very slightly sweet with a faint perfumed flavour that he could not quite place.

He would now have to wait several minutes to see if the larger intake of the fluid would react on his metabolism.

Making his way back to the rock-pile, he climbed up to the top and sat down to await the results, if any.

Kal noticed over to one side of the bamboo clump, another 'tree' that bore a strange crop of finger like fruits, at least he supposed they were fruits or seed pods.

It looked as though someone had strung up a series of large dark brown hands all over the tree, and it gave the whole thing a very sinister look indeed. He thought that the 'fingers' might be a possible food source.

The bamboo juice didn't seem to have had any bad effects on him, so he went back to the clump, and cutting the tops of several small shoots, drank his fill. He could hardly believe his luck at finding this source of water, and generally felt a little better towards this apparently hostile world.

He went over to the 'Finger' tree, and knocked down a clump of the brown fruits with his pole. Nearby was another odd looking growth which bore a number of bright yellow pear-shaped objects, and one of these was added to his collection. On his way back to the copper rocks, Kal also collected a few of the bright red berries he had seen earlier, as they reminded him of a fruit from his home world.

The light level had dropped perceptibly, and Kal reasoned that the safest place to spend the night, if indeed there was a night, would be on top of the copper stained rocks which he had discovered when he first arrived.

He thought that he would feel a lot more secure in the comparative safe haven of the rocks, when he tested his fruits. Kal was aware that his collection may well contain some powerful drug-like qualities, and decided to make sure he did not go wandering off in a dazed state, to match the fate of the caterpillar like creature.

To this end, he undid the belt from around his waist, and jamming the buckle in between two rocks, he tied the other end around one ankle. At least, he could not wander too far.

The first item to be tested was the bright red berry. Kal sniffed it, and found there was no odour that he could detect, and he had to admit, it did look inviting. Breaking the skin with a finger nail, he immediately wished he hadn't.

The smell that assailed his nostrils was the most revolting stench he had ever experienced. His stomach tied itself in knots and he tried to be sick, but this was rather difficult as he hadn't eaten for so long, but it hurt just the same.

Exit one sample, as far as he could throw it. It took some minutes for Kal to get back to normal, and he was a little reluctant to try any of the other produce he had gathered.

He knew it was no use putting the moment off, as he must find something to eat because the emergency rations would only last a day or so. Mentally gritting his teeth, Kal broke off one of the brown finger like things from the little bunch he had collected.

That smelt all right, but try as he might he could not break through the tough skin. Perhaps a tooth on the jaw saw would do the trick. It did, after a while. At last he managed to prise off the outer coating of the 'finger', to reveal a solid grey coloured compound inside.

Using a 'tooth blade', he was able to scrape a little of the compound off, and pressed it to his lower lip. He noticed a warm, not unpleasant, musky smell, and dreaded to think what it might taste like.

The lip did not swell after a few minutes, so he placed a few flakes of the 'nut' under his tongue, and waited for the reaction.

As nothing had happened for a full ten minutes, Kal put a little more of the compound into his mouth, and chewed it.

He was quite surprised to find it very much like a perfumed nut, both in flavour and texture, although a little tough.

Feeling a little more sure of himself, he swallowed the sample, and sat back to see if it would affect him.

Kal sat there some time, mulling over the events of the day, and he nearly drifted into sleep. So far the Finger Nut had caused him no harm, and as he was feeling hungry, he thought it was time to really put it to the test and try a mouthful. He tried biting the nut, but it was too hard, and he did not want to risk breaking any teeth.

Back to the scraper, and soon a small pile of flakes were ready to be eaten. The nut flakes were a little dry, and he wished he had brought a few lengths of the bamboo back with him to quench his thirst. All in all, the finger nut provided a satisfying meal, and probably contained a quantity of protein.

He toyed with the idea of trying the bright yellow pear thing, and as there was nothing else to do, he broke the skin open to reveal a pale cream coloured flesh, with darker streaks of deep yellow within.

Taking a sniff, he found it had a fruity smell, but to which fruit family it belonged, he was not sure. Again, taking a small sample on his finger, he applied it to his lip.

At first there was just a mild tingling sensation, with a warm glow behind it, and then his eyes went out of focus and he was floating about in the air, waving his arms and legs, and feeling very happy indeed.

He drifted around like this for quite a while, smiling at the beautiful plants, and waving at the many creatures of the forest as they went by.

Some smiled back and even waved, and he felt at one with the planet and its strange inhabitants, who were after all, really no stranger than him.

When he awoke, it was quite dark. His arms and legs ached from being twisted into unnatural positions, his head felt full of barbed wire, and he had fouled himself into the bargain.

Slowly, Kal regained some semblance of normality, and was very glad he had had the foresight to anchor his leg to the rocks; otherwise he would probably have wound up being a meal for something.

Kal spent the rest of the night drifting in and out of fitful bouts of sleep and their accompanying nightmares, and lying on the hard rocks, cursing his misfortune.

Dawn broke after about three weeks, or so it seemed. He had to admit that the rising of the sun was a beautiful sight, not just because he was glad to see it, but for the wonderful colours in the sky.

After getting some life back into his cramped legs by jumping, or rather stumbling, from rock to rock, Kal warily made his way over to the bamboo clump, and cut several young shoots. He found that if he made the cut near ground level, the end of the pole was plugged with a pithy substance, and the fluid did not run out.

He was now equipped with a water supply of sorts. After a quick wash of himself, and his lower tunic, which dried out quite quickly in the sun, he felt a lot better. A couple of finger nuts made him a satisfying meal washed down with bamboo water, and he was ready for the day.

No way was he going anywhere near the sandy beach and the sea, so inland seemed the only other possible alternative, unless he just stayed put.

Armed with the dead bamboo pole which he had sharpened to a point with the jaw-saw at a solid joint near one end, and a bundle of 'water sticks' tied up with his belt, he set off along the edge of the forest.

Every now and then, he came across a bamboo clump dotted about among the other tree-like growths, so water shouldn't be a problem just so long as the bamboo kept cropping up.

There were many other strange plants for him to inspect as he went along his way, some bearing fruits and others with what he took to be flowers adorning their branches.

Suddenly he came upon what could be mistaken for a track, leading into the thicker part of the forest. It was well defined and about ten metres wide, the ground cover being the ubiquitous gross, and nothing else.

On each side of the track the forest grew in profusion, but only to a clear cut edge where the gross took over.

That seemed even stranger than some of the plants he had found. One possible explanation could be that there was solid rock beneath the track, and the bigger plants could not grow on it, or perhaps there was a fault in the ground structure, and a chemical was leaching upwards, and only the gross could tolerate it.

He had no way of finding out for sure, so it was only of academic interest, but intriguing just the same.

It was now decision time, to follow the sparse forest along the shore line, or to go up the track with dense forest either side, and nowhere to run if the need arose. Kal had his sharpened pole and a good pair of legs, so he settled for the track, it might lead to something of interest, and he could always return if it fizzled out.

He had gone but a few hundred metres when he came across a little clump of white balls about the size of his fist, in a tight little group at the forest edge.

He gave one a poke with his pole, and it rolled away quite freely with no sign of roots beneath it, leaving a bare patch on the ground where it had been.

Within a few moments, the gross had curled over to cover the empty patch, as though nothing had been there before.

'That must mean these things come up very quickly, possibly over night', he concluded, and somehow it rang a bell in his memory.

Not wishing to go too near the forest edge, he rolled the ball towards him with the pole, and picked it up.

It was soft but firm, with no smell that he could detect. A possible food source? maybe, so he cut it in half to reveal a soft but solid centre, and again, no smell. Kal jammed a whole one into his bundle of water sticks for future investigation, and proceeded on his way.

He had had very few thoughts of the Star Search, or her crew, who would still be in deep sleep for months yet, or for that matter even of his own home world.

He put it down to being so preoccupied with his own survival here, but that did not really satisfy a nagging feeling of selfishness on his part. Somehow he was becoming part of this strange world, and he didn't seem to mind, and that worried him a little.

Up the track, some distance away, he suddenly noticed a four legged animal of about his size, eating the white balls as if they were just about to be taken off the menu for ever.

It had a beak-like mouth piece on a large head which in turn was attached to a rather small body, and so the whole thing looked somewhat out of proportion.

It mopped the balls up one after the other at great speed, and looking around for more, it spotted him. It froze, and then with mouth open, it advanced slowly towards him making a loud hissing sound.

Kal stood his ground, heart racing. This was going to be the first conflict between native and interloper, and would decide the odds of Kal's survival for the future.

They were only about three metres apart, when Big Head thought better of it, and just stood its ground, hissing as loudly as it could. Kal, sensing the slight back off, let out as ferocious a yell as he could muster, and the creature went silent, backing up a pace or two.

Having gained the advantage, Kal moved forward with his pole and jabbed 'Big Head' in the beak with it. It was enough, the little legs couldn't move fast enough to carry the creature to the forest edge, where it turned around and began hissing again.

Unfortunately for 'Big Head', it had not chosen a very good place to stand and bay its defiance, for just behind it stood what Kal later christened the 'Whip Tree'.

This particular nasty offering had a trunk as thick as two men side by side, and was covered with an olive green cotton wool looking substance. Several tendrils, as thick as an arm, swept up from the base of the trunk vertically for about three metres, and had hooked themselves onto the lower branches with the aid of a claw like protuberance.

Kal let out a yell and ran forward waving his pole. Big Head' took one step backwards, and one of the tendrils swept down, the claw embedding itself deeply into the creature.

The squeal of terror was soon muffled as it was drawn up against the trunk of the whip tree, and the cotton wool covering opened to accept it.

Within seconds the woolly covering had completely hidden its captive, and the tendril swung up to hook itself back onto one of the lower branches.

Kal felt saddened at Big Head's demise, for the poor creature was only defending itself and its territory from something it had never seen before, and he admired its bravery for doing that, as he had very nearly turned tail and run himself.

In the days of the Star Search, and considering the number of planets they had explored for minerals, there had been very little life in what Kal would call an advanced form.

There had been the odd few exceptions, and they had come across some humanoid type people, but they had only been of a primitive kind. None the less, they hadn't encroached on the humanoid's territory, and only mined when they didn't disturb the normal course of nature too much.

This planet seemed to be fairly well advanced in some ways, although the vegetation was a little odd, and he thought some of the creatures were going to be unlike anything he had ever seen before.

Kal moved over to the middle of the track, choosing the widest part he could see, giving the ground a good poke to release anything hiding there, and then sat down to rest.

Everything was still around him, an almost eerie silence pervaded the track way.

In the distance something snapped a twig, or whatever passed for a twig on this world, and there was a general soft scuffling sound in several directions for a few seconds, and then all was quiet again.

Taking a closer look at the gross, he was surprised to find it quite tough; a fair amount of effort was needed to pull a small piece up from its roots.

It had no smell that he could discern and felt more like a synthetic rubber compound than an organic plant. Taking a chance he knew he shouldn't, he bit a tiny piece, but there was no flavour to it at all. It did look a bit like the grass he was used to, perhaps crossed with a strain of moss.

Something moved to his right, he didn't see it directly, just a slight flash of light caught in his peripheral vision. Kal looked in the direction of the movement, but could see nothing in motion. And then there it was again, just a tiny sparkle of light falling to the ground.

Intending to ignore it until something more positive happened, another tiny flash occurred, and curiosity got the better of him, and he heaved himself to his feet.

First he took a good look in the direction of the light flashes, but all there was to see were the plants at the edge of the track, and they were motionless. And then he spotted it.

One of the bushes had at the end of its stumpy branches, a fine hair like growth, and it was from one of these that a small drop of liquid fell to the ground beneath.

Where the drops had fallen, the gross had turned a darker colour, and was much thicker, and probably tastier to eat, although that shouldn't take much doing, he thought with a silent chuckle.

Perhaps if he sat over on the other side and waited long enough, something might come along to eat it. But then that something might also like meat as well, and he wasn't going to chance that.

Bearing in mind what had happened to Big Head, he thought it best to give the plant life a wide berth until he had worked out which was safe, and which wasn't, and that in itself could be quite a dangerous occupation here. If nothing else, it would keep him on his toes for a while.

Kal thought he could survive here. He had found a source of water, and no doubt there would be other water bearing plants, or even an open pool or stream, and if he was lucky the water wouldn't be contaminated or poisonous.

His diet was a bit limited at the moment, and that too could be improved, but he would have to be very careful. He didn't think loneliness would affect him for a while, as there was so much to learn if he was to stay in one piece, but it would catch up with him one day, he felt sure.

He had food and water, next he would need shelter of some kind as it was going to rain sometime, and he didn't like the idea of getting wet when he didn't need to.

But the main thing was to find a place to sleep, where he couldn't be got at by anything that was hungry enough to want to turn him into a meal.

He would have felt a lot happier if he had brought a weapon with him, but you don't usually carry guns when servicing equipment, he thought wryly. A pointed stake was all very well for small creatures, but as yet he didn't know the extent to which the native creatures could grow.

If only the shuttle had survived, and not been consumed by whatever it was that lay beneath the sands of the landing beach. It would at least have been a home to go to for a safe rest and sleep.

He considered himself very fortunate to have escaped the dreaded sands in one piece, bearing in mind the speed with which the craft had disappeared from view.

The track continued in a straight line into the distance for as far as Kal could see, but up ahead, he could just discern a large rock formation on his left, towering above the surrounding greenery.

As this made a change from the jungle of bushes and trees around him, he hurried forward to investigate. The formation was a lot larger than he had first thought, and went back into the forest for some considerable distance.

There were no plants or other growing things on the rocks, and the gross went right up to where the rock surface protruded from the ground.

At first sight, it looked as if the ground had been weathered away from around the rock formation, so exposing it to view, but it was quite high, and erosion alone would have taken a long time to have done this.

Kal, seeing no obvious danger in the rocks, climbed up to obtain a better view of the surrounding terrain, and was confronted by more of the same forest into the far distance.

He did not go up to the top, as quite apart from the height, which was deceptive, there were fewer footholds above him.

While traversing along a ledge, he came to a cave-like opening, and as there was plenty of headroom considered that it might be safe to enter, but very carefully.

Kal had only gone a few metres into the cave, when he heard the drip of water. The light level was dropping the further in he went, but was just enough to shine on a small pool on the cave floor. First he poked his trusty pole into the water in case it contained something waiting for a meal, and getting no response; he knelt down and dipped his hand into it. It seemed like water, and had no obnoxious smell, so he did the lip test, and tasted it.

It was good, and as there was no unpleasant metallic after flavour or reaction to his test, he drank his fill.

'That'll supplement the water tubes' he thought. 'They could be kept for a reserve if more caves could be found.'

Although he was tempted to go further into the cave, the light level was not sufficient to make the investigation a safe proposition, and so he decided to withdraw and perhaps come back one day when he had found a method of generating a light, even if it was only a flaming firebrand.

This would also make a very good safe haven if he was attacked by something he couldn't overpower, and had to retreat from. 'A few well placed rocks around the entrance would make it defendable' he mused, as he returned to the world of the forest.

Kal walked on up the track, looking behind him every now and again, just to make sure that nothing caught him unaware from the rear.

He thought it strange that there were so few legged creatures about as the gross was so evenly cropped, something must have been eating it, and he wondered what.

'Maybe it all happens at night', he thought, but he was not too keen to wander about at night to find out.

Kal had been walking along for some time, when the end of the track came into sight. It just stopped, and he didn't like the thought of having to go all that way back again.

As he was so close to the end he thought he may as well see what had caused it to terminate. Maybe a clue as to what created the track in the first place would come to light.

Kal was surprised to find that the track didn't just end here, but took a sharp right angled turn to the left, and then went on into the distance.

The next unpleasantness to be presented to him was only a short distance after the turn he had just made. Beside the main track there was a small clearing, and in it what looked like a pool of muddy water.

The actual water was only about half a metre across, and it was skirted by a muddy patch of about the same width. The whole thing was quite a neat circle, and that aroused his suspicions straight away.

Somehow it lacked something that a pool of water should have, but he couldn't make out just what it was. He decided to sit down in the middle of the track and keep perfectly still to see if anything happened.

He was just about to give up on his vigil, when one of the caterpillar type creatures came into view, its head swinging from side to side. It must have sensed the water, for it made a straight line towards it.

The muddy section did not seem to impede it at all, and it left no track in the mud, and that was when Kal realized that the pool wasn't all that it seemed to be. The caterpillar reached the 'water' and lowered its head to drink - and was stuck fast in a glue-like substance.

The outer edges of the 'mud' then curled up to envelope the caterpillar completely, and a heaving muddy lump was all that there was to be seen of it. Only moments later the lump unfurled itself and the 'pool' was back to normal, with no sign of the meal it had taken.

Kal was getting used to the fact that very little here was as it appeared to be, but the last episode emphasized the point, and he resolved to be even more careful in future.

The track was now getting a little narrower as Kal progressed up it, and in the not too far distance it really did look as if it had closed in completely.

There was nothing for it but to go on and see what lay ahead, if anything apart from solid forest, and he certainly wasn't going to venture into that.

Kal could not help thinking about the huge bones he had seen in the thorn thicket. There had been no sign of any large animal, and because there was no bare earth to speak of, as the gross seemed to cover every piece of available open space, he had seen no footprints. Of course, this didn't mean that it did not exist, but he would feel a little easier if he knew a bit more about it.

The track had now narrowed down to about three metres, and he was beginning to feel a little uneasy. There was still room to manoeuvre if need be, but the closed in feeling was getting to him.

Fortunately, the sides of the path were not too densely populated with vegetation as it had been earlier, so did this mean that the track still existed as such, but the various trees and bushes were trying to encroach on the track itself?

He plodded on to a point where some larger trees had actually spread their canopy over head to make the track into a tunnel for a short distance.

Kal checked the tunnel forming trees for any hidden traps, such as the Whip variety, or anything else which could reach out to him as he went underneath them.

It all looked innocent enough so far, and he carefully ventured in a short distance to see if there was a change of circumstances ahead.

The uneasy feeling was getting stronger, and as he had got used to listening to his senses, he stopped, and looked around.

He could see nothing untoward at first, and then he noticed high up in an overhead tree a large greenish plate-like object, spread across several smaller branches.

He hadn't come across anything like this before, and he wasn't going to get too near it until he found out what it was or did, if anything.

A small pile of rocks, the first he had seen for a long time, lay to one side of the pathway, behind which was a bush of a type he hadn't seen before. It consisted of a series of thin stems atop of which grew large clumps of fluffy white fronds, as fine as hair.

It was a very delicate looking thing, but Kal was taking no chances, and gave it a poke with his pole. Nothing untoward happened, it didn't try to bite the end of the pole off, or wrap itself around it, so he thought it was of the non aggressive type, and was therefore relatively safe.

As Kal wanted to use the rocks as a place of safety to observe things for a while, and the white bush would be at his back, he would be hidden from that quarter and would be able to concentrate on what lay before him. He settled down to wait for whatever happened here when no one was around making a noise.

A closer look at the strange plate-like thing in the tree revealed it to be rather like a sheet of a leathery substance, about fifteen millimetres thick and spreading over an area of one metre in diameter.

Roughly circular in shape and a dull olive green in colour, it blended in well with the growth around it. A tiny sparkle of light caught Kal's attention, and he realized that it was a drop of liquid that had fallen from the thing in the tree.

Where it had landed, the gross had grown profusely, and was very lush and thick as it had beneath the other bush he has seen earlier. Maybe this was a lure for whatever the leather shape above had in mind for a meal, for he felt sure that a meal was involved here somewhere.

Kal must have dozed off for a while, for he awoke with a start and was aware of movement off to one side of the track, and it was not long before the creature hove into sight.

It was almost comical to look at, a pear shaped body supported on two stumpy little legs causing a wobbly gait to its movement. On top of the body, a small elongated head with large brown eyes, bobbed up and down, as it cropped the gross between the trees.

Two long thin arms completed the picture, and it brought a smile to Kal face, the first for quite a time.

Although he sensed something unpleasant was about to happen, it still came as a shock when the 'Leather Flap' detached itself from the tree, and glided down to land with a dull plop on top of 'Pear Shape's' head.

It promptly slumped to the ground as though stunned, as the Leather Flap wrapped itself tightly around the head and upper trunk of the poor creature. A few twitches, and Pear Shape lay as still as the rest of the forest around it.

After a few seconds the body seemed to swell almost to bursting point, and then deflated as the 'Leather Flap' grew larger, and then uncurled itself from the bag of skin and bone that was left, and wriggled a short distance away.

Having chosen a suitable site, the Leather Flap then proceeded to screw itself into the ground until all that was left to show its whereabouts was a small olive green tube-like structure poking out just above ground level. Even as he watched, the tube adjusted its height until it was only just visible, and then the gross curled around the top, hiding it.

Of all his discoveries so far on the planet, this was quite the most unpleasant thing that Kal had witnessed so far, and it was some time later, when he had time to spare, that he fully uncovered the true life cycle of the Leather Flap.

Although it was his policy not to take life unless it directly threatened his own, this revolting creation instinctively made Kal want to destroy every one he came across, and he had great difficulty in suppressing that urge.

It was some considerable time later when he managed to work out the complete life cycle of the revolting Leather Flap, and it was no less unpleasant than the way that it caught it's food.

Taking the life cycle from the point where it was up in the branches of a tree, the abomination sent a series of probing shoots into the living tissue of the branches, and withdrew moisture and any nutrients it needed.

From this, it manufactured a form of liquid fertilizer which it then dripped onto the ground beneath, and the gross in the treated area grew thick and fast, forming a tempting lure for any grazing creature that was passing.

Somehow the Leather Flap sensed the presence of its intended prey below, and glided or dropped down onto it.

As soon as contact was made with the quarry, a set of hollow claws on its periphery sank into the victim, and injected a paralysing fluid which was quickly followed by an injection of one or more enzymes, the purpose of which was to rapidly break down all internal tissues so that they could be ingested by the Leather Flap.

When this had been done, and it didn't take long, the creature left the corpse and located a soft piece of ground where it literally screwed itself below the surface.

Kal was not sure how long the next stage took, but in essence, the

Leather Flap underwent some form of metamorphosis, and in time disgorged about six or so replicas of itself, leaving behind an empty leathery bag underground, which, no doubt, something else found a use for.

The offspring were akin to very large grey slugs, about the length of his forearm and twice as thick.

These then found a suitable a tree, climbed up to the branches over a clearing and stretched themselves out to begin the repulsive cycle all over again.

Kal supposed that in time something would come along and make use of the sad remains of Pear Shape's skin and bone, as nothing seemed to go to waste for long here.

He sat for a while thinking about what he had just seen and wondered if there was a size limit to the creature that the Leather Flap would take. He supposed not, and resolved to be very careful indeed.

Kal scraped a quantity of Finger Nut flakes into his hand and followed his meal with a drink from his water sticks. He had seen quite a few bamboo clumps along the way, so he was not too worried about his water supply at the moment. It was time to head up the track again under the archway of overhanging trees, and he noticed to his relief, that the path was getting a little wider the further he went. It was not long before he was out of the tree tunnel again, and felt a lot better for the relative safety of the open.

A few kilometres along his way the ground changed, the gross getting more and more sparse as gravel and then fine stones showed through. The forest still continued on either side of him, and this gave the track a man-made look, although he doubted very much that it was.

There had been no sign of intelligent life so far, but then again, he had not travelled all that far, when taking the whole planet into consideration.

The vegetation on either side of him still provided the odd surprise, with different coloured fruits and odd looking shapes adorning the trees and bushes.

New types were tempting to try for food, but he reasoned that the brighter the colour, the more harmful they might be, at least they were according to his past trials.

The old faithful Finger Nut trees showed up every now and again, as did the Whip Trees, but he had not seen any of the drinking Water Traps for some time.

Occasionally he thought about the old Ship, and his fellow crewmen, but it all seemed a considerable time ago, as his attention was fixed on survival.

'Strange how one can adapt so easily to new circumstances if you have to' he thought, and promptly stumbled over a ridge in the track surface.

He staggered a few paces before falling down in a heap and that probably saved his life as a giant tendril as thick as his thigh arose from the ridge and thrashed about, no doubt guided by his body heat.

Kal rolled away from it as fast as he could, and then leapt to his feet to get as much distance between it and himself as possible. The snaking tendril having missed its intended prey, wriggled itself back into the ground, this time not leaving such a large ridge, and Kal began to worry that he would not see the next one.

Very carefully he walked on, looking for anything that was not quite as he thought it should be, but decided what should or shouldn't be on this world, was getting rather more difficult as time went by.

Up ahead the terrain was showing signs of change as the trees and bushes were becoming sparser, to be replaced with large and rugged rock formation.

At least without trees either side of him, he didn't need to worry about the giant tendrils, or did he? He never did see if the last one was attached to anything, or was a lone entity.

Kal stopped in his tracks, and thought a moment. If the area up ahead was all rocks and no vegetation, he might be short of water, and now would be a good time to stock up on his water tubes.

He turned back and retraced his footsteps, keeping a lookout for a bamboo clump. The other problem was the belt he used to hold the bundle of canes together with, which was not really long enough to secure a decent sized supply.

The Whip Tree could provide a tendril to use as a rope, if he could retrieve one without getting caught in the process.

A bamboo clump came into sight before long, and he set about cutting a pile of canes with the Jaw Saw. Getting a tendril from the Whip Tree was going to be dangerous, and he thought a small tree would be the safest to tackle, and would provide a more slender tendril.

The light was beginning to dim a little, and he wanted to get back to the rocky area before it got too dark so that he could find a safe place to sleep. Leaving the track, Kal made a note of the direction from which the light from the sinking sun was coming from, so that he would not lose his bearing and would be able to find the path to the rocks again.

He was about to give up his search, when he came across a denser area of strange growths, and sure enough the ubiquitous Whip Trees were among them. Finding a small one was not so easy, and he had to settle for one that was far too business like for his comfort.

Kal stood just outside the range of the Whip Tree's tendrils, and wondered just how he was going to get what he wanted without becoming a meal for the tree, and then he remembered the sharp teeth of the Jaw Saw.

It was a chancy idea, but it might work. To keep out of the range of the 'whips', he needed another dead bamboo pole to add to the one he already had, and went to get one.

Joining the two poles together with the belt was easy, but the difficult part of the operation was prising a 'tooth' from the Jaw Saw without cutting himself into the bargain.

Using a small stone, he chipped enough bone away to release a tooth, and marvelled at its sharpness even after he had been using it to cut the bamboo poles. Cutting a slot in the end of the pole, he carefully forced the base of the tooth into it, and was ready to get his tendril.

Kal approached the smallest of the Whip Trees, and making as sure as he could that his double pole was a little longer than he estimated the chosen tendril could reach, he slid the pole forward, lining it up with the base of the growth.

The first stab brought about an unexpected reaction from the tree, all the tendrils lashed out and writhed about, looking for the thing which had dared to attack it.

He waited for the tree to calm down, and tried again with the same result. Luckily, the tendrils did not go for his pole, as it did not give out any body heat, and he thought that heat was the key factor the tree used to sense prey.

At long last, after multiple slashing and stabbing, a tendril was severed from the base of the tree, and lay writhing about on the ground, seemingly with a life of its own.

Using the pole, Kal eased it away from the strike range of the tree, and waited for it to stop moving, not knowing if it still posed a danger if he got too close to it.

The claw on the end of it could inflict a nasty wound if it struck him, so he was very careful to watch it.

Kal put his foot on the severed end of the tendril, and applied a little weight. A thick brown liquid shot out, and the tendril gave a little wriggle.

The main length of it was only about half the thickness of his wrist, but this was still too thick to use as a rope. He applied a few more squeezes with his feet, and found that when the liquid had been expressed the tendril was reduced in diameter, and had become a little more flexible. This was what he wanted, and he set about squeezing the rest of the length to clear it of the unwanted contents.

It took a little while to clear all the thick liquid from the tendril, but having done so, Kal had a strong and flexible rope to tie up his drinking poles, and returned to the pile he had cut earlier.

By now the light had dimmed a little more than he would have wished for, as he still had quite a way to go to reach an area of rock that was completely devoid of vegetation.

Hurrying along, he got to thinking as to why so many of the trees were hell bent on feeding off animals, and the only conclusion he could come to was that this place was short of 'fixed' nitrogen, and this was the only way a plant could get a good supply, by taking it from something that had already obtained it.

When Kal reached the rocks, he was tired and thirsty, and set about finding a comfortable recess in which to spend the night. A good scraping of the Finger Nut washed down with the slightly sweet perfumed water of the bamboo pole and he felt a lot better.

As Kal lay in his rocky niche, he wished that he had had the foresight to have gathered up a quantity of gross on which to sleep, as it would have been a little more comfortable than the unyielding rock.

The sun finally sank below the horizon and the stars came out like twinkling jewels in a black velvet sky. He looked at them for some time, and was surprised to see so many of them were coloured.

Or was it a trick of the atmosphere? Finally he drifted into a dreamless sleep, and the night and its strange happenings passed him by, silently, as far as he was concerned.

Again, dawn was a beautiful sight, and stretching his somewhat stiff limbs he suddenly froze. A clatter of falling stones echoed around the rock pile, something was out there, and of a respectable size to have caused such a noise.

He was armed with his pole with the sharpened end, and another one with the tooth, but that would be little defence against a large animal, and he felt that something big and hungry was out there, looking for breakfast.

Kal thought that being on top of a large rock might be the best place to ward off an attack, but then he would be in full view and advertising his presence by so doing.

'So, what to do?' The decision was taken from him as he caught a fleeting glimpse of a large cat like animal disappearing into the loose rock formation below him. All he could see was the large general shape and a purposeful flowing movement as it slipped from view.

Kal lay motionless for some time, just to make sure that it had gone about its business and left the area. His breakfast was boring but nutritious, and he was surprised that he got so much energy from so little food, but that was just as well in the circumstances.

He must try again to find something else to add to his larder, if only to make sure that his diet was in balance.

The first thing he wanted to do was to reach a high point in the rocks to see if they went on forever, or if there was a return to an area of vegetation beyond them.

The track still made its way through the rocks and was reasonably straight, with odd large stones strewn about here and there. Eventually Kal came to an area where the track did disappear; his way was blocked by an upsurge of what looked as though it had been molten magma in the past.

Great pillows of fused rock were piled high one upon the other in all directions. There was nothing for it but to climb to the top, and see what lay beyond. He toyed with the idea of leaving his supplies at the base of the rocks, returning for them later if the way through was possible, but then realized that to do so would take a long time and much effort, so he collected up his belongings, and began the ascent.

The climb up was not as hard as he had expected, and soon he was able to see over the top and into the next section.

The region ahead was much the same as the one he had left, except that the high cliffs each side of the reappearing track were almost sheer, and would be impossible to climb if he should need to for any reason.

There was nothing to do but go on, as there were surely more things to discover, and returning to the forest he had left would be of little gain to him.

He made his way down the huge lava pile, and out onto the old track again. The cliffs around him seemed to be getting higher and were now almost vertical. He walked on for what he thought was about a kilometre when he noticed that it was getting slightly darker, and the pathway was now only half the width it had been at the start.

Within a short distance he suddenly realized that the rock lined track was only just wide enough for him to get through, and the light had almost disappeared leaving a menacing gloom. He had never suffered from claustrophobia, but was beginning to get an idea of what it must be like.

A flash of panic brought a rush of adrenaline to his system, and his head swam for a moment or two. Kal sat down to try and reason out if it was worth going on, or should he settle for that which he knew back in the forest, which now seemed to be almost friendly in comparison.

He decided to go on, and try to reach whatever lay at the end of the rift in the cliffs, if his nerve held out. He must have stopped at the midpoint of the narrowing section of the gorge, as the track soon began to widen and light flooded in to dispel the closed in effect.

An hour or two later Kal reached the end of the gorge-like valley, and saw before him a plain covered in areas of vegetation interspersed with sandy patches and the odd few rocky formations. With a sigh of relief, he trotted down the slope from the cliff gorge, and out onto the plain below.

The first thing to do was to restock with water poles and Finger Nuts, if any could be found. He needn't have worried, they were here in abundance, and he quickly set about collecting all that he required.

One or two new 'trees' were to be found on the plain, but nothing that looked as if it would provide a meal except for the round white balls he had seen in the forest yesterday, or was it the day before?

The white ball he had previously jammed into his bundle of water poles had long gone, so he picked up one of the smaller ones at his feet and split it open.

The same testing technique as before was applied, a rub on the lower lip brought no stinging sensation or swelling, and a small piece of the material placed under the tongue was similarly unspectacular in its reaction.

Did he dare try actually eating it? Kal made his way into a nearby collection of rocks so that he could hide away from anything that might take a fancy to him, and bit a piece of the white ball off, and chewed it.

It tasted quite good, and he took another bite. The texture was a bit like soft rubber, but it crumbled down after a bit of chewing and certainly made his saliva glands work. It was then that he remembered where he had seen something similar, the Puff Ball, which seemed to turn up under different guises just about everywhere.

Kal swallowed the pulp and finished off the rest of the Puff Ball, quite confident that it wouldn't harm him.

The track he had been following for so long seemed to end where the plains began, the only sign of it was at the entrance to the valley gorge.

There was something about that track which still worried Kal, but he couldn't think what it was. Pleased that he had now supplemented his diet with a new food, he felt keener to look for more. The criteria for so doing seemed to be choosing a drab or dull colour with an unattractive shape, as all the appealing looking fruits had proved disastrous.

This area of the planet didn't have as many of the attacking type plants as he had previously experienced, and Kal felt more at ease walking among the trees and bushes.

He was a little wary of the bare sandy patches and gave a few of them a poke with his pole. Nothing happened, but he didn't try walking on them.

'No point in looking for trouble,' he mused, 'if there's something life-threatening in the sand, it will show up sooner or later, hopefully at something else's expense'.

Being too careful would preclude him from many valuable experiences, so he was tempted when he saw a bush like plant bearing egg sized pale grey oval berries.

They were quite firm, and removing the stones he had earlier placed inside his tunic top, he replaced them with a dozen or so of the berries. These could be tried when he next settled down for the night and was safely ensconced in a rock pile. Things were getting relatively better, and he felt quite a bounce in his step as he went along.

As there was no path to follow or guide him, Kal just wandered about, taking in the sights and what few sounds there were.

'Funny that, very little in the way of sounds' he thought. 'Maybe things livened up a bit at night', but then he was usually asleep. There were very few insects, at least as he knew them. One or two little crawly things on some of the plants, and a worm-like creature that kept its head above the ground until he was a foot step away, and then disappeared.

He dug down on one occasion just to get a better look at it, but it must have retreated to some considerable depth, as he couldn't find it, and gave up.

Enjoyable as this meandering around was, Kal thought he should proceed in a relatively straight line so as to experience as much diversity as possible, for that was the only way he would learn about what to do, and what not to do, when he came up against forces greater than himself. He was mainly thinking of the large animal he had caught a glimpse of this morning and any similar cousins it might have.

The terrain he was now on undulated slightly, and apart from the rocky outcrops that dotted the landscape and the odd tree or bush which was different to those he had already found, it was much of a muchness for many kilometres.

One place interested him though; it was a long gully which suggested that it had been formed by running water, although no water was present at the moment.

Kal climbed down into it and dug around at the bottom just to see if a trace of water remained, but it was as dry as the ground above. He concluded that it must have been formed a long time ago, probably by a flash flood or particularly heavy rain.

Once more, the light was failing, and Kal began looking for a place to spend the night.

Without the rocks for protection, he didn't think he would have lasted very long, and that was a worrying thought as it would prevent him from going into any area where there was nowhere to hide. Some other means of protection would be needed to go into such places.

The Finger Nut flakes and a Puff Ball filled him up, and after they had been washed down with a drink of water, he decided to try the grey berries.

Removing them from his tunic, he tried to break the skin open with his fingernail, but it was too tough. The Jaw Saw did the trick. The little berry split open and exposed the pale grey flesh inside.

He put a drop of the juice on his lip, but somehow knew that it was safe to eat. Rigorous training at the academy had instilled a degree of discipline in him that overrode even his hunches, so he went through the whole testing rigmarole anyway. If he got sick, he would be at the mercy of anything which might come along.

The berry proved to be quite acceptable, and had a delicious sweet spicy flavour, and made a very good finish to end off the meal with.

The rocks Kal had chosen to use for the night had a copious supply of large stones, which he was able to lift or move and so was able to construct a shelter of sorts, utilizing a shallow cave like depression in one of the larger rocks.

He felt much better having done this, as it afforded a small degree of protection from anything large and hungry which might roam the dark hours.

The entrance to his abode had one of his poles across it, such that if it was dislodged, it would in turn release some small stones he had piled around its end, and so awaken him, he hoped.

The night passed uneventfully, at least as far as he was concerned. The pole was still in place along with the little pile of warning stones, and Kal got breakfast underway.

It was while he was chewing his way through one of the Puff Balls, that he remembered the ration concentrates he still carried. They would need dissolving in water but he didn't have a receptacle for this, and resolved to try and find something suitable.

There may well be some fruit that had a tough outer skin which he could dry, and so make a useful drinking vessel.

The hunt for a gourd-like object was not as easy as he had thought. Several 'fruits' looked promising, but all were brightly coloured, and he knew that they would contain one or more harmful substances, probably concentrated in the skin, knowing his luck.

A new stock of Puff Balls were gathered and stored in his tunic, but of the new grey berries he found none. About midday he found what he had been looking for on a tall spindly tree.

It was right at the top and well out of his reach even with his two poles tied together. Try as he might, the tree would not bend, and this left Kal with a degree of frustration he had not known for a while.

He ate his midday meal while pondering the problem. He had tried the Jaw Saw, but it made no impression on the trunk, and that was when he noticed how the uncooperative plant had achieved its armoured trunk.

The tree had exuded a form of resin from closely spaced vertical pores, and the resin had hardened in the sun or by exposure to the air. It was like glue by the way it stuck to the trunk, and try as he might, he could not even chip it off with a stone.

And then he had a flash of inspiration. He could use his belt as a sling shot. Collecting a good supply of stones, he stood back and took aim. The first few shots were well wide of the mark, and he realized this was not going to be so easy after all.

With patience running dangerously low, a few shots were reaching their target, and finally he hit the 'fruit' on the tree top squarely on.

There was a sharp crack, and it fell to the ground. When Kal retrieved the fruit, he noticed a sticky substance on the end of the stem, and experienced the second inspirational flash of the day.

It was the 'glue' the tree had used to cover its trunk with. Quickly he picked up his pole with the tooth on it, and applied the few drops of the glue like juice to the blade.

When this had hardened, it would take a lot of punishment to dislodge the razor sharp tip from the shaft of the spear.

Kal jammed his prize firmly between two handy rocks, and proceeded to apply the Jaw Saw to it. Fortunately, the fruit was not as hard as the trunk, as yet.

The top quarter of the fruit came away exposing a densely packed fibrous centre, and he could not believe his luck at how easy it was to scrape the fibres out. Kal now had a cup, and a good sized one at that. He washed it out just to be sure, although the fibres from the fruit when pressed to his lip had not rung any alarm bells.

Feeling very pleased with his days work, he took it easy, just wandering around and looking for anything new and useful, and the new grey berries.

Considering the way the gross was cropped, something must be doing it, and a lot of something's at that. Kal was determined to find out what was responsible, and he decided to try and keep awake for as long as possible that night.

The trees and bushes must shed their fruiting bodies, yet there was no sign of them on the ground, so something was taking care of that too.

How to keep awake was the problem, as he had easily fallen asleep as soon as he had eaten and the light level dropped. Perhaps that was it, don't eat until later. He now had his cup, and could prepare his food for later consumption. It was worth a try.

The rest of the day he spent pottering about near his chosen rock pile, looking for new growths but finding nothing of any great interest. The 'glue' on his spear had hardened, and there was no way the tooth was going to come out now.

He thought one more bamboo pole may well come in useful, and set about looking for a clump.

He would keep an eye out for another 'jaw' as the teeth could be used to make a few spare spears, which no doubt would be needed in the future. The big cat-like thing was still at the back of his mind, and every now and again, came to the front. He would be prepared.

Another thing he was going to need sometime was clothing. He was used to it, and did not think he would feel right running about stark naked while trying to fend off wild animals.

A plant that produced a fibre must be sought, the spinning and weaving was only a mechanical skill, and could be developed in time.

He would also need some kind of footwear, as he was sure he hadn't seen the last of those nasty little plants which had poisonous spikes just level with the ground, and who could say what lay just beneath the surface.

The sun was sinking, and night would not be long in coming to this land, and he was going to be ready for whatever it held. He hoped he was not going to get too great a shock.

Living in innocence was all right up to a point, but here he needed every bit of information that was available to enhance his survival status. Time to prepare the food for later and so Kal retreated to his rock house for the night and began his vigil to see what ate what in the darkness.

The sun did its usual dip towards the skyline, the shadows grew longer and denser and Kal got ready for his night vigil.

Like a flickering candle, the orb lit up the horizon in a multitude of beautiful colours, flickered once too often, and was gone.

Darkness raced across the land like a black velvet cape and the stars came out to prove that the universe had not changed very much from last night.

Kal could see outline detail of the area around him, and knew that with time his eyes would get accustomed to the lower light level, and more detail would then be visible.

He waited for something to happen, and it didn't. He felt tempted to tuck into his delayed evening meal, but knew that he would feel sleepy afterwards, and so waited.

Slowly his eyes were picking out more and more detail and he thought he saw movement by one of the trees. It must have been wishful thinking on his part, for it didn't happen again and the stillness enveloped everything like a gentle thick woolly mist.

He must have dozed off, for he awoke with a start to the shriek of something being taken apart by something a little bigger, or equipped with larger teeth. Kal strained his eyes into the darkness, but could see nothing moving.

Some while later one of the planets belonging to the same system, cast a little reflected light on the surroundings. Not much, but it did make a difference. Just below him, where the gross began at the foot of the rock pile, there was movement.

Dozens, no hundreds of little grazers were munching away at the gross. They were everywhere. A chorus of faint chomping noises drifted up to him and he knew he was going to be in for an entertaining night.

Suddenly there was a little muffled shriek, as though that which had made it was being drawn into a hole, to be followed by a whole series of them.

There was a lot of scampering about, and then complete silence. After a few minutes the chomping started up again, and Kal could see the little grazers had returned to their nights work. The chomping, shrieks and silence cycle continued well into the night.

There must have been a vast number of 'chompers' to sustain the losses, and an equally large number of 'eaters', or perhaps there were only a few 'eaters', and they were very hungry indeed.

There was the occasional thud, which Kal supposed was a fruit falling to the ground, but he could not tell in this dim light. He didn't doubt that by morning, nothing would be left of this night's feast, and he was right.

The rustling of tiny feet and the chomping stopped, but there was no shriek preceding the stoppage. Something new was afoot, and Kal waited with baited breath, as no doubt, did the little creatures below him.

Faintly, but getting louder by the moment, there was the soft pad, pad, pad of feet. Whatever was making the sound was of a good weight, and the time between each 'pad' indicated to Kal that the creature was fairly large.

A short yelp of pain rent the night air, followed by the crunching of bones and a smacking of lips. Then silence, except for the padding and another yelp.

This went on for several minutes, and then the padding sound grew fainter as the creature making it moved away. Shortly afterwards the scampering and chomping hurriedly started up again, as if to make up for lost time.

Later, Kal was to find out that the little grazers froze when threatened, and the 'eater' just walked among the paralysed bodies, picking out the plumpest until it had had its fill.

He thought it was about time to eat, as nothing new was happening, and having taken his fill in the dark, lay back in his little stone house with its booby trapped entrance and fell asleep. The stars circled around above his head, the grazers went back to where ever grazers go during the day and the dawn broke to show a tranquil and undisturbed scene.

Having eaten, and armed himself well, Kal set out to find any trace of last night's carnage. Not a sign of it remained. There were no tracks or marks where the grazers had been, no faeces from the 'Pad Pad', no holes in the ground to show where the subterranean consumers of grazes were hidden.

In fact, nothing to show of any activity, except that the gross was only a little shorter than the night before, despite all the commotion in the dark hours.

Kal was not going to be put off that easily, and began prodding the ground with his pointed stick. He had covered quite a large area before he got a result, and didn't much like it when he did. The stick dropped about half a metre into the ground and he nearly fell over.

This was accompanied by a slight heave in the surrounding surface, and a jerk on his stick as something recoiled in pain.

He pulled it out, and found it covered in a noxious liquid that smelt as though it had come straight from hell, and had taken no corners on the way. The end of the stick had been attacked by the fluid, and had lost its sharp point.

Kal had no compunctions about giving the underground 'thing' a good poking just to see what size it was, and wished he hadn't.

The pole was slowly getting shorter, but he managed to determine the size and approximate shape of the creature.

It was pear shaped, with the narrow end just below the surface of the ground, and the body a good metre in diameter.

The top of the neck sported a sphincter on which it had persuaded the gross to grow, so the camouflage was complete, and that was why he had never noticed it before.

Kal supposed that it was dormant during the day and that was why it hadn't tried to take his foot off, as he must have trodden on several during his travels.

As there was little more to do here, Kal noted where the sun was and set the course for this day's journey of exploration.

The night before had given him plenty to think about as he wended his way between the trees and out onto the clearer ground ahead.

Kal only walked on the gross, or a stony track, as anything else may well have hidden dangers.

A couple of hours into the morning's walk, and the ground began to rise a little. There were definite signs of water runoff here, and he was glad of that as it meant he would not be so dependent on the water sticks, which he still carried.

Ahead he could see a cliff-like formation with clumps of rocks breaking up the otherwise smooth landscape. The rocks looked a little different somehow and he went over to one formation to see why.

They rose about thirty metres above him, and the only way to see anything other than the outer ring of rocks was to climb up, which he did.

He was surprised to see a large pool of crystal clear water, and he could see right down to the very bottom of it. The water was a lot deeper than he first thought, and he wondered what dangers it might contain.

This much water and nothing using it as bait? Hard to believe. Very cautiously he reached down and scooped up a cupped handful of water. A drop on the lip, and he knew it was good. Kal drank his fill and wondered about having a swim to clean up and refresh himself a little.

That might be a little too risky, as he didn't know what might be concealed and looking like a rock. He was getting cannier as time went by, or was it just good old plain suspicion?

Kal climbed a little higher to check out the view, and thought that the ridge of cliffs, which he could now see more clearly, might be worth a visit later on.

It was very pleasant up here on the rocks, and he lay down in the warming sun for a while, and dozed off. Kal awakened to the sound of a stone rattling down the rock face below, and he froze. Movement gives most things away; it was quite surprising what would miss you, if you kept still.

Very carefully he rolled himself towards the edge of the rock, and slowly moved forward to peer over the edge. He could not believe what he saw.

In a group at the pool there were six little people drinking the water, with two more armed with sticks looking back down the rock face, probably in the direction from which they had come.

THREE:
The Tribe

It was difficult to judge height accurately from up here, but Kal estimated that they were only one third of his height at the most. They were naked as the day they were born, and covered with a deep honey coloured skin and a fine hair or down of the same hue.

High pitched squeaks and whistles drifted up to him, and he supposed they were conversing with each other.

Kal was tempted to make himself known to them, but for all he knew there might have been a hundred of them just around the corner, and they might have been hostile.

As discretion was always the better part of valour, he decided to follow the little people to see where they went, and find out just how many of them there were, before making any advances.

The drinking party had finished, and two of them took the sticks from the guards, and took up their position at the rocks edge, while the previous guards went to drink.

'That proves a reasonable degree of intelligence' Kal thought and felt a bit easier at once. The little troop climbed down from the rocks, one by one, and onto a rough path which Kal hadn't noticed before, a guard leading and one following, each armed with a stick. They too, were taking no chances.

Kal followed at a discreet distance, not wishing to show himself until he had learned a little more about his new discoveries. They may well turn out to be friendly, and he would then possibly have a few companions, although they didn't look very human to him. Perhaps less distance between them might prove otherwise.

Following the little troupe was made easier when they approached the cliff, as there were plenty of rocks about the place for Kal to hide behind, while he observed them.

As he got closer to the cliffs himself, he was in for another surprise. There were about one hundred and fifty of them. The water party was greeted with hoots and whistles and seemingly made very welcome.

Now that the cliffs were a bit closer, he could see that the little people had been busy constructing a wall of stones around a dark opening in the cliff face.

He assumed the opening was a cave, and this was their home. The wall was well put together, with an opening in it for the people to come and go.

They probably had some means of closing the entrance at night, to keep out unwanted guests. That would prove a higher degree of intelligence, hopefully.

He kept them under observation for the rest of the day, and retired to the big rock formation for the coming night.

Kal would still keep to his stone house with its alarm system of pole and stones until he was sure of the kind of reception he would get from his hoped for new companions.

He finished his meal, watched the sun go through its usual colourful ritual, and fell asleep. That night he dreamt peacefully for the first time, although he couldn't remember what it was about next morning.

The little people were up and about just as early as he was, and although his camp was high up in the rocks, he tidied away any sign of his being there except for his stone house. Let them make of that what they will, if they found it.

Shortly after sunrise a large troupe of them came to the watering place. Several guards with sticks went before the main group and some brought up the rear, in all it must have amounted to at least half the tribe.

Kal watched as they all had a drink and walked around the area of the pool, but none of them bathed. Perhaps they didn't wash, or didn't want to pollute their drinking water.

Later, when the troupe had returned to their cliff-side site, the others made their way to the pool. They seemed very orderly, with no rushing about as one would expect with animals, no playing or fighting.

Maybe they were somewhere between animal and humanoid. There was something about them that did not seem quite right.

When the little people had all returned to their site, Kal moved in closer to observe them. The rocks gave good cover, and he was able to get quite close to the stone wall they had built. They did not seem to have any tools or utensils of any kind, not even a drinking cup like his.

They just sat around in little groups, or walked about talking in their squeaks and whistles, the groups breaking up sometimes and reforming with different members.

Kal didn't want them to see him until he was good and ready, with a strategy of safe contact worked out. Although they were so much smaller than he, and didn't look aggressive or even very strong, enough of them armed with sticks could do him some serious damage, and that was chance he could not take.

This of course, limited the risks he could take in getting close to them. A small party of them suddenly appeared out of nowhere and entered the enclosure. They had been out gathering food by the look of it, as they were in twos, one on each end of a long bamboo pole from which hung clumps of fruit of a kind he had not seen before.

The usual guards with sticks accompanied the little group, and they were greeted with a chorus of squeaks and whistles as they entered the hole in their protective wall.

Kal thought a gift for the little people might be a good idea. They would then know that there was someone else out there, who didn't mean them any harm.

Later that day he left the pool rocks and made his way down to the area where he had seen several bamboo clumps.

The dead poles still had a growing point on them and after snapping several of them off, it did not take much effort to work up a good sharp point using a rough textured stone.

He then made his way back to his side of the rock formation, and climbed up to his stone house which was well out of sight of his neighbours.

Waiting for darkness to fall took forever, but he used the time well by working out a safe route from his position to their wall entrance.

Not only must he not be detected, but neither must he provide a meal for anything on the way. Kal prepared his evening meal in his cup, to which he had added two more cups that afternoon.

Things were getting a bit more civilized. At long last the sun dipped below the horizon with its customary scintillating display, the stars began their dance across the heavens, and Kal set out on his gift bearing journey.

Reaching the wall was no problem, but a guard had been posted near the hole in the compound wall. Kal wanted to place the bamboo poles at the entrance to make the point that he could get there undetected, and was pleased to leave a gift at the same time.

He took a chance, and picking up a small stone, took careful aim and sent it on its way to a point further along the wall. It had the right effect. The guard made a couple of low whistles to summon up help, and went to investigate the place where the stone had landed.

Quickly Kal slipped up to the entrance, placed his bundle of poles across it, and retired into the darkness.

He didn't think his gifts would be discovered until daylight so he retired for the rest of night, and he was right. Kal was up early next morning, ready and waiting.

The water party had just made it to the entrance when the poles were seen by the leading guard. They stopped, and a chorus of squeaks pierced the morning air. They approached the bundle cautiously, and there was much squeaking and waving of arms.

The fear they had shown was soon replaced by wonderment as they realized what had been done, and a few of them climbed up onto the wall to look around in all directions to see if the gift bearer was still in the vicinity.

The bundle of poles was distributed among the larger members of the group, and they ran around jabbing at imaginary foes, much to the delight of the others.

They caught on quickly Kal was pleased to see, and he thought a gift of cups may go down well. If they could figure out how to use them, then he would know that they really did have a level of intelligence that could be contacted.

He wondered why they had not armed themselves with the bamboo poles before, and then realized that they were probably not heavy or strong enough to break even the dead bamboos out of the clump.

Later that day, while he was hiding behind a rock observing the compound, he had a chance to see some of the little people at close hand.

A party of four were engaged on clearing stones from the path that led from the compound to the pool rocks, and a guard armed with one of the new bamboo poles was standing on the highest point of the wall overlooking the area.

One had a stick with which it prised up the stones that were making the path uneven, while another scraped the surrounding ground for loose sand and gravel to fill the hole left by the stone, and trampled it flat.

The third was placing the stones neatly alongside the edge of the path, so making the path more distinct. The fourth member of the party was keeping a general lookout for anything untoward that might appear. All in all, well organized, Kal thought.

As the little group worked their way nearer to Kal's hiding place, he was able to get a much closer look at them. They were definitely humanoid in having a head, two arms, hands with three fingers and an opposing thumb, a trunk and two legs complete with feet.

There was little or no head hair as he had, but the whole of their bodies were covered in a short dark honey coloured fine hair the same colour as their skin.

Facial features were a little strange, but they did have two eyes, a stumpy nose, a mouth slit as opposed to a full set of lips, ears that were more like holes with a fringe of skin around them, and a neck that was only just discernible where the head joined the main body.

They were not ugly or pretty, just different, and he was getting used to the idea of them as fellow beings. They were the only beings around, so he had little choice really.

Their bodies were well proportioned, and moved with ease. There were no signs of genitals or mammary glands, so determining their sex was not possible, at least not yet.

If the sexes were mixed, there was no clue as to which was which. Their speech was at such a high frequency that Kal could only hear it as the squeaks and whistles that had been going on ever since he had first seen them, so conversation between them was going to be a bit of a problem.

The little work party had now moved past Kal's vantage point, and he carefully retreated to the pool rocks.

The afternoon was spent in making some more cups, and at the same time using the 'glue' from the base of the pod stem to glue a few 'blade teeth' he had found into short pieces of bamboo, making a kind of knife.

He hoped they would figure out how to use a blade before they amputated their fingers, especially as they had one less on each hand than he did.

A few bamboo spears were added to the collection, and he was ready for another visit to the compound that night to deliver his gifts, and after that, perhaps he could take a chance, and make contact.

Early that night it rained for the first time and Kal quickly took off his clothes and tucked them under a ledge so that they would remain dry as he got wet.

The rain was warm and he felt refreshed afterwards, as this was his first all over wash since arriving, and he needed it. Just before dawn he crept down to the compound, and left his gifts outside the entrance.

Kal had his breakfast just as the sun began to light up the clouds on the horizon, and then made his way over to the view point to see what would happen when his neighbours discovered what he had left for them.

He didn't have long to wait. It was almost as if they had anticipated the gifts, for they came running over to the opening in the wall and gathered around the collection, showing no fear at all.

The gifts were passed around for all to see and touch and he thought that just about the whole tribe had gathered by the time the excitement had died down.

Shortly afterwards a small party of the little people left the compound, and began searching the immediate area, possibly looking for clues as to their benefactors whereabouts.

Kal felt pleased that a form of contact had been successfully made, and that the little people now knew that there was someone else around who posed no threat to them.

Feeling drawn to the next best thing to human company that this planet had to offer was a strong reason for not continuing his exploration, but he knew that he needed all the information he could get in order to increase his survival potential.

Who knows what lay just around the corner, so to speak. There may be other tribes, more advanced, maybe a whole civilization complete with space travel.

Somehow he didn't think so, it didn't feel as though there was anything more advanced than the little people, it was just a hunch, but his hunches were usually right.

Kal decided to press on a little further in the same direction as he had been going, and if nothing of value was found, then he could always return, and establish contact.

Collecting up his armoury and provisions, he set out early next morning, before the others were up and about. By midday he had left behind the pleasant rolling plains of gross, dotted about with their various trees and bushes, and arrived at an area of desert.

It was a clean cut break from one kind of country to another, with no gradation in between. Rolling sand dunes swept out to the horizon in all directions, and just to make sure there was nothing out there for him to visit, he returned to the nearest rock formation to gain a better view.

By the time Kal had reached the top of the outcrop he was feeling very tired. The climb had been a lot higher and harder than he had anticipated, but the view was worth it.

He was right about the desert, it was never ending as far as he was concerned, and he then remembered seeing huge areas of this world covered in sand when coming in to land.

There had also been great oceans of water, and he now recalled that the vegetation covered portions of the planet were not very large in comparison to the desert and water covered areas.

There was no point in going into the desert, and the only item of interest he could see was a range of high hills or mountains, over to his left.

They seemed quite a fair distance away, and he wondered if it was worth the bother of paying them a visit. But then if he didn't, he would never know what was there.

With that bit of philosophizing out of the way, he set out to satisfy his curiosity once and for all. As long as he kept to the fringe of the desert area, he could always obtain his provisions, although he knew that he must keep an eye out for changes in the vegetation, in case his food trees did not extend into this region.

The going was smooth and easy here on the fringe, and he only had to watch out on one side for unwelcome attention, as he felt sure that the desert didn't support much life.

It took several days of constant walking to get anywhere near the black mountains he had seen earlier, and as the land was beginning to undulate, the goal kept disappearing from view. He pressed on, and was rewarded for so doing by coming to the first running water he had yet seen. It was a small stream, a mere two metres wide and not very deep.

'The source of this water would be a good place to visit' was his first thought, and as he didn't come up with anything better to do, he set off to follow the bank of the stream, first placing a marker pole in case he returned this way.

The water was as clear as crystal, tasted good and as well as having no fish in it, was completely devoid of all life as far as he could tell, which seemed strange.

Running in an almost straight line with a bed of gravel and the banks covered in gross, it made travelling a pleasure.

The land here had flattened out, and the black stone of the mountain range was beginning to get closer.

It was not long before Kal came to great blocks of black stone. They were scattered about in random fashion to begin with, but soon there was little space between the blocks, and to continue he had to walk in the bed of the stream.

Ahead, he could see that the stream had disappeared into the mountain proper through a cave-like entrance.

Approaching the opening he was surprised to see there was a ledge of cut stone blocks, about two metres wide running along beside the water, right into the tunnel.

This was too perfect to have been the random work of nature, and certainly not the efforts of the little people. So who had done this? He left the stream bed, and continued walking along the stone block path beside it as he entered the black mountain.

In time, the light would not be sufficient to enable him to go forward safely, so he was surprised to find that the light level didn't alter very much, even when he was a few hundred metres into the tunnel.

The walls seemed to give out their own light, just a gentle glow, but enough for him to see to travel safely along the ledge. A gentle breeze blew towards him, cool and soft and with a fresh smell to it, not the sort of thing one would associate with a damp cave.

It was nearly half a kilometre later when Kal came to the cave. It was colossal, the sides curving away on either side, and the roof nowhere in sight. Hanging down from a ceiling he could not see, were huge crystals, water dripping off them onto the floor of the cave and then running in grooves cut in the floor to join the stream.

Kal continued to walk across the grooved floor of the cavern for a while, and was about to give up and return to the entrance, when up ahead he could see several huge black pillars reaching up into the domed vault above.

As they were not the same as the crystals in shape or colour, he assumed their function would be different, and that awakened his interest.

They were six or so metres wide, triangular in section, and the tops of them disappeared into the gloom above.

There seemed to be a pattern in their layout, and then he realized what they were, as the breeze he had felt earlier grew stronger. These were giant baffles to direct the breeze, or was it wind? For it got stronger as he approached.

Passing through the pillar baffles, ahead he could see the black opening of another huge tunnel, and a gale of wind was issuing from it.

Kal was intrigued, and would have liked to go down the new tunnel, but apart from being pitch black, the wind was too strong and nearly blew him over, and as yet he was nowhere near the actual entrance.

It took a while, but he had it figured out in the end. Somehow a moisture laden wind was forced into the tunnel ahead and came out into the cave, hit the triangular pillar baffles and was deflected around the cave.

Something must have drawn it upwards, because it was only a very gentle breeze in the stream tunnel. The moisture, for some reason, condensed on the huge crystals and dripped onto the floor, where it was directed to the stream and flowed on to the world outside.

It was one hell of a construction just to make a little stream of water, which didn't seem to go anywhere, or did it? That he would have to find out.

There was little else to do now, except marvel at the size of the structure, admire the beauty of the crystals hanging from the roof and have another drink of water. Having done that, Kal followed the stone ledge beside the stream back to the outside world.

He would like to have known where the stream led, as this might give him a clue as to its purpose, if any remained.

And so, with this in mind, he started his journey back down the stream bed and out onto the plains.

As he passed the point where he had first come across the stream, he moved the marker stake to the bank on the other side to remind him which way to go should he wish to return.

He was soon back into familiar country, with the odd rock clump here and there, and the ground gently undulating. The stream carried on, and sometimes the banks were very steep, as the ground rose and fell around the flowing water.

It was several days later when he came to the disappointing part of the trek, the stream disappeared down a large hole in the ground, and was no more.

Kal thought the only sensible thing to do was to follow the stream back to his marker, track along the edge of the desert and then make his way back to the cliffs and the tribe of little people.

He then realized he was not sure where to turn right from the desert's edge to find the cliffs, as he hadn't had the foresight to leave a marker at that point.

It was while he was pondering what to do next that he had another surprise. Up ahead there were three of the diminutive little people. He took cover behind some rocks at once, but needn't have done so, as they promptly turned, and were heading away from him.

'So there are more groups of the little people about on this world' Kal said to himself, and decided to follow them at a safe distance to see if their settlement was any different to the one he had seen by the pool rocks.

They had been out gathering by the look of it, as one had a big stick and the other two had their tiny arms full of something, but Kal couldn't see what.

They must have been the brave ones in the group, as it was some time later that they joined up with another small party, and they all headed off at high speed together.

He followed them at a safe distance for some time, and as he came around the edge of a large rocky outcrop, there were the pool rocks just ahead. He must have gone around in a huge circle, and spent days at it into the bargain. After the first fleeting feeling of anger for not realizing what he had done, he gave a little chuckle, and headed for home.

It was very pleasant to be back in familiar territory, and having regained the security of his rock cave above the pool, he settled down to get the evening meal ready. Looking back on the last few days, they hadn't been a waste of time after all, as he had found out a little more about this world, albeit not all of it was understood, but it was a little more data to fit into the overall picture.

First thing next morning, Kal set off to replenish his stores of food, and collect a few more items to make into gifts for the tribe. He wondered if they had any idea where the gifts were coming from, or how they explained it to one another.

It would have been interesting to overhear, if he could have understood their language.

Towards evening events took a turn to change the relationship of Kal and the little people for good. He had been out on one last trip to the bamboo clumps to obtain material for spear making, when he heard a commotion just ahead of him. Frantic squeals and whistles indicated trouble for someone.

Kal sprinted towards the sounds of panic, and rounding a corner was confronted by three of the little people and a cat-like beast which he had caught a glimpse of some time ago.

They were in a small dead end gully, with one of the little ones lying on the ground and badly mauled, the other two were frantically trying to beat the cat thing with a stick and one of Kal's spears.

The creature was nearly two metres long and must have seemed a giant to them, with its massive head and body supported by six legs and a long tail for balance.

Later, Kal found that only four of the legs actually worked as such, the two front ones were more like arms with two retractable claws for holding its prey, and slash attacking.

Fortunately he had his blade spear with him, and he rushed forward to drive it straight into the cat's mouth as it reared up at him.

As quickly as he lunged forward with the spear, he retracted it and dealt a blow to its snout. The cat creature screamed in pain and reared higher this time, and as it went up Kal drove the spear into where he thought the cat's heart would be.

The blade was very sharp and sank in deeply. Just as quickly Kal pulled it out again, and as the cat lowered its head to look down at whatever had caused so much pain, he put all his weight behind the thrust that sent the quivering spear into the cat's eye, and as it later turned out, it's brain.

That final blow must have been a mortal one, for the cat's screech faded as its huge body fell to the ground and lay there quivering and twitching in its post death throes.

The two little people stood transfixed in shock, as much at the death of the cat creature as at the giant person who had come to their rescue, while their companion lay in a jumbled heap just behind the still quivering cat.

Kal was shaking too, and stood still so as not to add more fear of the unpredictable to the state of the other two.

The wounded one was in a very bad way indeed, and needed medical attention at once, so Kal gently picked him up in his arms and looked towards the compound. The other two caught on at once and shakily tried to run on ahead to tell the others.

As they approached the wall, a small group of the little people came out and crowded around the party, leaving a respectable three metres or so of space between them.

He continued to walk on and into their compound, stopping just in front of the cave entrance. Eager little hands reached out for their battered companion, and Kal gently lowered him to the ground.

One of Kal's cups filled with water was brought to the wounded one, and Kal took it, trying to get a little of the fluid between the thin lips. The little one coughed and then swallowed a little of the water, opening his eyes wide in fright at the sight of the giant before him, and passed out.

Kal took a piece of cloth from his pocket, and dipping it into the remaining water, tried to wash away some of the brown fluid that covered the casualty.

The wounds were not as bad as they had at first looked, and had stopped bleeding. It just remained for Kal to clean him up, and then he didn't look too bad.

Kal stood back as the little one sat up, which brought a gasp from the others. Maybe they would have given him up for dead and the giant had brought him back to life.

'This is how legends start' Kal thought.

Soon the wounded one was back on his feet, although a little shaky, and joined his two companions in a chorus of whistles and squeaks, telling the tale, no doubt, of the brave giant who fearlessly came to their rescue.

Kal was not too sure just what to do now, so he slowly backed away, and the little crowd opened up to allow him to reach the opening in the wall and go down the slope towards the pool rocks. He looked back several times, but the little people didn't make any attempt to follow him, so he considered it best to retire to his cave.

On the way, he thought he might drag the cat creature up into the rocks so that it would not be scavenged over night, and with a bit of a struggle did manage to get it into a gap between two large rocks, and then covered it up with some flat pieces of stone that were to hand.

A well earned supper went down well, but he still felt a bit shaky, as his over tired body begged for sleep, and he then decided he had done enough for one day.

Contact of a sort had now been made, although it was not quite what Kal had in mind. He wondered how they would react to him when they next met, and tried to work out a scenario that would benefit all and dispel any possible magic element that the event might have brought about.

The morning was bright and clear, as were all mornings so far, and last evening's drama seemed long ago and somehow in a different place.

Kal went down the rock path to see if the cat had survived the ravages of the night scroungers, when at the bottom he discovered a little pile of gifts.

Several coloured fruits, a small collection of coloured stones which may have been precious or semiprecious, but in their uncut state he couldn't tell which, and what looked like a little bundle of dried meat strips, or they could have been leather.

No way was he going to touch the fruit, the colours were too bright and that meant he would react to their toxins. The coloured stones were very pretty, but that was all.

Kal felt cross with himself for his ungracious thoughts, and for not accepting the gifts in the manner in which they had been given. No doubt, to the little people, they were highly prized, and he didn't think that they had very much else to give anyway.

He collected up the offerings and took them up to his stone house. He didn't want to appear ungrateful, and who knows, he may need their help one day.

He was a little undecided as to whether he should go and visit his new friends or wait for them to come to him. Either way, contact had been established and they both knew about the existence of the other now.

Kal made his way down to the dead cat again and found that covering it up had saved it from the worst ravages of the night cleaners, as he thought of them. He then had one of his better ideas. Skin the cat, stuff it with gross and use it to show the little people how to defend themselves from it or anything of similar ilk.

The tooth blade made short work of cutting the skin of the cat, and it was not too difficult to remove it more or less in one piece. How he would sew it up was another matter, but no doubt he would find a way when the time came.

He laid the skin out in the sun to dry a little while he collected up some of the longer gross from around the edge of the rocks.

A small group of the little people had joined him and watched in silence for a few moments, and then, with squeaks and whistles, they set about collecting gross as well.

With their help he soon had a pile of the stuffing material and showed them how to push it into the empty skin. No volunteers came forward for that job, so he was left to finish it off by himself, watched by a fascinated audience.

Now he needed to sew up the belly slit he had made when he first skinned the carcass, so he cut a strip of skin from the side of the belly opening, and making holes with the tip of one of the smaller teeth of his Jar Saw, was able to stitch up the stuffed skin to make a very lifelike cat creature.

The party of watchers backed away a little, as he pushed it into a more realistic sitting position. Now the fun could begin.

Kal took hold of the cat creature by the tail to show his lack of fear and total disdain for it, and began dragging it towards the compound, followed by the party of onlookers who were twittering their heads off.

As he entered, the rest of the little people gathered around at a respectable distance to see what he would do next. Kal propped up the stuffed cat with stones from the top of the wall to make it take up the most realistic pose possible.

By now there was total silence from his audience, and a look of apprehension on most of their faces, or so he thought.

The next trick was to get one of them to attack the cat with a spear to see how they would go about it.

Kal held out one of the spears he had brought with him, but there were no takers. Either they didn't understand, or instinct made them too wary.

'Nothing for it' he thought, 'A little persuasion was needed' and he slowly walked up to one of the biggest members of the group and placed the spear in his hands.

As nothing much happened, he took him by the elbow and gently led him towards the cat. Kal could feel him stiffen up, and had to be quite firm for the last metre or so. He then backed away for a short distance, waiting to see if the spear carrier would do anything.

At long last the idea got through, and the spear carrier began beating the stuffed cat with the spear, egged on by the squeaks and whistles from the crowd. The encouragement really got him going, and he rained blows on the cat with the spear until he was exhausted, and then stopped to look at Kal for the next instruction.

As there was no way Kal could learn their language, let alone speak it, they would have to do their conservation bit by signs, and this was a good time to begin.

He gently took the spear away from the 'cat beater' and walked up to the cat. The first thing to establish was positive and negative, yes and no.

'Here goes' he thought, and began beating the cat. A few strokes later he stopped and made great play of shaking his head from side to side.

He then fingered the sharp edge of the spear blade, making great play about its sharpness, and then took up a position of aggression in front of the cat and gave it a good stab in the side of the neck, withdrew the spear, took a step back and nodded his head firmly.

Kal then repeated the action, this time positioning himself so that when he beat the target a fore limb flopped towards him, and he fell to the ground clutching his 'wounded' leg. Jumping to his feet, he looked around and shook his head with an exaggerated motion.

He then did a little dance in front of the cat, and gave it another good stab with the spear, stopped, looked around, and nodded vigorously.

Kal then handed the spear to the little 'cat beater' and waved him towards the cat. He walked up to the cat, did a very good imitation of Kal's dance, stabbed the cat, looked round at Kal and nodded his head.

A chorus of squeaks, whistles and hoots from the audience rent the air, and he knew that they had got the idea, and quickly too. It had been well worth the effort.

It wasn't long before they were queuing up to have a go at the 'cat stabbing' game, although he suspected they did not look upon it as a game exactly.

What really did impress him was when one of the smaller ones was given a spear and began hitting the cat with it, one of the others squeaked at him, shook his head and Kal watched fascinated as the little one then proceeded to stab at the cat. 'They really do cotton on fast' he thought.

The rest of the morning was spent watching the little people practice their newly acquired art, and when everyone had had a go, some of them came and stood around him.

Kal wondered what to do next, but the matter was taken out of his hands as two of the bigger ones came forward, took his hands in theirs, and led him across the compound and towards the cave entrance.

He had not been close enough to the cave opening to really see it in any detail, and now realized that they had carefully built up a considerable amount of stones around it, no doubt making the entrance a lot smaller than it originally was.

He was led inside and was surprised to find that there was a large system of natural tunnels which they had partitioned off into little rooms.

Fortunately for him, the height of the tunnels were just enough for him to walk upright without difficulty.

Another mystery was about to be solved. Kal had not noticed any very small members of the tribe, or any with stomachs bulging through pregnancy.

They were all here, in the caves. Most of the caves, which seemed to run along just inside the cliff face, had little holes cut in them, letting in a surprising amount of light, and there were the mothers and their offspring, safely out of sight, but able to see out.

Maybe they did come out at certain times, and he hadn't been there or near enough, to see them when they did.

The tour of the caves finished with him being shown into an empty one, the little people withdrawing to the entrance and nodding their heads.

It was quite obvious that they wanted him to stay, and he could see no reason not to. They were after all, more intelligent than he had hoped for, and would no doubt be good company. Well, company, at least.

Kal wanted to collect his possessions form the pool rocks and felt that he should make his intentions clear to his new hosts. He cleared a small space on the ground outside the cave entrance and scratched a crude picture of the cave and compound in the sand.

He then drew several little people and himself somewhat bigger. Over to one side he drew a pile of rocks and pointed to the actual pool rocks. Kal then pointed to the picture of himself, walked his fingers to the drawing of the rocks, went through the motions of picking something up, and walked them back again, stopping at the cave entrance, and nodded.

There was a slight pause, a few squeaks, and then they nodded also. Kal felt very relieved that they had understood so quickly.

On his way to retrieve his things from the stone house, he was joined by three guards equipped with spears held in the stabbing position; it seemed they were not going to lose him to any of the local predators now.

It didn't take long for him to collect up the odds and ends from the house and he almost felt a little sad at leaving it, but knew that his chances of survival would be much greater with the little people, and survival was what it was all about.

The cave which they had allotted to him was quite a good size, and his collection of tools, cups and spears looked a little lost in all that space.

He thought that he could now set about making a bed for himself, as they didn't seem to need one, or had not realized the comfort to be had from a soft resting place.

Kal had a little opening from which he could see the pool rocks, and wondered if the cave complex would yield a water supply. He felt it should, as the top of the cliff was quite high and there was a good spread of land above it.

That was a project for the future, when he had developed some means of lighting his way deep into the tunnels.

He would have to refuse any food offered to him by his new hosts, as it would seem that they could eat fruits that would probably kill him, and he would have to get this information across to them.

As the first day in his new abode drew to a close, he ate his meal of Finger Nut flakes and Puff Balls, washed down with the water from the bamboo sticks, which caused some interest from the onlookers, and retired to the sandy floor of his cave before all the light had gone.

'Must admit, it's a little more comfortable than the rocks' he thought, and drifted into a deep sleep.

Daylight came sooner than expected, so he must have slept very deeply indeed. The little people were watching closely as he prepared his breakfast, and must have taken note of what he used, for later a couple of them came in carrying Finger Nuts and an arm full of Puff Balls, which didn't amount to very many as their arms were so small.

Kal noticed that the little people had not developed fire, and thought that it might be useful to keep intruders at bay, and cooking some of the fruits might reduce or eliminate their poisonous content. Light would also be needed if he was going to explore the cave system.

'Today is going to be another good one' he thought.

There were several things about the little people which Kal felt didn't quite make sense. They were totally different to any of the other life forms he had come across here, and somehow, they didn't seem to belong or fit in.

Why had they not achieved a better system of defence than they had? They took to the spears quickly enough, so why had they not developed something along the same lines themselves? There was no sign of fire, tools, clothing, organized harvesting, or anything else that a seemingly bright people like them should have by now.

As far as he could tell, there was just the one group of them, when there should be several little groups dotted about the place, if past experience was anything to go by.

No, they didn't seem to belong here, and if they hadn't evolved here, and it didn't look as though they had, then where had they come from?

His presence here was self explanatory, but he couldn't imagine a ship full of them arriving in the same manner, and then forgetting everything they knew to appear as they now did. Or had someone or something dumped them here as an experiment, to see what would happen?

If that was the case, where were those responsible for that unkind act? Were they observing their handiwork? Would they interfere if Kal gave the little people a hand in developing their knowledge, and so bring them out of the dark ages? And should he interfere anyway?

He was getting more questions than answers, and that was not helping very much. Kal thought that he had better work out a very careful system of skill and information introduction, so that he could watch to see if they were able to extrapolate data from their experiences, as this would indicate any latent abilities they had.

The first thing to do was to establish a better method of communication, and to that end he decided to use the good old method of pictures. Drawings in the sand would have to do for now, as paper making skills were well down the line of developments.

They had quickly understood the concept of his going to the pool rocks to fetch his things, so he thought it should work well enough for them.

The little people did not seem to have a leader, so he chose the biggest and oldest looking one to address. Soon he had a little audience around him, eagerly watching his every move, or so he thought, as facial expressions were not their strong point, and they might have been thinking anything.

First he drew a picture of himself to one side of the square of sand he was using as his drawing board, and pointed to himself. Then he drew a group of little people on the other side of the square, and pointed to them.

A series of eager nods indicated that they had got that message. A sketch of the sun rising and falling again soon got the idea of a day across to them.

He spent the whole morning doing sketches of various things, and by midday, they were joining in, a little crude in their drawings, but adding to the overall picture of events.

Kal stopped for food about then, and the concept of different foods for each of them had already been understood.

He was making more progress than he ever thought possible, as they were very bright, and he couldn't understand how they had not developed further than they had.

From the data he had managed to extract from them, it seemed that left to their own devices, they would not have survived much longer, as their numbers were falling faster than they could be replaced.

By late afternoon, and feeling a bit shattered from prolonged concentration, Kal had assembled a good picture of the events that had befallen his new friends.

It would seem that they had been here for about fifty to sixty years of equivalent time on this planet. They had no memory of anything before this, and in the beginning, their numbers were decimated by the local life forms.

There had been about three times as many of them as there were now, and they knew that their numbers were dropping, but could do nothing about it except be very careful and keep in their compound, going out only when really necessary.

Kal soon realized that combining his skills and their quick learning curve, they could both survive much better.

Not only that, he would have company of a sort, and the more he thought about it, the more he realized it was necessary for his survival also. Kal finished the day's work by collecting a good supply of gross, and made a bed of it in one corner of his room.

The others caught on with their usual speed, and several, but not all, also made 'beds' He was willing to bet that next day they would all have more comfortable sleeping arrangements.

Kal learnt that occasionally a cat creature or some other large predator, would come over the wall and take one of them, so he decided to reconstruct the wall next day, perhaps using more of the natural contours of the land to their advantage, and also make the compound a little larger for the things he had in mind for the future.

After his evening meal, accompanied by the day's closing display of coloured cloud effects, Kal laid his head down on his new bed and had the most comfortable night's sleep he could remember for a long time.

They were willing little workers, almost to a point of embarrassment, as Kal found out next morning. He had surveyed the compound from several view points, and then marked out where the new wall would go.

This would make the enclosure nearly three times as large as it was when built originally, and they didn't query his decision. Once he began to build, they joined in with a ferocity that was hard to believe.

The larger rocks Kal moved, levering them into place with the thicker of the bamboo poles, and not to be out done, they tried the same and succeeded by using more of their numbers. Considering their size, he was very surprised to see how strong they were, and almost tireless.

The new wall was nearly three metres high in the places where he thought a large cat creature would likely try to jump it and a little lower where natural rocks and the contours of the land would make it difficult for an attacker to gain entrance.

It would take quite a while to complete, but when finished would afford them full protection, unless something else he had not yet met, came along.

Once the wall building had got under way, apart from the very big rocks, he was able to leave them to it. They seemed quite happy to carry on, and unless he was mistaken, showed a deal of pride when he did his evening inspection of the day's work.

A large stock of tooth bladed poles were made, and placed in groups at intervals along the wall as it progressed.

Practice sessions with the poles was enjoyed as far as he could tell, for they went at it with great enthusiasm although the stuffed cat was now in tatters, and would have to be replaced with a replica made from something else.

Kal wanted to improve the efficiency of the food gathers by supplying them with some sort of carrying device, as they brought it back in their arms at the moment.

He gathered a small group around him who were not on wall building, and using sand sketches showed them what he had in mind.

The idea was to use the tendrils of the Whip Trees as rope to bind things together, and perhaps crudely weave an open bag that could be slung between two poles, and then carried. The little party set off, complete with guards.

They would not let him go anywhere without at least two spear bearers, and sometimes more.

They had to go some way to find a small Whip Tree that was suitable for their purpose, and then set about severing the tendrils one by one with two poles tied together with a tooth blade at the end.

Once he had shown them how to squeeze the liquid out of the tendrils, he left them to it, while he tried to work out a more efficient way of gathering the tendrils. Kal wanted to try one of the larger trees, as they had many more tendrils, and were much longer.

Two poles would not give them the needed safety margin, and three poles were too difficult to manoeuvre into the cutting position. And then he had an idea.

'It'll be risky, but worth a try' Kal thought, as he made up the necessary equipment. Several tendrils were knotted together and a running noose was made, the eye of the noose being large enough for the knots to pass through.

A second noose was then made, and a group of the little people spaced themselves around the tree just out of range of the tendrils with the second noose suspended on the end of their poles.

The first noose was eased around the tree as close to the trunk as possible, and the end threaded through the noose loop which was then lifted on the end of triple poles to a height of two metres. The tree did not react during this time as the ropes were not hot blooded and so didn't give out any heat, which was what the tree seemed to react to.

At his signal, the first rope was pulled tight around the tree trapping the base of the tendrils, and as nothing much happened except for the odd twitch, he gave the signal and they all rushed forward, lifting the second noose on their poles as high as they could.

That noose was then pulled tight and made fast. The tree did react to that manoeuvre, but it was too late, as the tendrils were lashed to the trunk top and bottom, and could not descend in their normal sweeping arc.

Tendril cutting then began in earnest, and it was not long before they had as many as they could carry. The material was a bit like leather, but the tendril Kal had cut many days before was still as supple as the day he had cut it.

The rope party made their way back to the compound, and Kal showed them how to split the tendrils and weave the ropes into an open mesh sheet, string it on two poles and load it with fruit that had been gathered earlier by the others.

They liked the idea, and soon there were no tendrils left, but many fruit gathering bags.

A few Jaw Saws had been found over the last day or so, and when Kal showed them what they could be used for, the collection grew rapidly.

Pole cutting and tendril gathering took place several times next day, with Kal making sure he was with the tendril party every time, although once they had got the hang of it, he needn't have bothered.

Stocks of material were building up in the compound and Kal felt it was time some new ones were added to their collection, if anything suitable could be found.

He remembered the Frond plant behind the rock back in the forest track where Pear Shape met his end, and wondered if it would be possible to spin the fronds, and make some form of cloth.

As it was a long way back he did not think it worthwhile going just yet, as they may find another one nearer home. Home? Yes, it was getting to be one.

Fire seemed to be unknown, as no burnt plants or charcoal had been seen. Lightening often caused fires, but perhaps there was no lightening here, which would account for the lack of 'fixed' nitrogen to some extent, and the number of plants that obtained their nitrogen by ingesting animals.

Kal thought he would try making fire, but first he would need a supply of dead wood, or what passed for wood here. It was too difficult to try and explain to the little people what he was about to do, so he just set off, with four guards armed to the teeth.

Dead bamboo was too useful for making into spears and shafts for other tools to use it for firewood, that's if it would burn. The party tramped on for some time before they came to a densely wooded area, not at all like the plains they were used to.

Kal tried to make them aware that innocent looking trees could be a danger, but they already seemed to know that, and moved about with caution. Steady progress was made albeit a little slowly, but they did find what they had been looking for after a very long search.

Several trees in an area of about fifty square metres were as dead as they were ever going to get.

Whether it was nitrogen starvation from being too close together and not being able to catch enough prey, or just old age, Kal didn't know, or for that matter care much, here was the wood he needed.

He tried snapping off a few branches to see how hard they were to break. Tough enough, but just possible, and Kal had to stop the rest of the work party from stripping the trees of their smaller branches.

He selected a tree of medium thickness with regard to its trunk, and applied the Jaw Saw. Soon a deep groove had been cut into the dead trunk, and when he made another cut on the opposite side it did not take much effort from him to bend it back and forth quickly to build up momentum until it snapped and fell to the ground with a resounding thud.

Soon they had all the wood they could drag, and made their way back to the compound. A crowd gathered to see what wonders Kal would produce from this useless pile of dead wood. To them it was not even suitable to make 'beating sticks' with. Kal was more interested in food at the moment, so they had to wait for a while.

As he ate his meal, Kal wondered if he had bitten off more that he could chew with regard to fire making.

He had never made fire, as there had been no need to, and the survival courses somehow missed out on that one or he had.

'This should be fun, but tomorrow' he thought, as he was tired now, and he needed to think out a method of doing it.

'When you are looked upon with such high esteem, you have to produce the goods' and he drifted into sleep.

By morning he had several ideas with regard to the fire making caper, and after a meal he sorted through the wood, separating it into piles of soft, tough and darn right hard.

The idea was to make a small shaft of very hard wood with a point on one end, which could be rotated very fast in a depression cut into a softer piece.

The friction generated, if he could spin it fast enough, should cause it to catch fire or at least produce a few sparks.

It took quite a while for him to find a natural stone with a depression in it to use as a bearing for the top end of the stick.

A strip of tendril leather affixed to a bow shaped piece of thin branch completed his equipment for the experiment. Using a tooth blade, he scraped some very fine shavings from one of the softer pieces of wood, and he was ready.

A little group of his new admirers stood around him, the rest seemed to be out of the compound wall building, so if it didn't work he wouldn't lose too much face with the whole tribe, although he suspected the word would get around sooner or later.

'This had better work' Kal thought, as he assembled the pieces together.

The larger soft wood block was held firmly down with his feet, the point of the sharpened stick was placed in the middle of the block and the stone placed on top of the stick so that pressure could be exerted downwards, driving the hard stick into the block below.

A little pile of the shavings surrounded the place where the stick impinged on the soft block, and with the bow string already looped a couple of times around the stick, he was ready for off.

Kal pressed down on the stone, played the bow back and forth as fast as he could, and nothing happened except a faint squeaky noise which the onlookers didn't seem to find amusing, by the look on their faces.

It must have hit their resonant frequency, or was maybe an insulting sound. A desperate feeling was beginning to form in his mind, how was he going to explain this energetic rigmarole should he fail?

The perspiration was beginning to bead on Kal's brow, when the first tiny wisps of smoke appeared bringing a gasp from the audience.

He 'bowed' even harder, and was rewarded by a larger plume

of smoke and a few sparks, some of which obligingly fell onto the shavings. He stopped 'bowing', and gently blew on the tiny glow in the shaving, and a small flame appeared.

Carefully sliding the ignited shavings onto an already prepared bed of fine twigs, a little more blowing and he had fire. Larger sticks were then added, and he sat back, hot, sweaty and relieved that it had worked.

What the little people made of it, he was not sure. They had backed off a little, and then come forward, fascinated by the apparent life of the leaping flames.

Someone must have squeaked rather loudly, as before long he had the whole tribe around him, chattering away excitedly and watching the flames in awe.

By demonstration and pictures drawn in the sand, Kal managed to get across the danger of fire, its use to give light in the dark, and as a deterrent to hungry intruders.

The next thing to do was build a fireplace from stones, which would allow slow burning of the wood and so keep the fire in at all times. He got this idea across to them and received the usual nods of understanding, and watched as a fire detail was selected for duty.

Again, Kal marvelled at the very quick comprehension of these people, and wondered what it would lead to in time.

If he could find a source of fat or oil, then lights of some kind could be constructed, as flaming fire brands were a rather clumsy way of obtaining light and have a short life.

So far, there had been no apparent source of supply, although some of the nut like fruits might yield oil if he could press them, but of mineral oil there had been no trace.

From memory, animal fats were another possibility, but catching enough of them to make it worthwhile didn't seem like a viable idea. With a light source, they would be able to explore the cave system, and maybe find their own water supply therein, so removing one of the inconvenience and dangers of the twice daily trip to the pool rocks.

Kal still had the idea of trying the frond trees as a supply of fibre to spin and weave, but had seen none in the vicinity of the compound. Sooner or later he would have to find some form of material to make clothes from, as those he had wouldn't last forever.

But did he really need clothes? The others didn't seem to, so why should he? Old habits die hard, and he still liked the idea of covering his nakedness.

The wall was coming on well, and he was thinking of some form of gate or removable barrier for it. They now had a good source of timber not too far away, although cutting it was a bit of a chore without a proper saw.

What he desperately needed was a means of making metal, so that in turn they could manufacture some really useful tools. Kal remembered the copper stain on the first rocks he had seen, and reasoned that there should be more of the same somewhere; it was just a matter of finding it.

If they could locate an area where gross or any other plant wouldn't grow when it looked as though it should, then copper might be responsible.

Trying to get over the concept of what he wanted was beyond his means at the moment, so he settled for the idea of a search party to look for new things, but that was not so easy to explain either.

They set off early next morning, carrying a supply of food and water, and with the guards armed to the teeth.

The first place to look was around the local area, but that didn't produce any promising results, so they made their way up into the rock formation that skirted the cliff.

The going was hard, more so for the little people than Kal, and they were half way up the jumble of rocks when they came to a track, not unlike the one Kal had found in the forest. The gravelled surface made travelling a lot easier, and they wound their way upwards and onto the cliff top.

The view from the top was stunning, and it was easy to see why the little people had chosen the place they did for their camp, as it was the only place as far as the eye could see that could be defended.

The rocks up here were of a different type to those below in the cave complex, and Kal began his search for the telltale signs of metal ore stains on their surfaces.

It was while they were rummaging about in the broken rock formations, that Kal realized that these were not naturally formed. He didn't quite know how he knew this, but they just didn't seem natural somehow.

This meant that someone else had been here, and had turned the place over looking for something, and if the something was the same as that which Kal wanted, there may well be a little of it left for him. He was right, for a while later they came across a cleared area with a quantity of smaller broken stones scattered about, as though left over from loading onto something.

It was just a feeling he had, and his feelings were usually right. Some of the stones had green and bluish bands running through them, and these he began collecting, quickly joined by the rest of the party.

In anticipation of making a useful find, they had brought some of the woven food carriers with them, and these were quickly loaded with what he considered to be too heavy a load, but the strength of these little people far belied their size, and the party set off for home at a good pace.

Going down the lower rock formations proved a trifle difficult, but they made it in the end with only a few bruises, and returned to the compound triumphantly.

Smelting the copper ore, for that was what Kal thought it to be, would be quite difficult, but not impossible if only he could get enough heat from the charcoal he was going to make from the wood stock pile retrieved earlier.

Charcoal making was the easy part, and before long they had a large pile, although trying to explain what it was for wasn't so easy. Once Kal had used a hard stone to break up the ore bearing rock, the others joined in, and separated the green ore out into a pile on its own.

Before Kal could use his furnace, he would need to make a crucible and a lining material for the fire box; otherwise he would not be able to pour the molten metal, if he managed to get any. Without a lining, most of the furnace heat would go into the stones from which the furnace was constructed.

This needed some careful thinking out. The crucible especially, and lining, would have to be fairly strong, be able to withstand high temperatures and the shock of a sharp rise and fall in temperature.

It seemed to Kal that one problem when solved, always led to other problems, and the sequence was never ending.

First he would have to locate a supply of clay, or whatever passed for it on this planet. Next he would need quartz sand, and a supply of fine organic material which would burn out, so making the 'fired' material porous.

It took nearly all of one day for the team to find eight samples of what might turn out to be clay, and Kal set about making test blocks of each to see how they would harden.

He moistened a good handful of each sample in turn and made it into a flat block, about ten millimetres thick and these were laid out in the sun to dry, with a symbol on each to denote which sample they came from.

The quartz sand was no problem, as he had seen a quantity of it in one of the water worn gullies earlier. The fine organic material, which would burn out in the firing, so leaving tiny holes in the finished material to make the lining less likely to crack and give it good insulating properties, was made by rubbing a piece of the soft dead tree with a rough stone, producing a wood flour.

To test the clay samples in order to find out which would be most suitable, he built a fire box of stones, filling it with charcoal and placing the test samples on top.

The fire was lit from the bottom, and as it burned through, more charcoal was placed on top of the samples so that they would be surrounded with heat. The fire took all night to burn out, and next morning the opening ceremony was attended by all those who had been involved with the mining and charcoal project.

All the others went about their other tasks such as wall building, food gathering and whatever else they usually did.

Kal raked out the test samples from the ash, and found that one sample had melted to a black glass like substance, and thought that it might have been a lead bearing ore.

'Could be useful later on' he thought. Most of the other test pieces had broken up into bits and showed no sign of fusing together, which was the main requirement.

One sample however, must have been the clay he had been looking for, as it had fused into a very hard block, without shrinking too much. He could still read the symbol he had scratched on the surface, and sent a team to fetch more.

Now he was ready to make his crucible. Kal made a mixture of the clay, sand and a little fine wood flour, moistening it with water so that he could work it up into a very stiff paste.

This was allowed to dry a little, until he was only just able to squeeze it into long strips about ten millimetres thick.

These were then rolled out on a flat rock, and he began to make a 'coiled pot' by running the long coils of clay mixture around and around upon each other, pressing the coils together as he went.

He finished the pot off by making two handles and sticking them on the side of the pot, making sure that they were properly joined on, and of adequate strength.

The pot was dried out very carefully in the sun, and the next day it went into the fire box. Next morning he had his crucible. Kal wondered just how much of the operation the little people had understood, and if they would now be able to do the same for themselves.

The design of the smelting furnace was a bit more complicated. It needed two fire boxes, one to actually smelt the ore, and another one below to keep the crucible hot when the molten metal hopefully dripped into it.

Kal set about constructing it up against the cliff face where it sloped backwards slightly, so that a tall chimney with a good draft could be laid up against the cliff, and be supported by it.

Once the main fire boxes had been built, he lined them with a similar mixture to that which had been used for the crucible, but adding a lot more wood flour to it for extra porosity, and then the stone chimney went on up to about ten metres, using the bamboo poles for scaffolding.

Unknown to Kal, a team of 'miners' had set out earlier that day, and had returned towards evening with a collection of many different coloured rocks.

They must somehow have worked out that he prized the pretty rocks, and had done their best to satisfy his liking for them. Kal did not have the heart to disregard the gift, and so carefully looked through the samples to see just what they had found, and was very surprised to see ores of lead, tin and silver among the collection.

The tin ore he could use, as mixed with copper it would make bronze, and this would be much harder and tougher that the raw copper he was hoping to make.

First, the furnace had to be made ready. After letting the liner of fire clay mixture dry out, a small fire was lit in the lower section and as the steam from the chimney decreased, the fire was made hotter and hotter, until the inside of the furnace glowed red. The fire was then allowed to go out, with entrance blocked up so that it would cool slowly.

Kal had chosen a slightly sloping sight for the casting of the molten metal, so that he could pour it into the top end of the sand moulds, and the metal would then run down to fill all the depressions he would make by pressing wooden shapes into the sand.

He flattened the site, and covered it with a mixture of damp sand with a little clay added to it, so that it would hold any shape pressed into it. He would have liked to add a 'binding agent' but at the moment, he didn't have any.

The mining gang watched the mould making in silence, with only the occasional squeak now and then, and Kal supposed that this was one of the brighter ones explaining something to the others, but this was only a guess.

Carefully carved wooden shapes of the things Kal wanted to make were prepared, and these included large spear heads, knives of several sizes, an axe head and an attempt at the two blades of a pair of scissors.

After the wooden masters had been completed, he pressed them into the sand such that an imprint of their shape was left, carefully clearing away the expelled sand from around the depression so formed.

Kal repeated the pressing process until he had a number of the shapes he wanted, and then joined them up by pressing straight sticks into the sand to leave little channels joining all the mould depressions up to a central channel.

The whole area was then carefully covered with thin slate like stones so that the molten metal would be forced to flow from one shape to another until all the depressions had been filled, he hoped.

Among the samples the mining team had brought him was a quantity of what looked like felspathic rock, and he knew that if this was added to the furnace at smelting time, it would act like a flux, and help the metal to run cleanly down into the crucible.

Kal had made some 'fire bars' from the same material as the crucible to put into the bottom of the two furnaces, and a supply of spares, as he didn't know how long they would last in the intense heat.

It was light up time at last, and with diagrams drawn in the sand he tried to show the assembled crowd what he was going to do, and why.

He was not sure that they understood it all, but would not have been surprised if they had, as the rate at which they comprehended things seemed to be increasing each day.

The furnace was lit, and as the heat increased more and more charcoal was added, until the inside of the top furnace was a glowing red hot mass.

The crushed mixture of tin and copper ore was then added, layer by layer, alternating it with charcoal. The second furnace was then fired up, and the crucible placed inside to await the first drip of molten copper.

There was a soft roar from the furnaces, as the temperature rose, and it was a full time job keeping them topped up with fuel, which was going down at an alarming rate.

Anxiously Kal waited for the metal to flow, but there was no sign of it. They kept adding more fuel until at last something like thick red hot treacle dripped down from the upper fire bars, and into the crucible.

Kal was disappointed until he realized that the treacle was the molten flux, and the metal should soon follow. Sometime later they had a crucible full of glowing metal, and the fires were let down a little so that they could push the crucible out of the side of the lower firebox.

His helpers were a little afraid of the pot of molten metal, as they could feel the heat from it, and they had remembered Kal's warning when he had explained fire to them earlier.

Very carefully the crucible was manoeuvred with poles to the moulding area, and the molten metal gently poured into the receiving hole at the top of the mould run, the bamboo poles suffering somewhat in the process.

It looked as if they had made enough metal to fill all the moulds, but wouldn't know for sure until it had cooled down enough for them to remove the capping stones.

The metal work party all stopped for a meal and a cool down, with a great deal of squeaky chatter going on among the little people. He wondered if they realized the momentous changes that were about to be brought about to their way of living, if he had been successful.

Waiting for the metal castings to cool down took a lot longer than Kal had expected, but in time they were able to lift off the flat slates and there were the bronze castings for all to see. A squeaky gasp issued from the crowd which had gathered for the opening event, and Kal could hardly believe his luck at having got so far with only the most rudimentary equipment.

Although the castings were still quite hot, they were able to remove them from the sand moulds in one big unit.

The next problem was how to cut them off from the linking bars or sprues, so that he would finish up with just the castings. The bronze turned out to be a lot tougher than he had expected, and this was going to be quite difficult to achieve without cutting tools.

Kal had anticipated this problem and had slimmed down the sprues where they joined the cast objects, but the bronze was still too tough to break easily.

In the end, he had to resort to jamming the block of castings in between two rocks, and with a lot of effort bent the main frame of castings back and forth until the trapped casting broke off.

It was very tiring and time consuming, but by evening they had all the little castings separated from the frame, and the frame broken up ready for re-smelting in the next session.

The means of removing the remaining sprue and general shaping up of the castings, he had already worked out in theory, and hoped it would work in practice.

A grinding wheel would be made from the quartz sand, which was very hard and contained sharp particles, mixed with clay, and fired in a charcoal fire.

Since receiving the gift of the fluorspatic rock, he thought a little of it added to the mix may help the grains of sand to adhere together better; anyway, it was worth a try.

The wheel was made by pressing the damp mixture into a sand mould, letting it dry out, and then very carefully refining the shape to be as truly round as possible.

A hole was cut in the centre for a shaft, and the whole thing fired off in a simple furnace built alongside the smelter, so that the same chimney could be used.

A simple wooden frame, pegged together, held the wheel and shaft, and with willing hands to turn it, the grinding wheel was trued up by holding a flint like stone against it, as it was turned.

Now they could begin cleaning up the rough bronze castings which had taken so long to produce, and in very little time the first shiny spear head was finished. Kal drove the shaft end of the head into the end of a bamboo pole, added a little 'glue' and showed the result to the others.

This was a formidable weapon, and would make short work of most attacking animals, and with a little care and strategy, the cat creature.

Kal got on with the job of finishing his scissors, although he had not yet worked out how to make the swivel joint in the middle.

Meanwhile the 'smelters' had of their own accord made several more grinding wheels, and of different sizes, but what surprised Kal most of all was that they had made one wheel of very fine grains, which acted more like a polishing wheel than a grinder.

He was constantly amazed at the comprehension of these people, and wondered when they would over take his ability in working things out.

The bronze wood saw caused a great sensation, and although it worked very well, it needed sharpening rather a lot, and resetting the teeth was not the easiest of jobs. With so many eager workers, Kal found that doing a job once was all that was needed, as they soon picked up the idea, and he was then free to go onto the next project.

Bronze nails brought about a whole new range of things that were previously impossible to make, and the introduction of the wheel was an earth shaker.

He had made a long bronze strip with cast holes in the tapering ends, which would take a rivet when he had bent it round to make the outer rim of the wheel.

Wood blocks were shaped to form the inner sections of the rim, and spokes posed no problem at all. The hub was of cast bronze and the central hole was 'cast in' with a core piece, and polished to a smooth finish with fine sand later.

A cart was constructed with shafts that would steer the front wheels, and that made food gathering and the shifting of materials almost a pleasure. There was great competition among the little people to be the 'cart pullers', and this was the first time Kal had noticed any form of envy, although that was perhaps not the right word for it.

As yet they had not invented anything themselves, Kal wondered just how long it would be before they did. They were quite good at modifying things once they had understood the basic principle, but innovation was not their strong point, at the moment. Time, no doubt, would alter that, and he wondered what would happen to this planet when they really did get under way.

At long last, a heavily armed search party went out to look for the frond tree. Kal had managed, or so he thought, to give the members of the party a good description of the tree, and set about oil extraction from a new kind of nut which they had found, while the search party wandered far and wide in their quest.

He had constructed a crude press, and after breaking the nuts up into small pieces did actually extract some oil. He tested it to see how well it would burn and was pleased to see that it did so with a clear yellow flame, and would give out a reasonable amount of light in the darkness of the caves.

In anticipation of the oil, fired clay 'lamp pots' had already been made and the only thing missing was a good wick.

The frond party returned that night, but without finding the frond trees he so wanted. But they did bring back something else that would possibly do the same job.

It came from a plant or tree that had a fibrous stem, which when it died had left a giant bundle of fine fibres in a clump, and the searchers thought it might do.

They also brought back a small version of the living tree, and later on, that was able to provide the material for spinning, making a rough but very strong cloth. The living tree somehow kept the fibres supple, and therefore manageable for the spinners.

Once the tree had died, the fibres became hard and almost brittle, as though something had been extracted from them in the dying process, and so had limited use.

Once enough of the fibre trees had been collected, the job of separating the fibres from the trunk and washing them kept the team busy for a while. Spinning the thread was done by using a spinning bob weight on a stick in one hand, while feeding the fibres to it from the other.

The thread produced was not very good, but it was at least proving that it could be done. The spinning wheel was much better; Kal could not help but admire the dexterity of the little spinners, as they were producing much thinner and more even threads than he had been able to.

Weaving the thread into cloth was a project for the near future, when he had worked out how to make a heddle for the loom, meanwhile the lamps had been improved, and an expedition formed to explore the cave complex.

Early next day, Kal, with ten of the little people, set off into the deepest of the caves as yet explored. They each carried a lamp and a spare oil bottle, food, water sticks and an assortment of weapons, just in case.

The tunnel seemed to have been water formed by the marks along its sides, but there was no sign of water at the moment. Eventually it leads out into a large cave from which many more tunnels led off.

Which one to go down? It seemed best to choose one that had a draft of air in it, and the wavering lamps soon indicated the best choice, and they set off once more.

Every once in a while there were other branches adjoining the main tunnel, and they were very careful to mark the walls to show which one they had come from so that there would be no confusion on the return journey. Once lost in the complex, it would be a lucky person who found the exit without guidance.

Time was difficult to judge in the tunnel system, and they let their stomachs guide them as to when they should take a break. It was while they were all resting that they heard a distant rumbling sound, very faint, but just audible. If it wasn't the hoped for water, Kal dreaded to think what it might be.

A little further on they came to a large cave off to one side of the tunnel, and went in to explore. The sight that met the gentle glow from their lamps was unbelievable.

Giant mushrooms, almost six metres high, stood before them. They were pure white, on long thin stalks, and with a canopy some two metres in diameter. They had seen no sign of life before this and he wondered why they had not spread to the other caves.

And how did they get here in the first place? Before he could stop them, one of the little people had gone up to one of the growths and attacked the stem with a Jaw Saw. The whole thing came crashing down almost as soon as he had touched it, and he was covered in the debris.

The little one crawled out from under the shattered mushroom and shook off the broken fragments which had stuck to him, while chewing on a portion of it. They seemed to know instinctively what they could eat or what was poisonous to them.

'Very useful' Kal thought, wishing he had acquired the same skill. The fruiting body of the fungus supplemented their food stocks, and when everyone had collected as much as they could carry, they returned to the main tunnel, and continued their journey.

The rumbling sound had got noticeably louder as they penetrated further into the tunnel, and they expected to see what was causing it soon. But not as soon as they did.

In a cave off the main run, something was moving or breathing. They all stopped in their tracks and waited for Kal to make a suggestion.

His instinct was to run, but they were armed and so should be able to defend themselves. But not against what the oil lamps revealed.

It looked like a giant maggot, a full three metres high with only the rounded end of its body showing in the cave mouth.

This was the rear end by the look of it, and that meant there must be another way into the cave, as the huge white shape couldn't have got through this entrance.

Should they look for the other way in? To have come so far, not found water and been confronted by this monstrosity was too much, of course they would check it out.

The tunnel was peppered with side openings for quite a distance ahead, and they systematically checked every one. Most just finished in a dead end, and then they found a longer passageway.

Cautiously they moved ahead, lighting up every nook and cranny to make sure they weren't taken by surprise, and then they found the entrance to the main cave. It was huge, the roof was nowhere in sight from the feeble light of the oil lamps, but they did light up the monster in the middle.

It was a colossal white maggot-like creature, with no eyes and only a slit like mouth. The skin was translucent and the internal organs could be clearly seen.

It must have sensed their presence, for it turned, and emitting the low rumbling sound, humped itself slowly along towards them.

The rush for the exit would have been funny if it hadn't been so serious. They were all out in the main passageway before the creature could move one more 'hump' forward.

As it turned out they were quite safe, as the monstrosity couldn't get out of the entrance they had used, and was probably too large to have gone down any of the passages they had travelled so far.

So what did it eat? How did it mate? Where were the others? That was far more worrying.

There was little more to be gained from this section of passages, except inviting any other giant maggots to get curious, and that was not considered advisable.

The little party carried on, paying a little more attention to the side openings than they had previously done. There was dampness in the air, and a very faint breeze.

Could this be what they had been looking for? The tunnel opened out into a similar colossal cave to that which Kal had seen when he had followed the stream into the mountain.

Could it have been the same one? He was not sure until he realized that the other one had a faint light of its own to it, and this one didn't. Or did it?

Using signs to convey his meanings, Kal had the little people go back around the first bend, leaving him in darkness. They were reluctant to do so, but he was adamant, and they finally gave in.

As the oil lights receded, the cave gave up its own light, and Kal could see the huge baffles in the distance and the crystals hanging from the roof. If it was not the same cave, then it was a very good replica of the earlier one, and Kal called the little ones back in.

He could have walked outside to see if the stream was there, the grooves in the floor certainly were. But so what? They had found water, and that was the main thing.

Because of the distance they had travelled, it was going to be a difficult and lengthy task to get water from here to the compound, and Kal reluctantly gave up the idea. Without the sand to draw on, he found it difficult to explain to the others what he felt, but they seemed to understand.

Nothing for it but to go back the way they had come. They could have explored a few more caves on the way, but all wanted to return to their friends and take a well earned rest.

Fate, or call it what you will, plays some strange tricks sometimes, and the team got lost despite their careful marking of the outward route.

They knew they were in trouble when the passageway began to get narrow and Kal had to bend down a little to give himself headroom. Lower and lower it went, until it was a hands and knees job for him, and the only thing that prevented them from going back was the gentle wind in their faces. If air was getting through, then maybe they could.

A slow drip, drip, caught their ears, and despite the lack of room, they all looked around and began squeaking in anticipation. The next few metres rewarded them for their long journey. Where the passage had widened out, there was a pool of water on the floor.

It was quite large, and when tested, deep. It was not so much a pool, rather a well, for they couldn't find the bottom, even with two of their poles tied together. They had found their water, but it was just as inaccessible as the first lot.

Moving around the edge of the pool they reached the other side, drawn by the faint breeze and hoping it would lead them out of the system. Once again Kal had to stoop down in order to get through the narrowing passageway.

A light ahead caused a great squeal of excitement, and they were out in the daylight in a few metres. They took it in turns to look out of the cave mouth, straight down onto their compound.

They called to their friends below, but couldn't reach them as the drop was at least fifty metres. Now what to do?

Kal squeezed past the group by the exit and had a look down. From the far side of the compound a group of the little people were bringing a bundle of bamboos to the cliff face, and a scaffold was soon under way.

The little people had anticipated the extra weight of Kal, and had built the framework accordingly, but it took a little while for Kal to feel secure on the spidery contraption.

The height didn't seem to worry his team mates, but Kal didn't like the look of the scaffolding one little bit. Because of the height, it seemed to taper away to nothing at the bottom and swayed about all over the place as the little ones climbed down.

Now it was his turn, and easing himself out of the small hole in the cliff face and onto the framework was not the most pleasant thing he had ever experienced.

Once on the frame it was not too bad as long as he didn't look down. And here he was, used to going outside in a space suit, and swimming about in no gravity.

When he reached the ground he was trembling and not feeling very well, while the others were just as normal, and he envied them their calmness in the descending exercise.

By now it was time for the evening meal, and he joined them as they all sat around twittering away, no doubt retelling the tale of their adventures in the mountain and of the awful monster they had encountered. He wished he could have joined in.

'A good night's rest should put things to rights' were his last conscious thoughts as he lay down to sleep.

Next day a gang was working to reinforce the scaffolding and he wondered what they had in mind, and then remembered the water.

Perhaps they were going to get it down here somehow; he would wait and see what they did. He didn't have long to wait, the leader of the team came up to him and took his hand to guide him over to the sand drawing area. They had worked it out all by themselves.

Join a long line of bamboo's together, dip one end into the pool above and let it run down to the base of the cliff. This was the first original idea they had come up with, as far as he could tell. Except it was not that simple in practice.

The pipes could be joined end to end if they put the smaller or top end into the base of the next one, but the bamboo's had a web going across the inside at every leaf joint, and this would not let water pass.

He showed them this, and they nodded sagely. Kal then showed them how to heat a stone or a chunk of bronze to red heat and drop it down the tube, burning out the web as it went. They got that all right.

One thing Kal had noticed was that if the green bamboo was cut and kept wet, it didn't seem to decay as the dead samples had done.

So live bamboo must be used, and the water flowing through them would keep the pipe system in good condition, at least for a time.

Another problem needed solving, and that was that the exit from the cliff face was some way above the level of the water pool, and they had no means of pumping it up.

He would check it with measurements, but it looked as though the siphon effect would just about work for them, as long as the initial rise was not too high.

Kal set a casting team up to make three right angled hollow bronze fittings for joining the bamboo's at the point where they would turn to dip into the water, come out of the cave, and at the bottom of the cliff where the tap would be.

He made the wooden pattern himself, and then set them the task of casting the parts for a bronze tap, the mating surfaces of which would be ground together with the finest sand, so that they fitted perfectly.

Kal had suggested that the scaffolding be reinforced at the top such that it was keyed into the cave mouth, and extended a little way above it. Also, using bronze spikes, that it be locked at intervals to the cliff face for added stability. This was willingly done, and although it still looked flimsy, had a strength that belied its frail look.

The casting team produced the parts for joining the bamboos and the others had collected a huge pile of 'green' poles of a length that Kal had not seen before.

These were stood up in turn against the scaffolding, while one of the little ones climbed up quickly and dropped a red hot piece of shaped bronze into the top of the pole, whereupon it burned its way through the 'webs' and came out of the bottom, when it was returned to the furnace to be reheated for the next pole.

It took several days to get everything prepared for the water supply system to be ready for assembly, and then everyone gathered to see what would happen.

The first task was to join enough lengths of bamboo together to reach from the cave mouth to the pool inside, and then fit an 'elbow' of bronze to the end that would dip into the water. Another pipe was then joined to the elbow such that the end of it was below the water level in the pool.

At the cave entrance an elbow was fitted and the bamboos were extended down to the bottom of the cliff where they went into another bend and a short piece of pipe to which the bronze tap was fitted.

Now the tricky bit was about to be performed. Kal had found that the rise in level from the pool's surface to the point where the pipes left the cave mouth was such that it would be impossible for him, let alone the little ones, to suck the water up to start the siphon action.

He wondered what they would make of the next trick he was about to demonstrate.

Kal had given instructions to the 'water team' and drilled them in what to do. The pipe that dipped into the pool was withdrawn, and a bung fitted in its end complete with a cord of tendril attached and a lever system, such that when the cord was pulled, the bung would be released.

The team at the cave mouth disconnected the lower end of the first 'down' pipe and swung it up vertically, so that it pointed to the sky.

Armed with pots of water taken from the pool, a group then passed water to the others at the top of the now extended scaffolding, and the water was poured into the pipe until it was full. There was now a solid column of water from the top of the vertical pipe to the end of the pipe which dipped into the pool.

At his command the upright pipe was swung down and quickly plugged into the pipes that ran on down the cliff face, and at the same time the cord was pulled in the cave, and the bung came out.

The upshot of this was that the water in the down section of the pipe tried to fall on down through the lower pipes to reach the ground, but could not do so unless it was replaced with more water drawn from the pool, which is what happened. A few seconds later a fierce jet of water blasted out of the tap at the bottom, and sprayed everyone in its path.

If they could have cheered they would have, but they did their best with the biggest chorus of squeaks and whistles Kal had ever heard. He then showed them how the tap worked, and using the sand drawings, the reason for not having the water flowing all the time, as he didn't know how much constant drainage the cave pool would take.

He had assumed it was replaced, as it was sweet when he had tasted it, and that meant there was a flow involved. But there was no point in wasting it.

Kal had noticed a small bush like growth that the little people highly prized as a food source. It was a little like a cactus in so far that it produced short lengths joined to each other that rose upwards where they terminated into a seed pod. The sections were broken off before the pod stage was reached, and new sections then grew to replace them.

As the compound was now so much bigger, he thought that a little farming would be a good idea, and to this end, he sent a team out to try and dig up a few of these bushes, and plant them in a section near the wall.

An underground pipe was then run from the tap area down to the bushes, so that any spilled water would find its way down to the plants, and they would have a self replenishing food supply on site.

All in all, things were going very well. They had a good water supply, a series of wagons for moving things around, a foundry to produce a range of bronze tools, food grown on site, to which the little ones had added several other plants which flourished well, and a secure wall to keep out unwanted guests.

Fire and light made a great deal of difference to their comfort and most caves now had their own lamps, as a nut pressing team had gone to work of their own volition and supplied copious amounts of oil. Things had come a long way from the day Kal had landed on the shuttle devouring beach, and he was enjoying himself into the bargain.

Wheel making had been improved considerably when Kal found out that the early ones fell apart after a while, due to the rough ground they sometimes had to travel over.

The inner rim of wood and spokes were assembled along with the central hub, and the outer 'tire' of bronze was made slightly small than the rim. The bronze tire was then heated in a circular fire to make it expand and was then dropped onto the wheel assembly, and quickly quenched with water.

The wood creaked and squeaked, which the little ones didn't like, as the shrinking tire pulled all the sections tightly together. None of the new wheels had failed, and another engineering principle was absorbed by the tribe.

One day, Kal gathered a group of his engineers together and explained to them that he wanted to test the water supply from the cave to see if it would sustain a constant drain on its source.

The reason for this was that he wanted to build a water wheel, which could then power a stamping mill for crushing ore and a hammer mill for beating out the metal they had refined.

The mill wheel was constructed and the water turned on for the first time amid loud squeaks and hand clapping, a habit they had learned from Kal, and which was strictly reserved for occasions like this to show their wonderment and appreciation. It didn't seem to matter how much water they drew, the supply still provided more.

The stamping mill soon followed as did the ore crusher, and several other useful tools. Kal wanted to build a large bellows to force air into the furnace, so that he could smelt some of the ores that would not respond to the natural draft version they had used up to now. He sketched out the general principle and left them to it to see what they would come up with, and was very surprised indeed. Once they got hold of an idea, there was no holding them, and they were getting better at extrapolating other data from it.

The bellows, when completed, was a work of art. Using the 'skin' from some giant tendrils they had found, they had cut them open to make what amounted to a series of leather-like sheets.

These were then stretched over circular wooden frames and the seams stitched and sealed with a sticky substance they had extracted from a plant.

A stack of these frames was assembled and sealed one above the other, and then set in a vertical main frame, the whole contraption being driven up and down by an eccentric cam, which was in turn powered from the water wheel.

Kal wondered how they had managed to stitch the seams, and found that the foundry team had made needles of bronze for the occasion. The method of so doing was a revelation in itself.

They had made a two part clay mould of the shape they wanted, and placed a very fine clay piece in position to represent the eye of the needle. The mould was blackened over a smoky fire to give it a coating of carbon which would help the metal to flow.

A long reinforced clay pipe was connected above the mould and the metal poured in from above. Gravity plus the momentum of flowing metal then filled the mould exactly, and all they then had to do was break out the clay eye hole and polish the casting up to have a very serviceable needle.'

Kal was always being surprised by the things they got up to, but this one shook him to the core. This showed, without any doubt, that they were thinking out their problems in a very efficient manner, and getting it right. He wondered how long it had taken his own people to arrive at this stage in their development, and thought it was probably a lot longer than 'The Tribe'

It was time to go to work on making cloth. A loom was not too difficult and now that they could cast finely, a heddle for the loom was a possibility. The design for one was sketched out, and the foundry team went to work.

Polishing all the rough edges off it was the most difficult task, but they did it, and the loom slowly took shape.

By now the thread makers had got it down to a fine art, and dyes had been introduced much to everyone's delight.

Some of the plants produced some astounding colours, and it was interesting to watch the experiments done by the thread makers as they sought new colours.

The loom was finished, and the reels of thread fed through the heddle plate and wound onto a drum. The shuttle was loaded and competition to pass it back and forth was very keen, but orderly.

Before long the first piece of cloth was produced to a round of the usual sounds and a bout of hand clapping. It was not long before a deputation, doing sand sketches, asked if the loom could be powered from the water mill.

'They're getting lazy' he thought, but changed his mind, 'They were just using their work force efficiently.'

An expedition into the cave complex produced a collection of crystals which were brought back for Kal, as they were still convinced that he liked the pretty colours.

As it turned out, they were very hard and it was not long before they had a drill using one of the sharp ended crystals as a drill bit.

It was crude, but Kal had no doubt that the engineers would soon have it refined to produce an accurate drilling machine capable of drilling holes in the bronze castings before long. With the principle of the drill understood, engineering would really take off.

Kal thought it silly, but he longed to make a steam engine with which to power a vehicle so as to be able to roam about the planet without using foot power. He considered it a bit too ambitious for now, but he liked to dream.

The collection of food plants had grown, and the wall builders had now constructed another section outside the main compound, and the growers were busy stocking it.

It had been a long time since Kal had collected his own food, as they had insisted upon doing the collecting for him.

New types of fruit and berries were offered to him, and they had soon learnt that only the dull coloured ones were acceptable. The variety of his diet was such that it took at least ten days before he had to return to a food that he had eaten before, which made mealtime a lot more pleasurable.

At first, Kal thought that the little people had considered him to be a God, or something like that, but looking back upon events, he was not so sure.

They were too bright to be fooled by mysticism, and although they were in a sorry state when he found them, they had developed in leaps and bounds since, as far as culture and survival were concerned.

The mystery of how they had got there, and why they weren't able to work things out for themselves in the early days was something he may never know, but it intrigued him all the same.

Kal now felt at home with the little people, and couldn't imagine life without them, as there was none of the usual human traits to spoil the very pleasant relationship which had grown up between them.

In fact, if he had the choice, he wasn't too sure if he would return to his own people, such was the co-operation and harmony that existed here.

He sometimes wondered how long it would be before they advanced ahead of him, and he would have to ask them for advice. That was something he was not looking forward to.

The length of time Kal had spent on this planet seemed to be of little interest to him, as he was surprised to find out one day when trying to get things into chronological order.

So much had happened, with so many things having been reinvented and modified, that it was all getting a bit confusing trying to get them into sequence. He gave up in the end, and mentally just sat back and enjoyed the view, as they say.

The weavers had done themselves proud, and most caves sported pretty tapestries on their walls, but as yet clothing had no appeal to the little people.

His own clothes were wearing out, and replacements manufactured from a fine fabric, some of which had been made from fibres he had not seen before, were more comfortable to wear than his old ones.

The population of the tribe had grown to nearly double the size it was when Kal joined them, as there had been very few deaths from animal attacks due to the improved weapons and an understanding of the planet's dangerous life forms.

The steam engine was still a dream, but he had discussed it with them. They were either unusually thick about the concept, or had little interest in it, for there was none of their usual enthusiasm shown for the new idea, which was contrary to their normal reaction to such things.

The sand drawings had been replaced by a several large sheets of a white slate like material, placed in strategic positions, complete with pencils of very hard charcoal. This made fine detail very easy to accomplish, and the slates cleaned off very easily for reuse.

It was getting more and more difficult to keep up with the newest developments, as they came thick and fast. Kal realized that the little people were now totally self sufficient, and could well do without his help.

Feeling a little left out of the leading edge of technology side of things, so to speak, he realized that it was inevitable, sooner or later.

The tribe had organized themselves into a very efficient hierarchy, with a top council of the best thinkers supported by those who had experience in their own fields.

Everything was carefully talked over, and decisions were based on facts, and facts alone.

Vested interest just didn't come into any of their calculations, unless it was for the betterment of the whole tribe.

'We could learn a thing or two from them' Kal wryly thought, as he watched a meeting taking place to decide where to set up the next garden unit.

Kal considered that he was only invited along to the decision meetings as a courtesy. But he was in for a shock that would rattle him to the core this time.

The little one who came for him and extended the invitation to the meeting looked a little apprehensive, or so Kal thought.

It was difficult to tell how they felt, as their flat faces did not give very much indication of their inner feelings.

He went along to the meeting, and took his usual place of honour among the leaders of the council. The meeting had an unusually large number of members and Kal wondered what was afoot. It didn't take long to find out.

A drawing slate had been placed before him, and one of the council began drawing. The picture showed Kal on one side of the board, a gap, a selection of the native animals and next to them a group of the little people.

A line was drawn from the top of Kal's head and extended across the board. The same was done for the other two groups, which indicated that the little people were the smallest group on the board, and planet.

In the gap next to Kal, the leader then drew a 'person' which was taller than they were, but not quite as tall as Kal.

The next drawing showed Kal with one of the little people touching each other; a line was drawn from them and pointed to the new person that had been drawn next to the first picture of Kal.

It was blatantly obvious to one and all that they wanted him to mate with one of their kind, and so produce a new race that was taller, and would be more able to survive here. He was shocked to say the least of it, and shook his head.

There was a stony silence, and the leader gravely nodded his head very firmly, looked towards the other members, and they too nodded.

Kal took up the drawing pencil, and tried to show that they were of such different sizes and totally different races, that it wouldn't work.

He drew frantically, expressing every possible reason why it was not possible, and finally running out of ideas, looked up at the council.

The leader pointed towards the 'couple' drawn on the board, and they all nodded again, looking him straight in the eye. This was a tricky one, and Kal didn't want to insult them, but no way was he going to get involved in something as outrageous as this.

They were his friends, and he liked them, but he considered them to be nearer the animals than they were to him, until he remembered their learning ability and the things they had produced, albeit with a little help from him.

He didn't like doing it, but he rose to his feet, shook his head vigorously, and left the meeting. As he walked back to his cave, he wondered what they would make of his refusal, and what action they would now take.

He had long noticed that when a resolution was passed by the council, it went ahead, unless the facts later showed it to have been a mistake. In his case, there was no way of proving it to be a mistake, so he was now looking out for some clever move on their part.

No further approaches were made in the coming days, and there had been no change of attitude towards him, so he was on the point of forgetting the whole unpleasant incident when he received a visit from three of the little people.

One of them was the council leader, but the other two he didn't recognize, as they all seemed to look the same except for a very few, and that was by bearing and presence rather than physical differences.

They all had a purposeful air about them, and he wondered what they were up to. The little group came closer and Kal was about to rise from his chair, when there was a barely audible hiss, and a fine mist that was only just visible drifted towards him.

As he was on the point of taking a breath, he inhaled a little of the mist before he could stop himself. They had timed it to perfection.

It could have been that they had brought a new perfume for him to try, except that they didn't use perfume as far as he knew. But it did smell very pleasant. And it had a relaxing effect, so he sat down again as his legs did seem a little unsure of themselves.

Kal smiled at his lovely visitors, as they wavered like ripples on a pond before him.

How kind of them, they must have known that he was rather tired and wanted to lie down for a while.

They were very persuasive, and he could feel the strength in their little arms as they helped him from his chair.

The room was getting bigger, and so were his dear little friends, and the perfume they were wearing was like a soft sweet scented cloak that swept over him.

And then two of them slowly drifted off and disappeared, the remaining one was smiling and showing the most beautiful teeth. Her face lit up with joy for having found him and her long dark hair flowed down to caress his cheek.

Soft gentle hands massaged his tired muscles and he could feel himself relaxing in a haze of sweetness.

Suddenly he felt a stab of pain somewhere, he was not sure where, and again, but it was getting less and less, and then a lovely sensation that he could only vaguely remember having once known, but could not place it.

His heart was racing; his pulse pounding and then he seemed to explode in a shower of beautiful sparks....darkness, peace and sleep.

Kal woke up at last. It must have been night, for someone had thoughtfully lit his three lamps, and the room was bathed in a gentle pale yellow glow. He went to sit up and found that a certain part of his body was very sore, and then he remembered.

At first he felt a surge of livid anger; he was going to break heads over this violation.

Slowly he came to his senses, and looked at the facts, as they would have done. They had carefully worked out what they saw as the best course of action for the betterment of the whole tribe, which meant its extension into the future.

They had tried to get his co-operation and had failed.

Their basic goal still remained, so they went for it using the next most subtle thing they had, skill. Someone somewhere, must have noticed a slight reaction on his part to something, and putting two and two together which they were getting a little too good at, came up with a solution to their problem, the sleep mist.

It would be interesting to see how they felt towards him after their rather cheeky ploy. After all, 'do it yourself' was one thing; 'help yourself' was a different matter.

As he suspected, it made not one jot of difference when he went outside next day. It was as if nothing out of the ordinary had happened, and from their view point, it probably hadn't.

Kal felt he had to admire their single mindedness directed at achieving their goal. There was no maybe or perhaps, they just went ahead and did it. This kind of attitude would make them a very powerful race indeed, if all went well for them in the future.

Kal decided to forget the whole incident, it wouldn't work anyway, so was not likely to be repeated, and holding a grudge wouldn't get any of them anywhere, and was totally non productive.

There were some more metal ores he wanted to experiment with, and see if he could make iron, and then refine it to steel. That really would be something.

Steel would open up a whole new range of things to make and opportunities to be exploited. He swallowed what he thought was his hurt pride, took a deep breath, and went out to the mineral piles, to look for a possible iron ore sample.

A few days later after the unfortunate mating incident, a couple of the little people came to him and indicated that they had found something they wanted him to see.

A group of them had been exploring the cave complex, and had stumbled across a strange white powder which they thought might be of interest to Kal.

They had brought a little of it out with them, but Kal couldn't make out what it was. It was definitely not organic, so therefore it must have originated from decomposed rock, or a mixture of rocks, or maybe something caused by a reaction of one mineral with another.

He had seen nothing like it before, but would enjoy finding out what it could be used for, that's if it had a use.

Kal had by now collected together a small selection of chemicals which he could use for analysis, in a crude way. The sample was broken up into several units and the testing began. He got a reaction to weak acid, as it fizzed, so that meant there was a carbonate present, but nothing else seemed to make any difference to it.

It was only when he put a small portion onto a clay plate and put that into the bronze casters furnace, that the miracle happened.

The white powder fused into a clear liquid, and when they withdrew the plate, the liquid solidified into a glass-like substance. It had also fused itself onto the plate, and they couldn't get it off.

Kal had never come across a natural mineral that was in effect glass in a powder form, but then he had never been here before.

He asked to be taken to the source of the material, and a small group of them set off later that day armed with carry bags and a small wheeled box, and the usual weapons.

They had gone quite some way into the system of tunnels before they came to the cave from which the mysterious powder had been collected.

It was in an off-shoot from another cavern, and had only been found when one of them had got lost, and had called for rescue.

The back wall of the cave had a small hole high up at roof level, and the powder had cascaded down to form a pile on the floor. They loaded up the carry bags and the box trolley, and then began poking the hole to see if any more was ready to come out. A little did, and they collected that too.

There must have been a strange chemical process going on up there in the section beyond the cave roof, but there was no way they could get to it from where they were.

After returning to the compound Kal, gave instruction for a long bronze tube to be made, using a sand and clay core to make the hole up the middle.

A new crucible was also made, and two days later they were ready for the experiment. He had not told them what he was going to attempt, as it was likely that it wouldn't work, but he thought it was worth a try.

The crucible was filled with the white powder and placed into the furnace, and after a while they could see that the powder had melted and was bubbling.

More powder was added as the material went into its liquid phase, and eventually the crucible was withdrawn. Kal took up the bronze tube, dipped it into the molten mass. Gathering up a quantity of it on the end of the tube, he proceeded to turn the tube and blow at the same time.

The blob on the end of the tube expanded, and before long a bottle-like container was formed. Kal let it cool awhile, gave it a tap at the point where it joined the tube and had made the first of many glass containers to come. The sharp broken edge where it had joined the tube was ground smooth on one of the old grinding wheels.

Several days later, Kal went one step further using a specially made box-like crucible, dipping a half metre long bronze blade edgewise into the glass, and slowly withdrawing it.

A sheet of glass was formed as the blade was lifted, drawing up more of the semi-liquid material as it went. After several attempts, he got the withdrawing speed just right, and a very respectable glass sheet resulted.

It did have a few bubbles in it, and there were a few ripples as well, but that was a minor detail as far as he was concerned.

The concept of windows was something new to the little people, but they accepted it with delight, when they found that it kept insects out, although there were not that many to start with.

A team of glass blowers was soon formed, and speedily had the art of blowing containers of all shapes and sizes at their finger tips.

The main problem was finding more of the white powder, as it was a little slow in producing itself in the cave.

Kal wondered if there was any way to speed up the process of powder formation, but as he didn't understand how it was formed in the first place he didn't have a lot to go on.

They explored the cave from top to bottom, but all they could find was the mysterious hole near the roof and a slow trickle of powder every now and then.

Caverns each side of the powder cave were looked at very thoroughly, but to no avail, and then they found a narrow tunnel which went upwards in the general direction of the powder cave, and in they went.

It seemed to go on forever and the air was getting hotter all the time. Suddenly they came to a point where it opened out to a small cave overlooking a vast cavern below.

The little team stood in awe as they were bathed in hot air and steam, with a strange chemical smell to add to the weird effect of the place.

The whole cavity was lined with a crystal formation, as though a huge bubble had been blown in the earth, and the walls had crystallized out like sugar frosting.

There were wisps of steam or smoke rising up from several places, and the whole area was lit with an eerie light coming from the crystals on the floor of the cavern.

Water dripped occasionally from the roof onto the crystals below, accompanied by a faint hissing noise and that was generating the heat and light as it reacted with the crystals, or so Kal thought.

It was only a matter of adding a little more water to the system and they could have all the 'glass powder' they were likely to require. Nobody enjoyed the journey up to the glass cavern and back, but the little ones didn't seem to mind when Kal explained what to do and why.

They were going to have to be careful not to add too much water at a time, as it was possible that there could be an explosion, so violent was the chemical reaction.

'What else might lay hidden in the labyrinth of tunnels and caves under the cliff? It must be worth a look at sometime' was Kal's instinctive thought, never one to miss out on a good opportunity. He was so busy these days, finding the time to do all that he wanted was getting difficult, despite all the willing help of the little people.

Kal suggested that they try adding small amounts of some of the strange minerals which he couldn't identify to the glass, it may well be that these could add some colour to the finished products. Some samples were crushed, and added to the molten mixture in the crucible.

They were a little disappointed with the result in the melting pot, as it didn't seem to make any difference, but much to their surprise, when the glass was cooled the colours were there, full and vibrant.

The making of refractory material for the furnaces led on quite naturally to ordinary ceramics, and everyone had a set of plates and cups of different sizes before long.

Store jars were very popular, as they could help to keep food fresh, and any uninvited insects, were kept at bay. Once the knack of adding a glazed finish to the pottery had been achieved, then decoration soon followed.

Kal was surprised that the little people went in for such a frivolity as decorating their pots, as they had shown no sign of it in any way before. He thought that they were developing in all directions now, and wondered when the first paintings would appear.

That reminded him, paper making was a possibility, as they had now found a plant similar to the fibre tree that yielded short but fine fibres that were not suitable for spinning, but may well do for paper.

As there was no verbal language between them, and apart from the slate drawings, which was their only form of communication, he had not bothered with the quest for paper. Now might be a good time for it.

They may develop their own written language, but he didn't see how, as there was no initial base to work from, and he could only teach them his own.

Weaving the very fine sieves on which to catch the paper pulp was the most difficult part of the whole project, and having achieved that, with the customary time and patience, the rest was comparatively easy.

Making a press or rollers to compress the rough paper sheets so that they were made smooth was well within the abilities of the paper gang, and they set about the task with keen interest, as far as he could tell.

Kal was never really sure, as their faces showed so little emotion, and he could only judge by the way they went about their tasks.

There were plenty of sources for the dyes and pigments required for making the paint, should they want them, and once he had shown them what could be achieved, they were all for trying it out for themselves.

The first efforts were not too inspiring, but as with most things which they tried, it soon improved, and he was surprised yet again at their learning ability.

The days rolled on into months after the mating incident, and Kal had forgotten all about it, which was not too surprising, as he had been rushed off his metaphorical feet, thinking up new ideas to keep the little ones fully occupied and stretched to the limit of their abilities.

One day a large gathering in the compound had caught his attention, and as he went over to investigate he was turned away, politely, but turned away just the same.

'What the hell are they up to now' he thought, as he stood there imagining the worst. Shortly afterwards, he was beckoned over, and he was sure that some of them had a grin on their faces.

In the middle of the quite large group, was a clear space, and in the space was the oddest looking contraption he had ever seen. Smoke and steam was issuing forth from a chimney, and he was gently taken by the hand and lead over to it. There was total silence as a lever was indicated to him, and they invited him to move it.

Kal pushed the lever down, and with a hiss and a few clanks, a wheel, which he hadn't noticed before, began turning. Faster and faster it went, until the whole thing threatened to shake itself to pieces.

'Good God, they've done it' he cried out loud, and clapped his hands as enthusiastically as he could. Everyone else joined in the clapping, and it was really evident that they were enjoying the moment.

It rattled and clanked with clouds of smoke and steam gushing out all over the place, but it worked, and that was the main thing.

Somehow he felt very proud of his prodigies for that was how he now thought of the little people. What an achievement, considering how they were when he had found them so long ago.

With a little refining, and a set of wheels, the planet was open to them, and he was looking forward to it immensely. The first thing to do was to see just what principles they had based their machine on, and improve it without giving his friends a loss.

The wheels were no problem, and crude springs for wagons had already been developed. He wondered what would have happened if they had discovered light based mineral oils, but they hadn't, so steam power would do for the time being.

Next day, after a good night's sleep and an early breakfast, he went to join the steam gang who were already there waiting for him.

The strange thing was that the little people expected him to add his ideas to refining their machine, and this was quite evident from the way they presented themselves, the steam engine and the way they reacted to him. His worst fears were allayed, and he set to work.

The sketch slates were presented for Kal to draw on, and work commenced to improve what had been a marvellous breakthrough in engineering to a superb self powered vehicle, bearing in mind the limitations imposed on them by the tools and materials they had to hand.

Many days later, the steam driven, charcoal burning monster of a vehicle powered up for the first time, with much hand clapping and general noisy approval from all assembled, and that was just about everyone.

This was a machine which would carry about forty of the little people and Kal complete with provisions and a selection of weaponry. Unknown to Kal, the weapons had also been improved somewhat.

He had shown them other possible uses for the bow which he had used to make fire, and it had been developed into an effective long bow, once the principle had been understood, and it was then taken a step further and became an even more deadly cross bow.

The great machine was going to make exploring a lot easier, and Kal noticed that the driving seat had been made big enough for him to sit on.

Obviously he was intended to drive it, and after a practice run in the compound, as many as possible climbed aboard and the gates were flung open for their first powered journey into the unknown.

It was not a great journey of discovery really, but it was well into evening before they returned, a bit dusty, but very happy and excited.

The machine had been a great success, and although a few

modifications were desirable, it had performed very well indeed, although the speed of travel on rough ground would have to be improved.

Kal suggested that after a few alterations, they really should go on an expedition, just to see what else the world had to offer, and this was agreed upon with great enthusiasm by one and all. The rest of the evening was spent with the crew telling tales of the adventure and the things they had seen, at least he supposed that was what they were doing, judging by the attentiveness of the audience.

He had been on the planet for some considerable time now, but he had not noticed any change of season. This must mean that the world rotated in a stable circular orbit around its sun, and had no axial tilt, as the sun always rose and set in the same places.

The plants seemed to have worked out their own way of coping with this, as he had observed that while some were coming into fruit, others of the same species were over their fruiting cycle and were resting before producing another crop.

This meant that there were no fruiting seasons as such, and crops could be produced at any time throughout the year, except that there was no year as he knew it. Time measurement had no meaning that he could discern with regard to the little people, and he certainly had no use for it any more.

The metal smelters had been experimenting with the various ores, and blending them to produce some interesting combinations that were unknown to Kal.

Combining their skills with the glass makers, who had developed coloured bead manufacture, they were making a form of neck jewellery and an assortment of beautiful ornaments to adorn their caves with.

This was the first real sign that they were developing an aesthetic taste, for the ornaments had no utilitarian use that he could see.

Some of the shapes bore no resemblance to anything Kal had ever seen, but they were very pleasing to the eye, and it was not long before he was presented with some, but how they knew he wanted them, he didn't know.

The wooden gates to the main compound were replaced with the most impressive and elaborate design of bronze scroll work he had ever seen, and he then knew they were into 'art work' in a big way.

If only he could speak their language or even understand what they said, but there was no way his voice could duplicate their high pitched squeaks and whistles, let alone interpret what they meant.

The drawing system was very good for getting ideas across, but it was feelings that he was missing so much now. He felt sure they had more emotion in their lives now than ever before, and he wanted to share it with them.

It wasn't until he really thought about it, that he realized just how much he longed for conversation and a verbal exchange of thoughts.

They did their best to include him in everything they did, except for the odd meeting, and that was withheld intentionally just to give him a surprise later he felt sure.

Several days after the triumph of the steam driven vehicle, there was a commotion in the compound, and Kal was sent for. He entered one of the inner caves and saw a group of elders clustered around one of their kind, on a bed.

They parted for him to come through, and motioned for him to sit down on a bench against the cave wall.

He couldn't see any great detail of what was going on with regard to the person on the bed, as so many others were clustered around, but thought that all would be revealed to him in their own good time.

After much squeaking and whistles the leader of the council came towards Kal, bearing in his arms one of their newly born offspring, and presented it to him.

He reached forward to take the little bundle when he noticed it was not so little, and very nearly dropped it when the full significance of the event hit him.

This youngster was really well built and twice the size of their normal babies, and must have given its mother a very hard time of it indeed.

'So this was the result of cross breeding with the natives', he thought. The elder gently unfolded the arms and legs of the little one so that Kal could appreciate the length of the limbs, and the head was different too.

It looked more human and had more finely defined features than normal. The little creature gave a cry that was well within Kal's audio range, and he then knew that this was going to be the company he had longed for.

Kal arose from his chair, and carrying the new arrival walked over to the bench-like bed upon which lay the mother of the new race.

He had to admit that she looked tired, and not a little uncomfortable, but she looked him straight in the eye and the thin lips parted in what he thought passed for a grin among the little people.

He felt strangely drawn towards her, and took one of her hands in his, holding it tightly for a few moments. A gentle sigh like sound came from the others present, and they all slightly bowed their heads.

Normally, telling the sexes apart was more by luck than observation, as the male equipment seemed to retract out of sight when not in use, and mammary glands didn't show on the females until they were about to give birth.

This one was definitely a female, and Kal's heart went out to her for her bravery at attempting the cross breeding project, and going through the trauma of delivery.

He handed back the little bundle in his arms to the mother, and noticed the tender care she showed to her offspring. Kal wanted to say something, or do something to mark the occasion, but could think of nothing appropriate. The entourage left the cave, and Kal was at a loose end as to what to do now.

Should he follow the elders or return to his own cave, or just go about whatever he was going to do anyway?

He went back to his own place, and it was just as well that he did. Shortly after entering and sitting down to recover from the shock of it all, he burst into an uncontrollable flood of tears, as the locked up emotions of what seemed like years flowed out of him.

How long he sobbed for he didn't know, but as the tide of emotion lessened and he looked up with a tear stained face, three of the elders were standing rock still in the entrance, with bowed heads.

He knew then that they could at least share some feelings between them. Silently they turned as one, and discretely left Kal to his thoughts of what the future was to bring.

After a meal, he felt a lot better, and went off to the new team of jewellers who had set up a workshop in one of the caves near his.

Using his sketch slate, he indicated that he wanted the finest necklace they had, and when it was handed over, he felt sure there was a grin on the face of the craftsman who had fashioned it.

Kal made his way to the cave of the mother and child, and as he entered her companion quietly left, leaving them alone.

He gave her the necklace which she looked at for several moments, and then she took his hand and held it to her face.

Kal felt the tears well up again, and as he looked her full in the face he saw her eyes were also moist. They stayed like that for some time, each thinking their own separate thoughts but unable to fully share them, but the emotional flow had brought about a strange bond between them.

Eventually she released his hand and closed her eyes as if to sleep, and Kal silently slipped away.

The impact of what had taken place, the way it had been achieved and the consequences of the whole thing, left Kal a little shattered.

If only he had someone he could talk it over with, but he didn't, and that was another load of emotion that one day would have to be released.

FOUR:
Into the Mountain

THE FINAL MODIFICATIONS to the steam wagon were completed, and provisions placed aboard. Although they could live off the land, they were not too sure what land they might have to travel over, and so were taking no chances.

They set off early in the morning and received a great send off by those who would have liked to have gone, but for whom there was no room on the wagon.

At first they covered ground that was familiar to them, as the colony had expanded out from the original compound for some distance. There were well laid tracks joining up the various new compounds where crops were grown, and the wagon travelled smoothly along for some time.

It was when they ventured out into virgin territory that the new spring suspension came into its own. There were no maps of the area, as no one had ventured into the hinterland very far, so map making on stiff paper boards was done for future reference.

They headed out towards the black mountains where Kal had first discovered the water cave, and the stream that ran from it. On the way, they passed the point where the stream disappeared into the ground, never to be seen again.

This intrigued Kal, as it should have made an appearance somewhere at a lower ground level, except that there wasn't any lower ground, so where did it go?

They halted at the place where the water went down, and took a break. Kal went to the edge of the hole, but all he could see was the water going in and nothing else below it.

There wasn't even the thunder of water hitting rocks below, so maybe there weren't any, but then what was there?

It was too much, and he decided to go down on a rope and see what went on. The team were not too keen for him to do this, but they too were curious as to what the water did in its sink hole.

A safety rope was lowered into the hole, one end of which was tied off on the steam wagon, and another rope with a sling on it was passed to Kal, who put it around his waist.

The other end of the rope ran through a couple of pulleys which were also attached to the wagon, so that the team could lower and lift him as needed, the pulleys taking the hard work out of it.

Down he went into the darkness, not getting wet as there was a small gap between the water and the side of the hole.

His lamp light glistened like a cascade of falling diamonds in the water column, and gave an eerie light to the wall of the hole, which, as far as he could tell was a vertical tunnel, and as smooth as glass.

This didn't look as if it had occurred naturally, and so he was on the lookout for any other odd things which might be down here.

Every now and then Kal noticed there were large openings in the wall of the shaft, and a gentle draft was issuing from them, but he hadn't noticed a draft at the top where he first entered the hole.

The end of the rope must have come at last, as the winching down had stopped. He looked around him and saw that the volume of water was only about half what it was at the top of the fall. Where had the rest of it gone?

There were no signs of it having been diverted off anywhere on the way down, but the volume had definitely decreased compared to that at the top of the chasm.

It looked as though he would have to give up the descent, when off to one side he could see a ramp spiralling on down with what looked like a short flight of steps at the top. It began just above his head, and if he swung across carefully, he should be able to reach it.

He tried calling up to the team, but the distance was too great for them to hear, and they wouldn't have understood him anyway. He tugged the safety rope, and they began to haul him up. It took a little longer than he had expected, as the distance he had travelled down was deceiving.

Once back at the top he explained that he intended to detach himself from the rope at the bottom, and then go on down via the ramp.

They were not very happy about this, but didn't try to dissuade him too much. Kal descended again to the full extent of the rope and then swung himself over to the place where the ramp started, getting a foothold on the solid rock.

Somehow he would have to secure the rope at this side, as he couldn't risk jumping across the gap to where the rope would hang naturally if it was let go. But there was nothing to tie it to.

There was only one thing for it, and that was risky. Taking all his clothes off he held them in the diminished water flow until they were soaking wet, and then used them as a weight to hold the rope on the ledge.

Luckily the water didn't impinge on the rope as the flow was so much smaller here. Kal stood there for a while ready to grab the rope if it should move, but it didn't, and so he took a deep breath, and started on down the ramp.

It was a very long way down, and he began to wonder if there was an end to it. The water still fell, although it was only a very small amount now and seemed to be disappearing before his very eyes.

A few minutes later there was no water falling, just the ramp going on down into the blackness. He just had to find out what this was all about, and went on down against his better judgment.

At last the ramp stopped. He was at the bottom of a circular shaft that was as dry as a bone, and no sign of it ever being otherwise.

So now what? He was at the bottom of an empty shaft and nowhere to go, but up.

Kal felt that there had to be something down here and began a thorough search of the wall. At last, in the dim light of his lamp, he saw a silver disc about the size of his hand set into the rock of the circular bottom of the shaft.

It was too much, he pressed it, and a section of the wall slid to one side, revealing a passageway ahead. As there was nowhere else to go, he went in. The lamp lit the way fairly well as the walls were shiny and not too far apart, and the floor was flat and smooth.

This meant that it was meant for walking on, not for water, and that was a comforting thought.

All of a sudden he was in a circular chamber about two metres across, and no sooner had he stepped inside, when a section of wall slid across the entrance, and he was trapped. Now there was nowhere to go.

The floor was solid beneath his feet, the walls felt as though they were carved out of the heart of the planet, and a solid looking ceiling was just one metre above his head.

He wondered how long the air would last as the chamber was now totally sealed.

It was not the most pleasant of feelings, but he remained calm and reasoned that there must be some way out, as the chamber was purposeless without one.

His control paid off when he was least expecting it to. The wall he was leaning against dropped away from him and he nearly went sprawling.

The floor of the lifting device was going up the shaft at a considerable speed, while the ceiling still remained the same distance above his head.

The wall was fairly streaking downwards now, or to be more precise, he was going up very fast indeed. Suddenly the floor stopped moving, and he nearly floated as his momentum tried to carry him upwards.

A section of the wall slid back, as he somehow knew it would, and he was out into another passage, as quickly as possible.

This one didn't go very far, and terminated in a blank wall with another silver coloured disc set in it. Pressing the disc he waited for the next surprise.

It was not slow in coming. The wall slid back and a short ramp lead up towards a jumble of rocks, which he hastily climbed, and there below him was the little stream, the steam wagon and his friends.

He let out the loudest whistle he could, which they heard, and came running over to him. He helped them climb the rocks and go down the ramp, but there was no sign of a silver disc on this side.

The ramp just ended against a flat wall of rock, with no sign of a door or anything else. It was obvious that they were very pleased to see him again, and were soon making saucy comments about his nakedness, of that he was sure.

They were definitely getting a little too cheeky, but he was so relieved to see them, that he didn't really mind. It was then that he realized the tension he had been under.

They made their way back to the wagon, and while taking some refreshment he explained what had happened as best he could. One of them made ready to go down the rope to retrieve Kal's clothes, but he explained that if they pulled the rope up it might dislodge the clothes and they would fall to the bottom of the shaft.

This did not deter the volunteer, who chose to use the safety rope instead, and when it had been hauled up, tied it around his waist and disappeared from sight. It was a long wait, but at last the signal to haul up was received, and the little fellow complete with clothes came to the surface amid a good hand clap from all present.

The 'clothes collector' had found that the clothes had indeed fallen on down the shaft, but he had the foresight to take a big stone down with him and so was able to secure the rope, go down the ramp, climb up again, give the signal and return to the surface.

He explained no way was he going to try the 'lift' as Kal had done, which caused a bit of leg pulling from the others.

It was decided that they all had had enough excitement for one day, and a proper meal was taken.

After their meal and a general chat via the drawing pads about the day's happenings, the protection shields were raised around the side of the wagon, and they all retired for a good night's sleep.

Kal kept thinking about the shaft. A lot of work had gone into making it, and so it had to have a useful purpose. And then he remembered that on the way down, some of the openings in the wall seemed to have air coming out of them, and some had air going back in.

If there was enough air flowing like that it could cause the water to evaporate, hence the dwindling column of water the further down he went.

'There must be something more to it than that', he thought, and then he recalled the vast hole in the cavern inside the black mountain with the blast of moist air coming out of it. It seemed to make sense, of a sort.

'But why go to all that trouble to recycle water like that?', he mused, 'how could so much water be evaporated like that as there didn't seem to be enough holes to supply enough air, but yet it worked'.

There was still something else missing from the equation, and he was determined to find it. Someone or something had gone to a lot of trouble to construct the water recycler, and they were not much bigger than him if the size of the passageways was taken into consideration, and then there were the steps, so they had feet, but why the ramp then... He fell asleep and dreamed of waterfalls and gentle breezes blowing around him and...

The sun rose on another glorious day as the crew of the steam wagon fired her up, and an early breakfast was taken so that they could get under way as soon as possible.

There had been no disturbances during the night, so all felt refreshed and eager to go on with the exploration.

The events of yesterday still held Kal's attention to some extent, as he didn't like loose ends, and there were plenty of them lying around after their escapade of the disappearing water. However, that would have to be put aside for the time being, as they were about to continue their voyage of discovery, and no doubt find many more strange things.

As soon as they had enough steam pressure up, and everything had been stowed away, they were off. The general idea was to skirt the black mountains and see what lay beyond them.

The wheels of the steam wagon were massively built, and wide, so quite rough terrain could be negotiated without much trouble, only large rocks and deep gullies could hinder their progress.

There was the occasional lurch, which left a depression in the ground and Kal thought it might be caused by going over one of the underground plants that caught the croppers, as it only happened when going over gross covered terrain.

The wagon was quite able to cope with it, but a really big hole might cause a problem.

About midday they came to a long upward slope in the ground, and upon reaching the top, the mountains hove into clear sight. They were certainly majestic, and were an impenetrable barrier for the steam wagon, so they chugged along at the base of the massive rock formation for the rest of that day.

As dusk approached they decided to make camp for the night. There didn't seem to be any dangerous creatures in the area, and as the ground was clear for some distance around, they set up oil lamps and had their evening meal out in the open. The lamps had been improved beyond all recognition, with a specially formed glass chimney.

The flame was steady, even in a light wind, and the lamp produced a lot more light due to a shiny metallic reflector.

It was at moments like this, in the restful quiet after an evening meal, which Kal sometimes thought about his old crew aboard the Star Search.

They would probably have reached their destination by now, and discovered his absence along with that of the shuttle. If they couldn't repair another of the old shuttles, then they would have to go back to base.

He knew that a search party would not be sent, as the possibility of finding him was so remote that it would not even be contemplated. He wished he could tell them that he was all right and enjoying life, but there was no way that he could do so.

Once more the safety shutters were put up, and the crew retired to sleep and dream their dreams, that's if they did dream. Kal thought he would enquire one day, although how he could get that concept across was beyond him at the moment.

As he thought about it, he drifted into sleep, and dreamed that he and the little people were talking together, later he could not recall what they had been saying, although he seemed to understand it at the time.

When they awoke next morning, they found that they had camped at the foot of a long smooth track that ran up into the mountain range.

The early morning meal was hurried as excitement grew at the prospect of the exploration, as it was quite evident that it wasn't a fluke of nature. The steam wagon had a hard time of it in one or two places as the gradient was quite steep, but with most of the crew walking beside it in the steepest places, she made it.

One thing they did have to watch out for was the width of track, as they didn't want to get into a position where they couldn't turn around if they needed to.

At last they came to a large flat space that once perhaps had buildings on it, or maybe was a transport parking area. It was clear now, and as the track ended here they turned the wagon around ready for the return journey down the hill.

Kal expected to see something up here to justify the presence of the track and the flat area at its end, but nothing obvious could be seen.

The crew split up into small parties and began exploring the sides of the flat space for clues. They were surrounded by towering cliffs of rock on all sides and there certainly wasn't another way down than that which they had came up by, so what went on here?

A loud squeaking caused all to run over to one party who sounded as if they had found something. A pile of loose rock was just a little too tidy to have been naturally formed, and this was what had been spotted by the 'squeakers'.

Closer inspection proved them right. A tunnel or cave was carefully covered up by the rocks, and the crew set to with poles and a couple of bronze bars from the wagon to lever out some of the bigger rocks, so that they could see what lay behind.

As the last few rocks were removed, the entrance to the cave was revealed. Lamps were lit, and all went in except a couple of guards left at the entrance as a precaution, against what they were not sure, but no chances were being taken.

The featureless walls had been hewn from the living rock, and they were about to give up after a few hundred metres or so and return, when the light from the leading lamp sparkled on something.

Kal went over, and found a crystal of water clear material, possibly quartz, lying on the floor of the tunnel. Picking it up, he saw that it was a true cylinder with flat ends.

Kal didn't know of any material that crystallized out in this form, as most crystals of quartz were six sided, and he had never seen a naturally round crystal of anything.

He passed it round for all to see. Kal took it again and looked in the dim light to see if there were any signs of it being manufactured.

It was perfectly smooth, and holding it in his hand, he gave it a tap on the end with his bronze knife to try and get some idea of how hard it was.

He was not ready for the nasty electric shock he received for his pains, and nearly dropped the crystal. Now he knew what it was.

The phenomena had been known for a very long time, but the crystals were usually manufactured, although he had heard of them occurring in nature sometimes. The effect was known as piezoelectricity. Some crystals had it, and if struck in a certain place, would generate an electric flow.

Also if the crystal was subjected to an electric current, it would change shape slightly. This crystal certainly packed a punch, and all sorts of ideas flashed through Kal's mind.

They must find more of these crystals and bigger ones if possible. This was conveyed to the crew and they set off along the tunnel to find the main source.

Side caves began to appear, and this slowed down the advancement along the tunnel, as everyone had to be checked. Nothing more was found and Kal began to wonder if the crystal had been brought into the tunnel system and left here. A little further on, and they heard the first sound in the tunnels, apart from their own foot falls.

It was as though something was shuffling along, and the crew immediately formed up to surrounded Kal, with spears at the ready. He then realized that they had been told to protect him at all costs.

'It is very flattering to be of such value to the tribe, but could get in the way of progress if taken to excess' he thought. The shuffling noise grew louder, and two of the crew with lamps held out on long poles, advanced into the cave from which the sound was coming.

The sound stopped, and before them was another of the giant white maggot things they had seen before in the main caves back home. This one was not all that big on closer inspection, but too big for the little ones to fight.

Kal stepped forward pushing through the group of protectors, and flung his spear with all his strength at the maggot.

It landed squarely in the middle of the head, just above the mouth slit, and sank in so far that only a little of the shaft remained in view. The creature opened its mouth and uttered a soundless scream, and the crew dropped their weapons and clapped their hands over their ear holes to shut out the noise. They could hear it, but Kal only got the feeling behind the sound.

He felt sorry for the poor creature, for after all they were invading its domain, and attacked it without provocation.

His pity melted away faster than it had come when the end of the spear fell to the ground, the rest of it having been dissolved away inside the creature. He signalled a retreat, and they backed off towards the point at which they had entered the cave, but the maggot followed.

As it drew closer, and more light from the lamps illuminated the hulk, its true hideousness became more apparent to those huddled at the cave's entrance.

There seemed to be a tough outer skin which was translucent, enclosing a jelly-like substance, and the organs of the creature could be clearly seen within the mass. It had no eyes and only a slit of a mouth.

It was the transparency of the creature that made it so horrible to confront, all those bits floating around inside. Whatever internal juices it had, they were very corrosive, as the remains of the spear had indicated.

They would have to fight it to the death or find a tunnel which was too small for it to follow them into. The crew raced along the tunnel and entered a new one which was slightly smaller and on an incline, hoping the creature would not be able to follow.

Unfortunately it did, although it was a tight squeeze for it. As they had gained a little distance from the monster, and they didn't see any profit in running from it forever, Kal made a decision that they would fight.

He took two of the blade-like swords which were carried by some of the crew, and jammed them into a crevice in the tunnel wall such that they stuck out like knife blades, one on each side.

Kal didn't know if they would be long enough to do what he had in mind, but it was the only way they could stop the creature, apart from standing there and throwing spears and that didn't seem to be a good idea after what happened to the first spear he had thrown.

They bravely stood their ground as the maggot forced its way towards them. At last it reached the blades but didn't seem to notice them at first, and then it screamed again and stopped. The screams rent the air again and again, and the crew were almost paralysed by the sound as they held their hands over their ears and gyrated around in agony.

Kal could only detect the sensation of the sound, almost like a vibration, felt but not heard. He had never experienced anything like this before, and was relieved as the sound died away.

The creature seemed to be shrinking as they watched, the head section lowering itself to the passageway floor and a gap appeared between the main body and the tunnel roof.

It took some time for the corrosive fluid that made up most of the maggot to drain away, but it did eventually, and they were left with a pile of skin with a few lumps and bumps in it, which they supposed were its internal organs.

A gentle draft was flowing down the tunnel taking the smell and fumes of the fluid away from them, or they would all have suffered the fate of the passage floor, which was being dissolved by the leaking juices of the maggot.

Once the bulk of the creature had totally deflated, they were able to carefully walk over the skin, avoiding any damp patches, to inspect the carcass.

There was not much of it left really, apart from the skin, the lumps that contained the internal organs, and the head section, and that proved an interesting piece of equipment.

It had been furnished with a set of jaws that appeared to have moved in and out rather than up and down, and rows of what they assumed to be teeth.

At the rear end of the carcass was the greatest surprise of all. In a big bulge they could see a collection of the crystals, and being very careful, were able to cut the skin, hook out what seemed to be a transparent bag containing the crystals, and drag it clear of the body.

Once on safe ground the bag was cut open, and the contents washed with a little of their precious water supply to remove any of the corrosive fluid which might have remained.

A selection of the cylindrical crystals glittered in the light from their lamps, and were gingerly picked up and stowed away in one of the carry bags they had brought with them.

Some time later, Kal was able to work out what the maggot was all about. He was not totally sure of his finding, but they seemed to make as much sense as anything else did.

The original 'miners' had either brought the creature with them or had found it here, and possibly altered it to suit their needs. The crystals, which were the key to the whole operation, were held in a matrix of an unusually tough stone-like material, and breaking it up damaged the crystals themselves.

Somehow, the creature was quite happy to eat this particular kind of stone, and in fact thrived on it, the crystals being of no use for some reason, and probably a form of irritant, were 'saved' in a skin bag inside the creature.

Whether they were expelled, or the creature had to be slain, Kal never found out. It was certainly the most unusual mining operation he had ever heard of, and the whole concept of using a live creature to do the work of selecting what you want from a pile of rocks, amused him.

They didn't like to risk going back down the tunnel past the remains of the maggot, as the corrosive fluid was still attacking the ground over which it had flowed, so another way out of the complex had to be found.

They went up the passageway until they came to a large cavern with many openings leading to a myriad of caves. Some looked as if they had been carved out of the rock, while others looked natural, possibly water worn.

A vein of the crystal bearing rock could be seen in one case, and Kal tried unsuccessfully to extract a crystal, but damaged it in the effort, so he abandoned the idea.

They chose a tunnel which was leading down towards the level from which they had started after the first encounter with the maggot, and followed its twists and turns for a distance that was far longer than they calculated it should have been.

Kal was getting worried that they were about to get lost, despite the fact that they had marked their way as they went along. The temperature was rising, and there was no longer a draft from behind them.

What little air flow there was, seemed to be coming from ahead of the little party, and it had a dusty metallic smell about it, which irritated their noses.

A feeling of unease soon pervaded the little troupe, and progress was much reduced, as every nook and cranny was closely scrutinized.

Suddenly the tunnel took a steep downwards dip, and faced with the option of going all the way back, which they thought they may have to do, or go on to see if there was a way out ahead, they chose to press on.

It was almost like going down a steep stone slope, except they were hemmed in on all sides by the rock walls. It was getting hotter, and although they could still breathe, it was most unpleasant and dried their throats.

Water, or the lack of it, was going to be a problem if they were not careful. Small regular drinks were taken, mainly to lay the dust which they were inhaling.

The tunnel opened out in a huge cavern just ahead of them, and a vast crater was in its centre.

They gingerly crept forward, ever watchful for any sign that the floor would give way, until they reached the rim of the crater. Looking over the edge was a bit like looking into what most people thought hell would be like.

There was a dull red glow engulfing everything. A hazy mist or smoke drifted up from holes in the base of the pit, accompanied by the occasional fierce jet of steam or gas.

At the bottom of the giant pit, the ground was covered in strange tree like growths with what appeared to be the odd limb attached here and there, but it didn't look like any form of vegetation he had ever seen before.

The only conclusion Kal could come to was that it was a mineral formation of some kind, caused by the gases rising from the holes in the crater floor, and being deposited rather like stalagmites in a limestone cave.

No one was going down to find out, so he only had his theories to go on.

Opposite to where they had entered the cavern was another tunnel, and as this was the only way out, apart from going back the way they had come, they took a chance that the fates would be with them, and entered it.

Before long it had narrowed down and was a tight squeeze for Kal, although the rest of the party got through all right. He could feel the heat of the rock walls on his flesh, and realized that if they stayed here too long, they would probably cook in their own juices.

The passage opened out after what seemed like several kilometres, but it was in fact only a short distance, and they were on their way upwards again.

The hot dusty air still blew from behind them, and they longed for the fresh clean air of the open plains, which at the moment seemed a long way away.

Kal thought it strange that what appeared to be volcanic action in the crater had shown no sign of its existence on the surface of the planet. This was unusual, but then so were most things here.

The climb up was getting harder, and the possibility of losing one's footing and sliding all the way down again was causing some concern. They reached a point where the tunnel was almost vertical, and had to use the spear poles to enable them to reach the next ledge up.

This was the most frightening part of their journey so far, and with a sigh of relief, they reached a section of the tunnel where it had levelled out a little, and they all took a break for food and a drink from their fast diminishing water.

They had reached a point from which they could not return the way they had come, and survive. The water situation was getting serious and all were feeling tired.

The heat had taken a lot from their energy reserves, and progress was slow and painful to say the least. It was at this point where they were not paying sufficient attention to their surrounding, that the first casualty of the trek occurred.

One of the little people who seemed to have more energy than most, had gone up ahead, and in so doing probably saved the lives of the others.

The passageway ahead took on a different appearance to that in which they were travelling, and the energetic one had stepped into the darkened area which immediately enfolded him in copious layers of what looked like dangling flesh.

He was gone in an instant, remaining as a slight bulge in the wall of the tunnel for a moment, and then was no more.

The rest of the party skidded to a halt just outside the range of whatever it was that had take their companion, in sheer disbelief and horror.

The monstrosity that lined the walls of the tunnel did so for several metres, and as there was no way around it, they were trapped unless they could come up with some way to fool it or remove it from the walls.

Kal advanced until he thought he was just outside its range and offered the tip of a spear. It was grabbed instantly and wrenched from his hands so quickly and with so much force, that he nearly followed it.

The spear was rejected by the creature and lay on the floor of the tunnel just outside their reach. Not wanting to lose a valuable weapon, Kal reached forward with another spear, and managed to hook the fallen one back.

The bronze end had been corroded with a brown slime like liquid, and they were very careful not to touch it.

A serious impasse had been reached. They wanted to go up the tunnel, and the thing on the wall wanted a meal. They prised a few rocks away from the tunnel wall, and threw them at the creature, which, after the first one or two, ignored the rest of the bombardment.

The sketch board came out and ideas flowed back and forth, but none seemed to be worth trying. Kal wondered if fire would cause the creature any concern, and poured a little oil on a piece of fabric torn from one of the carry bags. Attaching it to a spear end, he applied a light from one of the lamps, and advanced towards the thing on the wall. As the smoky flame touched the fringe of the creature, it shrank back, and Kal knew that they had it beaten, if they had enough fuel.

He took two of the precious oil containers, and removing the bungs, threw one of them up the passageway so that it landed in the middle of where the creature hung, and sloshed the other one around the entrance of the danger zone and up towards where the other container lay.

The flaming spear was then applied to the oil moistened edge of the horror, and they all moved back to see what would happen.

The flames leaped, and a thick black acrid smoke curled up from the writhing lengths of the entrapping tentacles of the creature as it caught fire. It crackled and popped as the flames and smoke spread rapidly up the tunnel, and luckily away from them.

It must have contained a high degree of fat or something like it, for it was truly ablaze in seconds, and the crew had to retreat back down the tunnel some considerable distance to get away from the heat.

There was a dull whoosh accompanied by a gush of flame and sparks, as the second oil container disgorged its contents into the inferno that now raged in the tunnel.

They waited for a time after the flames had died down, just in case some vestige of life remained in the creature, but all was still except for the odd little twists of smoke that drifted up from the remains on the passage floor.

The group advanced slowly until they were about half way through the mess, and then they all took to their heels and fairly belted up the passage to get clear of the nightmare.

Kal noticed a sadness had fallen over the little group, as they mourned the loss of their companion, and he too felt the loss.

The little people seemed to not only advance in their ability to learn and think things out for themselves, but their emotions and appreciation for things was growing.

This was a development that usually took many generations in other races, but with these people it was speeded up considerably, to a point which was very noticeable.

The climb up the tunnel was getting steep again, and frequent rests had to be taken. Just ahead the ways divided into three separate exits, and the dilemma which now faced them was which one to take.

Kal saw that one of the openings showed markings as thought it had been cut or enlarged, and so that one was chosen as it probably led to the workings above from which they had descended earlier.

They didn't know where they would come out, or even if they would reach the surface for sure, but as they had no option other than to press on, they did so.

The passageway now took on a definite look of having been cut, so this cheered them up considerably and the pace increased accordingly. Kal wondered, as they forged ahead, what other strange creatures these mountains held within them, and whether it would be worth their while setting up a special expedition to explore the tunnels.

There was great excitement as one of the party recognized a mark on the wall that they had made on their way into the tunnel complex. The only problem was, which way to go, as the mark on the wall was at an intersection which they had just come out of, and there was no indication as to the direction the party had taken when the mark was made.

They remembered the air flow on the way in had been behind them for some distance, but they couldn't feel anything now. While they all stood around wondering what to do, one of the little ones gathered up some fine dust from the floor of the passageway, and holding his hand in the light of the lamp, let the dust gently trickle from it.

There was a slight drifting of the dust in one direction, so they knew that the way out must be the opposite one, and set off as fast as their weary legs would carry them. Kal thought that the 'dust test' was yet another example of the brightness of these people, as he had not thought of doing it, and yet again wondered just how advanced they would get in time and with the right stimuli.

As they progressed along the tunnel, more of the markings came into view, and they knew for sure that they were on the way out of the complex.

It had been a difficult journey, and they had learned a lot from it, but the relief when it was over was very evident.

The main tunnel was entered at long last, and they positively hurried along and out into the bright light of day, or evening, as the sun had dipped towards the horizon.

The greeting they received from the rest of the crew of the steam wagon was quite overwhelming, and a surprise to Kal. It was as if they had been away for many years and the rumour had gone around that they were all dead.

This was another indication that the little people were changing, or maybe, hidden or repressed feelings were now coming to the fore.

The evening meal was an almost joyous occasion, and went on for a long time interspersed with much story telling. Kal wished he could have joined in more fully with it, but was limited to his sketches of events, which were looked upon with what amounted to reverence.

'There's no substitute for a good old chat' he thought, and wistfully watched the others squeaking and whistling away for all they were worth.

That night they all slept very soundly, and were not disturbed by the visit they had from something very large and possibly hungry.

The safety shields had been put up as a matter of course, and it was just as well that they had been.

Pad marks deeply impressed in the areas of sand denoted something heavy had come this way, and one of the bronze safety sheets on the side of the wagon had been bent back, as though something very strong had tried to force an entry.

The bronze sheets were very tough and it must have taken a lot of force to have bent the damaged one so out of shape, and Kal was surprised that no one had heard the attempt to get at the wagons contents.

This was something new to them all, and caused some consternation on the part of the little ones, as to them the visitor must have seemed colossal.

Kal was not too keen to meet it either, and set about following the tracks with an armed guard, to see if it was still in the vicinity, but the trail faded out as it crossed a rocky area, and could not be picked up again.

Extra guards were to be posted at night now, and would work in shifts, sitting in the driving seat of the wagon as this gave the best all round view from the vehicle.

As no one wanted to go back into the tunnel system for a while, it was decided to go back down the track and continue along the base of the mountain range; to see what else there was of interest.

The bag of crystals interested those of the crew who had remained on the wagon during the expedition, and a small crystal was used to demonstrate the electric effect for those who were willing to try it.

Kal thought that it might make some of them think up some uses for the crystals, although thinking back to his academy and training days, he had already got some ideas on the subject.

The journey down the track was mostly uneventful, except for two places where the steepness of the slope gave them a little more forward speed than they would have liked.

This meant that there was going to have to be a modification to the braking system, as soon as they returned to the compound.

The vegetation was beginning to get a little sparser as they travelled along, and the food stocks were topped up and water levels checked to make sure that they had the maximum quantity on board.

The steam engine used up quite a lot of water, and without a renewable supply the wagon would have been as much use as a fishnet in the desert. Fuel for the engine was not limited to charcoal, as wood could be used, but it did make a lot of smoke, and the crew much preferred the almost smokeless charcoal.

Midday brought them to the first area of open water they had seen since the pool rocks back at the compound. It was only a small lake, but made a pleasant change from the usual surroundings. It was fringed with an assortment of growths, all jostling for premier position at the water's edge, and quite a few new varieties were to be seen.

Kal stopped the wagon in a clear space well away from the water's edge, as anything new had to be checked out for safety before liberties were taken.

Some of the crew began collecting water for the main storage tank, while others stood guard on the water party. A few dead trees were found, cut up, and added to the fuel supply, before a meal break was taken.

Kal wanted to have a swim and tried to get the concept over to his friends. At first they seemed horrified at the idea of actually going into the water, but gradually interest was shown in him going in, but they thought water was only for drinking.

The idea of washing the body with water was something new to them, and Kal tried to explain his need to bathe. But as they didn't, and seemed as though they didn't need to, there was little understanding of the whole concept.

He had noticed without thinking much about it, that they didn't have a body odour as such in his terms, only a slight musky smell that was not at all unpleasant.

After the area had been checked out for carnivorous plants and other unwelcome items, and the water closely looked at and poked with a spear, Kal took off his clothes and slowly walked in.

It was very pleasant and cooling, and as he could see the sandy gravel that formed the bed of the lake, he felt fairly safe. By the time the water was up to his waist the onlookers were beginning to get a little nervous, and signalled for him to come in.

The bottom was still in clear view, there were no fish or anything else moving about in the water, so he lowered his body and began to swim. The look of sheer horror on the faces of his friends was something to behold, as it must have been the first time that they had seen such a spectacle.

Kal swam on until he was well out of his depth and dived down for a metre or so, surfacing some distance away. This did cause some concern, and he was sorry to have caused the little ones such an unnecessary fear.

He turned and swam as fast as he could for the lake side to demonstrate his prowess as a swimmer, not that it cut much ice with the audience, but he felt good about it.

As he stepped ashore there was a small tidal wave racing across the waters towards him, and he turned in disbelief as a vicious set of jaws set in a very ugly head broke surface a mere three metres away from him.

The water monster was all head, or so it seemed. There was a very small body with a disproportionately large set of driving fins, and a tail that looked as if it was capable of cutting him in two with one flick.

The creature had, in its enthusiasm to convert him into a meal, beached itself, and was not able at first to return to water deep enough to swim in.

As it thrashed about in its frustration, they all had a good look at a very proficient killing machine doing its best to take it's revenge on the shallows, as if were their fault that lunch had got away.

Somehow Kal had lost interest in the water, and didn't think he would go for another swim just yet. He was still shaking some minutes later after the monster had churned its way out into deep water, and swam off.

After things had returned to as near normal as they were going to for a couple of hours, the leader of the crew came to Kal with his sketch block, and very sternly forbade him to go swimming again.

There was no mistaking the authority displayed in his manner, and Kal felt for the first time that he was no longer the boss of the expedition.

In a way it was nice to know that they felt that much for him, but it also drove home the point that they were looking after their own interests in no uncertain manner, and would brook no nonsense.

A meal seemed to put things back into perspective, and the local vegetation was checked out for new edibles to add to the food store. They somehow knew what they could eat safely, or they had a sense that Kal didn't recognize.

He found only one new item, but it was worth waiting for. A large melon-like growth was found in the middle of a collection of the most vicious spine covered leaves he had ever seen. It took a while to strip enough of the leaves away to enable them to get at the fruit, which was a dull grey colour, and therefore possibly safe to eat.

It proved to be not only edible, but of the most delicious flavour he had ever tasted. He could not believe his luck, and was on the lookout for the hidden catch, but there didn't seem to be one, as yet.

The troupe got underway for the afternoon stretch of their quest, and followed the edge of the mountain range as before.

After the lake, the vegetation diminished considerably, with only the occasional small area of gross and its accompanying plants.

It would seem that water was getting in short supply as far as the ground was concerned, and only when there was an up welling from the subterranean water table could plants survive. Of course it could have been that the underlying rock was very near the surface, and didn't give the plants much of a chance.

On the horizon there was a large dark shape. They couldn't make out what it was from this distance, but thought it might be a lone rock or possibly a clump of trees. It looked out of place because of its size and isolated from anything else.

The steam wagon puffed along its way, eating up the kilometres as it went, and the dark shape drew nearer.

They had stopped, for no reason that anyone could understand, except that it had seemed a good idea. There was an area of very inviting sand just off to the side of the wagon, and the crew disembarked to go and investigate it.

Most had gathered a metre or so from the edge of the 'sand lake', for that was what it looked like, and Kal joined them.

There was something compelling about the sand. It was clean and silvery and looked soft and inviting and it would be nice to touch it and we would all feel so much better if we did and .... Kal let out a shriek at the highest frequency that he was capable of.

They were all going into a trance, and who knows what they would have done if all control had been lost. He had seen a movement out in the middle of the sand area, and this was quickly followed by several slight quivers of the sand in many different places.

Kal motioned them all back a few metres and a dazed huddle of travellers looked at him for the next instruction.

A few seconds later and the effect had worn off, and they all realized what had happened.

It was the first time he had seen what he thought to be anger displayed on their faces. Kal went back to the wagon and picked up a small selection of food stuffs.

Throwing the collection as far as possible out across the sand, they saw the whole area became alive as hundreds, possibly thousands, of 'something's' wriggled their way to the food.

Except that wriggle was not the right word because of the speed involved. It was about as fast as he could run, when going at full tilt.

In seconds there was nothing left to indicate that anything had ever been there, except the lovely inviting sands which.... here it was again, and Kal shook his head as though there was something nasty in his ear.

The others cottoned on quickly, and shook their heads to clear them. This was one of the most dangerous things they had yet come across.

It was one thing meeting a six legged tiger, a plant that caught you in its whip like tentacles or something that tried to make you think it was a pool of water in order to catch you, but when something could get at your mind and override your conscious thoughts it was time to take note, and clear the area until you knew a little more about it.

There was something, or a lot of something's, out there in the sand that did just that. The temptation was too much for Kal, as he had to know what it was, and set about trying to catch one.

He tried to remember which bait had been taken the most earnestly, and decided it all was, so it didn't matter what he used as long as it represented food to 'them'. The sketch block came out, and he showed the crew what he wanted them to do.

A quantity of fruit was lashed to one end of a pole and a long rope attached to the other end. A team of the little people held the free end of the rope while Kal threw the baited pole out across the sand lake as far as possible, being very careful not to get too near the edge, and keep his mind on what he was doing.

They hardly had time to take up the strain on the rope before they had a catch. The rope was hauled in, and on the end of the pole was a collection of very unpleasant looking worm like creatures.

They differed in size and colour, although the colours were mainly dark greens and greys through to black. A large head with teeth out of a nightmare completed the business end of the creature while the body tapered off to a thin whip like tail with barbs on it.

As the pole came ashore most of the little horrors dropped off and wriggled back into the sand, but one didn't quite make it, as it had driven the barbed tail into a piece of fruit and couldn't release it.

The bright light must have caused it some discomfort as it tried to bury its ugly head in the hard ground. Kal grabbed the pole and holding the creature down firmly with it, worked his way along the pole to get a better view.

Waves of fear with a hint of pain swept over him and he was nearly sick. Kal realized that the nearer he got to the creature, the stronger the feelings were getting.

He forced his attention on what he was doing despite the strange impulses he was picking up from the creature on the end of his pole.

'If it can send thoughts, then it should be able to receive them' Kal reasoned, and he strongly thought a picture of searing white heat blasting down on the creature.

The light or something must have got to it, for it gave a final wriggle and then lay still. Kal was taking no chances and gave it a poke with his foot, but it was dead.

Closer examination showed that the barbed tail was driven into the prey so that the head end could get a good purchase and go to work with the teeth.

Having gleaned all the information from the carcass that he was able, Kal pushed it towards the lake of sand, and as it touched the edge something waiting therein grabbed hold of it, and it was gone.

A little of the sand had stuck to the pole, as it had been moistened by the juice from one of the fruits, and Kal took a good look at it. There were a few grains of genuine quartz sand particles present, but most of it was made up of crunched up bones. He gave a little shudder as he realized the potential of those teeth. He would steer well clear of any sand lakes that came into view in the future.

The team were badly shaken by the experience, as they had been so easily taken over, as it were, and were not likely to forget it for a long time.

If the sand lake could contain creatures like this, where else might they be? This was not a pleasant thought, and Kal tried to forget about it, but the idea wouldn't go away.

They all piled back into the wagon, a very quiet and sombre little group, thinking their own thoughts no doubt, which were probably not too far removed from those of Kal.

They chugged on for a few more hours, but all the jolliness had gone out of the expedition.

It had shaken the little people far more that Kal had realized, and so he called a halt to the journey as soon as they came to a pleasant and safe looking spot, although there was still plenty of light left for travelling.

A good meal seemed to cheer everyone up a bit, and soon things were nearly back to normal.

Kal had made a ball from some heavy fibres from a plant they had found at the stop before the sand lake, and using the sketch block, tried to get the idea of 'play' across.

It was a bit of a dead loss really, so he positioned several of the crew in a circle, and demonstrated throwing the ball from one to the other.

They soon caught on to the throwing and catching part of it, and were just as good at it as he was before long, but didn't seem to find it a fun thing to do.

And then one of them lost his balance while reaching out to catch a badly thrown ball, and fell flat on his face.

That did it, laughter peeled out across the stillness of the evening, or at least Kal hoped it was laughter, as the frequency of it was only just within his hearing range.

He assumed it must have been funny for them, or at least contained some entertainment value, because they now went at it with great enthusiasm and played on until it was almost no longer possible to see the ball.

He was glad that they could enjoy a joke or have a bit of fun, as they had shown no sign of it in the past, and he had realized that something was missing.

Night came and went, and the new day saw them on their way along the edge of the mountain chain again.

The dark shape on the horizon was nearly upon them as they rolled along on a relatively smooth piece of ground, making better progress than they had for some time.

It revealed itself to be a kind of tree, but the biggest tree Kal had ever seen. It must have been over seventy metres high, and the trunk, although not one solid piece, was probably twenty metres wide at the base.

It was made up of hundreds of smaller sections, themselves at least a metre in thickness, seemingly not joined, but packed very closely together.

Upper branches were very short and only projected out from the main trunk a mere couple of metres with no sign of leaves or flowers on them.

There was plenty of what looked like twigs, which from a distance had given it a hazy look. It was indeed a strange thing to find out in the middle of nowhere with no other vegetation around it. Kal thought it was probably dead, and had been so for a long time, as it had that abandoned look about it.

The crew disembarked and walked over to the 'tree' to get a closer look at it, and it was only when underneath it that it's true size became apparent.

They were unable to reach the lower branches to gather fuel for the wagon, so had to content themselves with walking around it, and one athletic type tried to climb up the trunk, but didn't get very far because of the lack of foot holds and something to hold on to.

The wagon had been parked a fair distance from the tree just in case, but they were not sure of what. No one was taking any chances after the earlier escapade at the sand lake.

That had taught them a good lesson in being careful of that which you don't know much about, and the lesson had gone well and truly home. It was decided they had gone far enough for that day, and a good rest was in order.

A team of two guards and a couple of collectors went off in a circular tour to see if there was anything worth investigating in the near vicinity, and returned in the late afternoon with a collection of jet black stones that were a lot heavier than they should have been.

Kal didn't recognize them for any known mineral, so they were placed in the collection box along with the other mineral specimens they had acquired along the way.

They took it easy that evening, enjoying a good meal, to which they were now adding the new food stuffs they had gathered the day before.

A game of ball somehow got started, and Kal joined in so as to feel part of the group. Of late, the oneness he had felt for the little people was wearing a little thin. They didn't seem to be distant from him, just a little apart, and he missed the dependence he once felt they had on him.

He sensed it would not be too long before they were totally self sufficient with regard to their abilities to learn and work things out for themselves.

And where would he be then? Just one person of another species, who could not even talk to them, and probably wind up not even being as bright.

Maybe they would keep him as a pet, or just take pity on him and let him stay for a while until he became a crotchety old nuisance. He was getting maudlin, and that would do no one any favours.

The night passed, and he felt better after a good sleep and the bright light of a new day.

As they took down the shutters they were in for yet another surprise. The wagon had somehow rolled towards the tree, and was now right up against it.

But this couldn't be. There was a great commotion outside, and then they realized what must have happened. The tree had somehow moved over to them, and was trying to encircle the wagon.

A few of the trunk sections of the vast tree were still in their original position, but the others, and that was most of them, were spaced out in a line as though they were marching towards the steam wagon, and some had actually reached it and were trying to get around the other side.

Kal jumped down, careful not to touch any part of the huge trunks, and surveyed the situation. How much longer it would take for the tree to completely encircle the wagon he didn't know, as the movement was very slow. He signalled for steam, but the fire crew had already got the boiler going, and hot gases with the odd drift of steam and smoke were issuing from the chimney.

The rest of the crew ate their morning meal as they went about the various jobs that had to be done before moving on, and Kal thought that they were taking it all very calmly, as the situation was really very serious indeed.

If the tree had managed to encircle the wagon he doubted if they would have enough power to push their way out of the blockade, and then what?

Squatting down, he watched one particular trunk to find out how it moved. He couldn't be sure, but it looked as if the trunk was somehow linked to the others around it, and by some means, the underground connections between the trunks were being used to form anchor points from which a trunk could push or pull itself into a new position.

In turn, it then formed an anchor for the next tree to use. The movement was very slow, as the disturbance of the ground around the base of the trunk was only just discernible.

The tree was now strung out in two lines running from the position where they had first seen it, right up to the wagon and around the sides, forming a huge 'U' shape, with most of the trunks close to the vehicle.

At long last they had enough steam pressure to move the wagon about twenty metres away from the encroaching tree, and at that point Kal noticed all movement of the trunks had ceased. The tree must have sensed that its prey had escaped, and was taking a rest before doing whatever it was intending to do next, so they watched and waited to see what would happen.

Slowly, and then a little faster, the tree began collecting itself back together to form the large collection of trunks which they had seen when they first arrived at the site.

It didn't go back to its original place, but seemed to rebuild its collection of trunks where most of them were when the wagon moved off.

Kal wondered what would have happened if they had been fully trapped by the tree. Did it ingest its captives? The thought was not a pleasant one. They could all have escaped, as long as they did so before the tree had closed ranks tightly around them, but without the wagon they would have been hard pressed to make it back home.

Once more under way, the wagon ate up the kilometres along the edge of the mountain chain, with nothing unusual happening for a while. The crew seemed relaxed and would appear to be enjoying the trip, but it was hard to tell what they really felt, except under extreme pressure, when their emotions began to show through.

A midday break was taken, and while they were all lounging around the wagon and chatting among themselves, the sketch blocks came out.

Kal couldn't see what they were trying to do until he saw the boards being brought together, and then he realized that these were the map plates, not the ones he had been making, but a set that the little people had drawn of their own accord.

The plates were different to his, and the symbols they had used seemed to belong to a set that seemed to go together, as though they had already existed in someone's mind before being used here.

There were a lot of questions he would have liked to ask his friends, but the information gleaned from the drawings was not enough to formulate them, so he was unable to ask the right questions in enough detail in the first place.

Kal was asked to join the map group, and was shown that their map indicated that they had been going in a curved path, whereas his map showed a more or less straight line of progress.

He didn't understand this, but could not refute it, as he had no compass or other means of fixing their position when the map sections were drawn.

He had gone by the sun's position, and had assumed that it was a constant as there didn't seem to be any seasons.

Perhaps he was wrong, and as it was too difficult to ask the correct questions by drawing, he just accepted their map as the one to go by.

The wagon rolled on, and by evening they had reached the end of the mountain chain, and a way around the last outcrop of rock was taken to see what lay beyond. Standing on the highest part of the wagon, Kal could see desert dunes rolling off into the distance for as far as the eye could see.

There was little point in going into the desert for any distance, as there didn't seem to be anything to be gained by so doing, and the wagon could well get bogged down in the fine sand.

They had their meal, and followed it with a game of ball, which they had modified to include working in pairs. This, in effect meant that there were now two teams, but how they scored he couldn't tell. Perhaps they didn't; it was hard to tell. Kal spent some time going over the events of the last few days and came to the conclusion that he was of value to them, but not so much as a source of data or reasoning, but something else, but he couldn't put his finger on it. Time, no doubt, would reveal all, as it usually did.

In the morning, it was decided to follow the fringe of vegetation that edged up to the desert, that way they would have the supplies they needed to hand, and could pick up any changes in the terrain at the same time.

There was no need to go back to the compound yet, as the land they were travelling through kept them supplied with all that they needed.

Steam was raised, and they set off again. The wagon had proved to be more robust than Kal had thought, and had given them no problems, which was just as well as they didn't have the means to do any serious repair work this far from home.

They had only covered five kilometres or so, when they came to a hard track which led straight out into the desert.

It was quite obvious from its appearance that it had been constructed, and they all agreed to explore it for a short distance to see where it went, and hopefully, why.

The wagon turned onto the track and headed out into the rolling yellow dunes.

The sand was very fine, and if a wind blew up, the track could easily be covered, and they would have no means of keeping on firm ground.

But why was the track so clear of sand now? There was a gentle breeze every now and again, but the track had remained clear. Something here didn't add up, and Kal had an uneasy feeling that they may be in danger of some sort.

Before long the mountains had disappeared from view, and Kal realized that they had been a comforting sight, as they could be used as a direction beacon should they lose their way among the giant waves of sand.

The feeling of unease grew the further they went into the barren wastes of sand, and he tried to get this across to the others, but to no avail. They didn't seem to mind that there was no means of deciding which direction was which, so he gave up the struggle, and kept a sharp look out for trouble.

All was going well, except it was a little boring, when they came to a large block like building. It seemed to be made of stone or some very hard material, and appeared to be one big solid lump.

The track ended here, so the block was the reason for the track, but why all out here in the desert? The crew let the fire in the wagon down, but not out, and began looking around the massive block of stone.

There were no windows, or even a sign of an entrance of any kind. It was too big to have been just a marker in the desert or some ornament, as it towered above them for nearly fifteen metres, and was fifty wide at the base.

After spending quite a considerable time going around the block looking for a way in, they gave up and came to the conclusion that entry was to be denied to them. Perhaps it was just solid, but to Kal that didn't seem right.

The top of the edifice was the only part of it they hadn't seen, and although they didn't expect to find a door up there, the view would at least show up anything else interesting in the area.

Kal had calculated that if the spears were joined up and placed on top of the wagon, they might just be able to get one of the little people up to the roof, but it would be touch and go as to whether the poles would reach that far.

The fire was stoked up a little, and the wagon slowly chuffed up to the block. This was what the block had been waiting for, and a section of the wall shimmered and slid to one side revealing the entrance.

They stopped the wagon, and cautiously approached the opening. The inside was brightly lit, and one of the little ones cautiously went inside the building. Nothing untoward happened, so the rest of them went in, followed by Kal.

In the centre of the floor there was a large metallic plate or platform, some six metres in diameter. And that was all.

The room was bare of anything else whatsoever. It must have a purpose, but they couldn't work it out.

Kal suggested that they pile up some sand on the plate and see if that did anything, for the plate was the only thing to do anything with. They agreed, and carry bags of sand were brought into the building and deposited onto the large metallic plate.

So far so good, but that was it. A pile of sand just sitting there. Kal began a close scrutiny of the walls to see if there was any hint of controls or anything else which would give a clue as to what it was all about.

He was just approaching the middle of the wall opposite the entrance, when a pillar silently rose up from the floor with a series of silver coloured plates set into its top surface.

The whole place seemed to work on the principle of someone or something being in the right position in order to activate it.

'An odd way to go about things' he thought, as he tried to make sense of the little metal plates that would do something if he could only work out the sequence.

Kal waved everyone well back from the central plate, and began touching the controls, one after the other.

Suddenly the roof of the building changed and an opening appeared through which the pitch black of the night sky could be seen, complete with its diamond bright stars.

This caused a few squeaks and whistles, and a gasp from Kal. His fingers played over the controls again and a deep and massive thump was felt rather than heard, from somewhere below them.

There was a shimmering of the sand on the main plate and it disappeared, the plate remained, but empty.

A few seconds later there was a series of metallic clicks and the roof was back to normal, the control column retracted back into the floor, and the lights slowly dimmed.

Everyone made a mad dash for the entrance and got outside just in time. The opening shimmered back into being and the wall was once again a solid block along with the rest of the building.

Kal reckoned that someone somewhere had just received a load of unwanted sand, and sent a message back to say 'no more, thanks very much' in the most positive way possible by shutting down the matter transmitter, for that was what it must have been.

He had heard of transmitters, but they belonged to stories of the future and no one had ever managed to make one, though many had tried. Someone had succeeded very well.

They spent the rest of the day trying everything they could think of to gain access to the building again, but it was not having any of it, and remained as shut as it was when they had first arrived.

They didn't like giving up, but there was no alternative that they could see, so they settled down for the night, a little disappointed but satisfied with a good day's work.

Next day, after a good meal, they fired up the wagon and began retracing their tracks to the point where they had left the plains area the day before.

The journey back seemed to take a lot longer, and some were beginning to get concerned that they had got lost in the dunes, when the mountains thankfully came into sight.

They followed the edge of the desert again looking for items of interest, but after the block, the odd tree or coloured rock did not exactly turn them on to any great degree.

Several days passed with nothing very out of the ordinary happening, and Kal was looking forward to returning to the compound and the pool rocks. He felt sure they were safe for swimming, and as they didn't need to use the pool for drinking water, surely no one would mind him having a dip.

They continued on with very little change in the scenery, the rolling sand dunes on one side and large areas of bare ground with the occasional patch of gross with its trees and plants on the other.

To some extent it was boring, but there was always the chance that something unusual would turn up or happen.

The map making of the little people impressed Kal, and made his map, which he had abandoned some time ago, look a very poor thing indeed. They were meticulous in their recording of detail, although he didn't understand all the symbols which they had used.

Every little detail which could be of use was noted, and looking at the maps, it was easy to see the changes in the terrain as they had progressed along their way.

They came across another sand lake, but when they threw a piece of fruit in just for the hell of it, nothing happened.

A second try produced the same result, so they assumed that the inhabitants had died or moved on.

There was very little other vegetation in the immediate area, so starvation could well be the answer. No one was willing to put it to the test by going into the sand, but it was noted on the map, as Kal thought it would be a good supply of bone powder if they should ever need it.

There had been no sign of another massive tree, like the one that had tried to engulf the wagon earlier, and Kal wondered if it was just a collection of single trees that had grouped together to enhance their survival by using their total mass to overwhelm their prey.

The little people, and their way of life, still left a lot of questions which Kal would have liked answered. Where were their dead? He had not seen one who had died from old age, yet they must die sometime.

Where did the strange symbols they used for their maps come from? It was unlikely that they just made them up as they went along; the whole thing seemed too structured for that. Why did they not have a strong body odour after working hard, as all creatures that Kal had known did? But most intriguing of all was where did they come from in the first place?

It was difficult to ask some of these questions of them, as they only answered those which they wanted to, concealing the other answers from Kal by displaying a lack of understanding of the questions, or so it seemed to him.

The little people he was travelling with today were totally different to those timid, meek and mild little creatures which he had met at the pool rocks so many months, or was it years ago? These people were confident, outgoing, deliberate in their actions, and their reasoning power was advancing almost daily.

Emotions, which were almost absent when they first met, were now showing through, and Kal wondered what was causing such fast changes. It was a very speeded up development as far as he could see, and one which should have taken hundreds of generations to achieve, based on the development of other races he had known.

The other thing which took up a lot of Kal's free thinking time was the other race which had been here. They had left behind a little of their science which was so totally different to anything that he had come across before.

The strange water recycling plant in the black mountains was a very odd way of doing a quite simple job, so was there something else involved? Where was the driving force for the wind that drew the water vapour from the hole in the ground and sent it to the cavern?

And after all that trouble, why let it just run in a stream to go back into the hole and cycle around again? There were too many things that didn't add up, unless he was looking at them from the wrong angle.

His reverie was brought to a halt by the sudden lurch of the steam wagon. They must have hit something, or a wheel had dropped into a large hole.

It was neither of these, but what had caused the break in his thoughts would really take some thinking about. The wagon was stable again, but the driver had stopped the forward motion.

The ground beneath them was on the move, or so it seemed. Kal climbed up to the driving position and looked around the area.

A piece of ground about fifty metres across was wriggling along in a series of small undulating waves, and they were on top of it. From his vantage point beside the driver, it looked like a giant pancake.

The first thing to do was to get off it as fast as possible, so Kal grabbed the steam control lever and wrenched it into the backwards position.

The wagon shuddered, and the drive wheels slowly turned without any reverse motion of the wagon. Something was holding them back, and they couldn't see what it was.

One of the crew jumped down to what looked like solid ground, and leapt up again a lot faster as a pseudo pod of flexible material left the surface of the pancake and tried to encircle his legs. This caused the first real sign of panic among the little people that he had seen as yet. They were really frightened, and showed it.

Everyone was leaning over the side trying to get a view of the massive creature which held them captive.

The lower half of the wheels were already covered in what looked like a writhing leathery complex of flattened tentacles, intent on covering as much of the wheels surface as possible.

If they didn't get free soon, it would be too late for the steam wagon, although they may be able to run fast enough to evade the pseudo pods that erupted from the surface of the beast at the first sign of motion or pressure.

Kal sensed that the little people didn't know what to do, and this was confirmed when the leader came to him with the sketch pad and a look of fear on his face.

Perhaps he did have a use after all, but this was no time for feeling important, and rubbing it in. Fire was a good choice to try, as there didn't seem to be natural fire due to lightening or other causes here, at least as far as he knew as he had seen no evidence of it.

Kal instructed that thin kindling wood bundles be attached to spears.

Fortunately a good head of steam was up, as the wagon had been stationary for some minutes and they would need a lot of power to break loose from the tentacles which the fire couldn't reach.

Everyone took up their stations, and the fire brands were lit. At Kal's signal, the little ones leaned over the side of the wagon with their burning bundles of wood and applied the flaming sticks to the encircling growths around the steam truck's wheels.

Again, that strange scream, felt, but not heard. The little people were affected by it directly, as some of them dropped their fire brands, clapping their hands to their ear holes.

But the unaccustomed intense heat had done the trick, and most of the pseudo pods withdrew to the main mass of the creature and Kal wrenched the lever to deliver full steam.

The wagon's chimney gushed steam and smoke as the wheels started to turn, and they began to move back to the real ground they had been on before the lurch had signalled their present predicament.

The wagon was taken a good twenty metres clear of the moving 'pancake' to be on the safe side, and then Kal and a few of the more brave ones went over to the edge of it to see just what it was.

Although the edge of the thing was very thin, there was a definite rise in the middle of the pancake and the centre must have been at least a metre or more thick.

It seemed to be composed of a very tough rubbery outer skin that had taken on the appearance of the ground over which it travelled, or maybe that was just its natural look.

It moved slowly over the ground, but could exude the entrapping tentacles quite rapidly when needed.

Looking around, it would seem that the pancake moved across the ground, devouring everything that it covered in its travels and anything that was unfortunate enough to walk or land on its surface suffered a similar fate via the grabbing pseudo pods.

Behind the pancake there was a clear stretch of ground denuded of all vegetation for as far as the eye could see which bore out Kal's theory of how it operated.

One of the little people fetched a bronze axe and tried to chop off a part of the edge, but the only result he got was that the edge curled away from him, and the axe bounced back nearly hitting the person standing next to him.

They lobbed a few stones onto the surface of the pancake, but it ignored them and continued its slow progress on towards the horizon.

'Just how vigilant does one have to be not to get caught out?' Kal asked himself. They checked the wheels of the wagon for any damage or corrosion, but could find none thankfully, and all piled back on board to continue their exploratory journey.

In the far distance they could see a band of green and brown vegetation, and it was decided that after restocking up on food and inspecting it for anything useful, they would turn for home.

Kal had no idea of how long they had been travelling, but in his time it must have been many months, if not a year, or did it just seem like that?

A pile of rocks came into view, the first they had seen for some time, and they stopped for a while to refresh themselves and stretch their legs.

Kal wandered over to the rocks, accompanied by two guards with spears, and found that the ground around the rocks was devoid of all vegetation. That rang a bell somehow, and he then remembered the copper stained rocks he had found when he first landed.

Sure enough, these rocks had the same tell tale veins of copper ore in them, and rain had leached a little of it out, causing the vegetation to retreat as before.

Every now and again, something flashed like a bright light over to one side of them, and the impulse was to go and find out what it was.

This was agreed upon by one and all, as it would not take them very far out of their way, and they were off once more.

Kal was looking forward to the journey home, as it should prove to be quick and fairly safe, since they had plotted all the hazards they had met on their outward journey.

They had not gone very far before Kal recognized the flashes of light for what they were. He was up in the driving seat again and therefore had a better view than the others, so he called some of them up, and showed them the sea.

As they approached the great expanse of water, Kal was reminded of his first experience of this planet's sea, and the very close shave he had had on the beach.

It looked as if there was going to be another very wide beach here also, and he told the others, via the sketch pads, what to expect.

It didn't take long to reach the edge of the sands, although the water was some considerable distance ahead. They halted the wagon, and got down to take a closer look.

A similar bank of pebbles fringed the deadly sand, as it had done before, so long ago. They thought it should be safe to walk on, and so it proved to be.

It just had to be done, and one bright spark fetched a large fruit and threw it as far as he could over the sand. The sand erupted in the manner to which it was accustomed, and the fruit disappeared. No one was going to build sand castles today, that was for sure.

The vegetation began only a short distance away, so they all climbed aboard and headed for it, as there was nothing else to do at the sand's edge, and they were not going to risk the wagon just to get down to the actual sea after Kal had told them what had happened to his escape shuttle.

All of a sudden Kal had a strange feeling, and he called a halt to their progress. The maps were brought out, and assembled into one continuous sheet for the first time. They had been going on a circular path all right, but no one had realized just how circular it had been.

Kal had to readjust one or two of the sketch boards, and then it all made sense. They were almost at the point where he had landed all that time ago.

This caused a lot of excitement, as they all realized that they were not all that far from home, and wouldn't have to spend the next few 'months' retracing their outward journey.

Kal didn't tell them of the deep and narrow gorge he had had to squeeze through, as he thought they might be able to go around it.

Time would tell if they were successful, and he was feeling lucky anyway.

The wagon huffed and chuffed its way along the coast until the track that Kal had used came into view. He couldn't believe their luck, as it was certainly against chance to have found it so easily.

They turned inland, and made very good progress, as the track was hard and the wagon was able to go at full speed, which actually didn't amount to a breath taking velocity, but it was a darn sight quicker than walking, and a lot safer.

When they came to the section where the vegetation had almost covered the track, they put up the shutters to protect themselves from tree dwelling leather flaps and anything else they hadn't discovered, and forced their way through.

As they went along, Kal pointed out all the odd things he had seen, or at least the places where he had seen them and what happened, so long ago.

The memories of his lone march through this strange land were as crystal clear as if they had only happened yesterday, and in an odd way, he felt at home here, despite the dangers.

They came at last to the point where the track would shortly go into the narrow gorge, and turned the wagon off to the right, hoping to find a way past the high cliffs, and so back to the compound.

To begin with it, looked as if they would have no difficulty in getting through, but as time went on the ground began to rise, and the engine was almost at the limit of its power.

In one place they all had to get off, leaving the smallest of them to steer, and the rest of them did their best to push the wagon on up the slope. They just about made it, but if a steeper slope was encountered, they would have to find another way around it.

The top of the plateau was gained at last, and they were back to full speed once more. But not for very long, as a rift in the ground ahead blocked their way.

It was only about two metres in width, but the wheels would have got jammed in it, and then they would be reduced to walking.

Kal took a good look at the situation, and suggested that they try to bridge the gap with rocks, but the others didn't seem to think that it would be possible.

He gave up trying to persuade them after a while, and left them to chat among themselves as he went to see if there were any loose rocks in the area which they could move with the limited means they had.

By nightfall, the little ones had not come up with a solution to the problem, and Kal just kept quiet.

'Let 'em stew in their own juice for a while' he thought, as he tucked into his evening meal. There were no ball games that night, and they all retired to the wagon in a rather sombre mood, with of course the shutters firmly up.

In the depth of night, something big and hungry rattled the bronze safety boards, and caused the wagon to rock a little, which woke everyone up, and that was the end of their sleep for that night.

In the early light of dawn they all went outside to see what the commotion in the dark hours was about. And wished they hadn't.

In the soft sand just over from the wagon there were paw prints of something very big, probably a relation of, or even an adult version of, the cat creature which had brought them all together in the first place.

Every one hurried back to the wagon, and looked to Kal for advice. Although they hadn't seen it, they could guess its size, and to them it would be a monster of a thing.

'Once again I'm useful' he thought, and tried not to look too smug, although he suspected that facial expressions were wasted on them. If it did not go away, they would be trapped in the wagon, and would not be able to bridge the gap in the rift, and eventually they would run out of water and food.

Kal didn't like the idea, but if it persisted in staying in the vicinity, they would somehow have to kill it. But how?

It was big, even by Kal's standards, and quite likely proportionately mean with it, so he was going to have to use cunning to outwit the cat, and draw it into a trap.

The rift itself might be the answer, if he could only get the cat near enough to it, and then topple it in.

The first thing to do was to persuade the rest of the crew that the plan was worth looking at, and then decide just how to go about it.

The meeting was held with the screens up, and every one looking a bit apprehensive, or so he liked to think. What they really felt was only known to them, and they weren't telling just yet.

The idea of using the rift was accepted as the only way, as it would take a lucky spear at close range to dispatch the beast, and no volunteers came forward for that one.

The tricky bit was how to bait the creature to come close enough to the edge to be of any use. Using the drawing pad, Kal sketched out his plan.

The wagon would be backed up to the edge of the rift, so that they could operate from the comparative safety of its bulk. Some bronze sheets would have to be removed from the back of the vehicle, laid down next to the rift's edge and attached to some powerful means of lifting them quickly.

The cat would then, after being baited to the edge, hopefully lose its footing and topple into the rift, and they could then dispatch it.

But what to use for bait? No one offered their body, but unfortunately someone would have to, as the cat was obviously a carnivore and wasn't going to take much interest in the fruits of the forest.

They would have to catch something which the cat would normally eat. The first team to go out hunting for the bait came running back and shot into the wagon.

The cat was prowling around in the trees not far away, and picking up their scent, came crashing after them. They were reasonably safe behind the screens, and waited for the cat to give up, and return to whatever it was doing before they evoked its interest in them.

Once the cat had gone, they placed two of the safety screens side by side and close to the rift edge, and ran a couple of ropes back to the wagon, first running them over a pulley hung from the roof.

Kal had reckoned that if enough of them, while holding the rope, jumped off the other side of the wagon, it should be enough to topple the cat over the edge as the plates were lifted up by the rope, and if it failed, would give some of them a good chance of climbing back up to the safety of the wagon before the cat could get around from the other side.

Volunteers for this were naturally going to be a bit shy, but he would handle that when he came to it.

The bronze sheets were covered with a scattering of earth and a few bits of pulled gross, so that it looked like natural ground and the scent of those who had handled them would be masked.

All was ready for the great cat now, except the cat itself. It was decided to have their evening meal a little early, so that they could concentrate on the job of getting the cat, which was more likely to come snooping around at dusk.

Everyone was waiting that evening, and the tension, which Kal hadn't noticed as a natural part of the little people's make up, was beginning to show. The light level dropped, and a hush descended over the scene.

Somewhere, something large and hungry was looking for a meal, and the meal was waiting, standing on the edge of the bronze plates with a rope tied around his waist.

The steady pad pad of the large cat like creature could be heard by the little ones before Kal picked it up, and he took his cue from them.

The cat came into the clearing, looking around for the thing that smelt of food, and seeing the little person at the edge of the rift, bounded forward to grasp its prey. As it launched itself for the final killing strike, Kal gave the signal, and the group on the rope threw themselves off the other side of the wagon.

The bait was also attached to the rope that lifted the back edge of the bronze plates, and as the plates lifted, tipping the cat into the rift, the bait was swung up into the wagon.

Kal jumped down along with several others, and ran over to the rift. The cat was some three metres down the cleft in the rocks and was sounding it's fury at losing its evening meal, and being jammed in the rocks into the bargain.

The sound alone would have put most people Kal knew off any further action.

It seemed a shame to do it, but Kal knew that it had to be done, and drove his bronze tipped spear hard down into the neck of the beast hoping to break the spinal cord.

His spear was followed by at least six others, not thrown with as much force as his, but putting the finishing touches to the death of the giant killing machine in the rift.

They were all shaking after the event, Kal more so than the little people. He did his best to tell them how brave he thought they were, especially the 'bait' and those who jumped over the side of the wagon; it was difficult using pictures, but he did his best.

They all slept quite well that night, but memories of the beast filled more than a few dreams.

Having made such a success of the cat incident, he thought it worth trying again to persuade the others to co-operate in filling in the rift, so enabling them to go on their way.

A team had gone along the rift to see if there was a point where they could cross, but came back without finding one. This was apparently the closest the rift got to a bridging point, and they had found it by pure luck.

Early next morning the rock filling began. The first thing to do was to roll the biggest rocks they could find into the rift so as to form a jam part way down, and then fill up to the top of the rift with more manageable stones.

The steam wagon, with the aid of ropes, dragged the largest rocks as close to the edge as possible and sheer manpower moved them the rest of the way.

By midday, the larger rocks had wedged themselves across the awful drop and the filling in had begun. It would be the following day before they would have enough material in place to risk taking the wagon over.

The time came for the great test of their hard work, and no way would they let Kal drive the wagon, so most of the crew including Kal assembled on the other side of the rift as the mighty wagon chugged into position, and they all held their breath as it slowly inched forward.

The wagon was halfway across when there was a loud crack, and the wagon gave a lurch, but the bridge held and she was safely over to the other side. The crew were overjoyed, and this time the emotion was unmistakable, as Kal joined in the merriment. Once again he had proved his worth, and felt more at one with the team than he had for some time.

The food stocks were checked, and water sticks added to supplement the remaining water supply in the tanks, and then they were off on the homeward trail.

Kal could not believe that they had travelled around in a circle, and not spotted the fact.

A compass would have shown this up, but even so, he thought it very strange that they had arrived at the point on the planet's surface where he had landed the shuttle. It could have been by chance, but somehow he didn't think so.

The vegetation was now changing to that which they were all a little more familiar with, and home didn't seem to be too far way, although the journey would take them nearly five days.

After leaving the rift behind, the wagon was on a downhill course to the lower plateau, and this meant a detour out of their intended way.

The going was good, and time rolled by without any mishaps, apart from the occasional bit of road building where gullies had formed from heavy rainfall.

Everyone was feeling much more relaxed, and the evening games began again, although Kal still couldn't make out how they scored, or even if they did score.

So far, Kal had not seen a drop of rain, and only a few clouds, usually towards evening.

'So when did it rain?' he wondered. There must be rain sometime, as the vegetation couldn't go on forever without water, and then there were those gullies, they had been cut by a strong water flow.

As there didn't seem to be any seasons as such, he couldn't put it down to being wet in the winter, or whatever passed for winter on this planet. It played on his mind from time to time as one of those little things that didn't quite add up.

One evening, in the far distance they could see the cliffs of the compound in the pink of the setting sun. Some of the little people were all for trying a night journey, but the oil lights were not really good enough for this, and common sense prevailed for the safety of all.

Next day was a different matter. The wagon had steam up at the crack of dawn, and the early morning meal was bolted down rather than eaten so that they could get away quickly, and hopefully be home by evening.

As they approached the area of the compound, Kal wondered just how long they had been away. The whole place had changed.

There were now quite good tracks linking the garden areas together, and a wide main road going up the middle to the compound. Even this had changed, as it was now much bigger, and a form of ornamental battlement had been added to the heightened encompassing walls.

Kal had to admit that it did look very impressive as well as being safer against just about anything he had seen in the way of wild life.

The whole area had been expanded to nearly three times the size it was when they left on their journey of exploration, and many other improvements made, which in time were to make Kal blink in astonishment.

The rate at which these people were progressing would have been a threat to any other race, had there been one.

With the chimney belching steam and sparks as they made their way towards the settlement under full power, a welcoming committee was on its way out to meet them.

A chorus of squeaks and whistles almost drowned out the noise of the steam wagon as it rattled along the last few hundred metres.

As they reached the beginning of the main track to the compound, Kal had to reduce speed as he was concerned for the crowd which had clustered around the wagon, waving and calling to those on board.

This was an overwhelming welcome if ever there was one, and the intensity of it surprised him as this was raw emotion in full flood, which he had never seen before in the little people.

At long last the steam wagon was back in the compound, the fires raked out, and the samples they had collected stowed away in the cave reserved for such things.

By now it was quite dark, but the compound was a blaze of light from oil lamps and another light source which Kal hadn't seen before.

Tonight was going to be one to remember by the look of things he thought, as he sat down at a long table on a raised platform along with the rest of the crew and some of the old committee. Below them everyone else had gathered, and the feast began.

For the first time since being with the little people, his food had been prepared for him, and he carefully checked it to make sure that they had only used things which he knew to be safe. As usual, they had got it right, so he tucked in to a meal that he would remember for a long time to come.

After the feast, it was time for the speeches, or rather for the crew to tell their tales of the long adventure.

Although he couldn't understand a word of it, he could get the gist of what was being said. The main elder made a welcoming speech which was roundly applauded, and this was followed by the leader of the expedition giving his reply.

All Kal could do was stand up and wave his arms about and smile, at what he thought were the appropriate moments.

Several other members of the crew then stood up and squeaked and whistled their versions of the various events that had taken place on the journey, with many references to Kal, who felt obliged to stand up and do a little bow every now and again when all the attention was focused upon him.

It was indeed a night to remember, and well into dawn before they all retired to get a little rest, if they could.

Kal found it difficult to sleep; the images of the evening and of the perilous incidents of their adventure kept coming back, running like a series of films before his closed eyes. Eventually he dozed off, only to dream, and that was worse.

FIVE:
Electricity

The next day seemed like an anticlimax to Kal, and he supposed it must have also affected the rest of the crew, although they seemed quite cheerful when he met then at the steam wagon.

He had not really taken a good look at the works of the new and improved steam wagon before, as everything had been a bit of a rush going out on the expedition, and their time was mostly taken up surviving the hazards along the way, or driving along recovering from the previous incident.

He was amazed at the simplicity of the whole thing, as it only consisted of a firebox and water boiler coupled to a steam regulator valve which sent the steam on to a pair of crude cylinders and pistons. These in turn, were linked up to a crank on the main drive shaft with a rather complicated system of levers and gears.

The main frame of the wagon was made from cast beams and riveted together, upon which the engine was mounted along with a water tank for the steam boiler and a fuel bin.

The steering mechanism would have won prizes for novelty if nothing else, but it worked, and had done them very good service indeed. His respect for the ingenuity of the little people went up several notches.

Accommodation was rather crude as it only consisted of benches of wood, placed wherever there was a space big enough to put them, and some were placed where Kal would not have liked to sleep.

Every nook and cranny was filled with a cupboard or storage space for the food and a simple collection of tools and weapons.

As they had been able to work out how to build the wagon based only on the very basic principles which he had demonstrated to them over the preceding months, what would they be capable of if they had access to a good scientific field of data and a fully equipped workshop.

'Space travel in about six months' Kal thought wryly.

As Kal moved about the compound looking at the new additions which had been made to the water wheel and foundry, he noticed that the workers, if it was possible, stopped work and stood respectfully by their equipment while he inspected it. He wondered what this new attitude of respect was all about, as they rarely did anything without a good reason. It was only just noticeable, but it was there, and he didn't really like it, as something must be brewing and he wasn't in on it, yet.

The glass makers had advanced their skills beyond anything he had ever seen, and as well as having taken the art of glass blowing to extreme heights, had now developed some beautiful glazes which were being used by the ceramics team.

As yet they had not gone in for building houses, but what they had done was to extend the cave system beyond all recognition, cutting back and up into the mountain.

The rooms were now on four levels, joined up by passageways such that each room looked out onto the compound and had top hung windows which opened.

It had been discovered that once the initial surface of the sandstone like rock had been broken into, the rock behind it was relatively easy to cut with bronze tools, while the new surface hardened over in a few days once exposed to air.

With so many willing hands, the system had been expanded almost to the level of a small city.

On the other side of the linking corridors, store rooms had been cut from the rock, so that every room had its own store for food and anything else that was not in daily use.

The steam engine idea had been developed to make small wagons that had a crew of five to ten and a box like storage space at the rear. These were used for food and material gathering, and a larger version for transporting people around the field system.

The new wagons were a little more sophisticated than the original one used for the expedition, and a lot faster.

Some days later, Kal was asked to a meeting of the elders and was presented with the child he had unwittingly produced. It had grown considerably, and was now walking quite well.

It was obviously a mixture of the two races, and Kal had to admit that it carried more of his genes than its mothers, and without wishing to be prejudiced, was more human like than the little people.

He had long ago dropped the idea that they were nearer to an animal than anything else, as they had developed mentally to such a marked degree. It was only their looks that had brought about that unfortunate simile.

Once the niceties were out of the way, out came the sketch blocks, and the benefit to all concerned for the continuance of the cross breeding program was illustrated to him in no uncertain manner.

Kal hesitated before giving his answer to the proposal, as it did make sense and would produce a much superior race. If they were willing to lose their racial identity for the sake of a new and more able breed, then he should also give it some considerable attention.

He indicated his thoughts on the matter to the best of his ability, and luckily they seemed to accept it. 'At least for the time being' he thought.

The smelters had not been idle while he had been away. They had successfully extracted silver, tin, lead and of course copper, and in quantity, which was stock piled for future use in billet and bar form.

The main problem with all this smelting was that they had to go some distance to harvest the wood for charcoal, and that was now holding back production.

Kal wondered if another means of producing heat could be devised, and toyed with the idea of electricity, but the problem with that was he didn't have any copper wire, or the means with which to make the copper billets into the wire needed to wind a generator.

He put the idea across to the smelters and forgers to see if they could come up with something, feeling sure they would, if past experience was anything to go by.

A meeting was held, and the sketch blocks flew back and forth for some time, but no earth shaking breakthrough was forthcoming. It would, no doubt, given enough time.

The water system had been improved, and every cave now had its own supply, complete with a tap. A waste system was also installed, and the contents were piped out of the compound and into a seemingly bottomless pit they had discovered at the edge of the field system. All in all, things were taking on a very civilized state of being.

The little people had not devised any form of barter or monetary exchange. They all had a job to do, or so it seemed, and no one person was responsible for asking them to do it as far as he could tell.

Every one of them proved to be a willing worker for the good of all. If a job needed doing, then someone would do it, without being asked. Some were better at some things than others, while some, he suspected swapped jobs every so often, and the whole system worked very well.

Whether they generally rotated their jobs around, Kal couldn't tell, as they all looked so much alike, with only a few having distinguishing marks that he could recognize.

There was no election of a leader or of the council of elders, as he liked to think of them. They just seemed to take on the post, and carry out their duties as if they had done it all their lives.

There may well have been some form of election among the little people, but Kal missed it if it had occurred, which he very much doubted somehow.

As there didn't seem to be any seasons here, there was no need to store the fruits, berries, and other foods for long, as supplies were always replenished as they were needed.

A few more foods that Kal could eat safely were added to his diet by his 'cave keeper' as he thought of her/him or whatever, and so far he had suffered no ill effects from the additions.

Life was settling down again to a nice steady routine, and although he missed the excitement of the expedition, it was very pleasant to relax a little, and think about things for a while, and there was a lot to think about.

But no matter how well organized one gets, such things don't last for very long, as he was about to find out.

If they were to make an electric generator, then they would need iron, or some other magnetic material. So far, Kal had seen no sign of iron ore, and that had been disappointing, but then he doubted if they would be able to smelt it, because of the very high temperatures required.

He was rummaging about in the cave containing the materials they had found on their various journeys, when he came across one of the very heavy black crystalline rocks which had been brought in some time ago.

Kal had found no use for it until now, and wondered what it was, as it didn't fit into any known ore group he could recall. It was very heavy for its size, and deep down in his memory, it rang a bell.

If it was magnetic, it showed no trace of wanting to cling to the other pieces of the same material, so maybe it was electromagnetic, taking on the properties of a magnet when in an electric field. But how was he going to generate an electric field?

This was the typical chicken and egg situation, but it would have to be overcome somehow if progress was to be made.

A visit to the forgers and smelters got him under way with his generator project with regard to the copper wire.

They had managed to beat out a bar of copper to a very thin rod, annealing it every now and again to re-soften it, and were in the process of drawing it through a hole in a piece of hardened bronze to reduce its diameter still further.

This was repeated several times using smaller and smaller holes, until he had his copper wire, not quite up to the quality he was used to, but serviceable none the less.

The next thing which had to be done was to coat it with an insulating layer of varnish, and he knew that was going to be a little more difficult.

One of the 'new material seekers' had found a tree like growth which exuded a sticky resinous liquid when cut, and had collected some in case it had a use, but the difficulty so far was that no one had found anything in which it would dissolve, to make it more varnish like.

A few days later they succeeded by mixing it with the sap from another tree, and this held it in a liquid state just long enough for them to coat the copper wire and so form a layer of insulation. It was crude, but would probably work.

The creation of simple battery cells to provide power for the magnetic test was quite easy, as they had dissimilar metals such as silver, tin and copper, and now they had refined zinc.

Fruit acid would provide the necessary driving force for the voltaic cells, and it was only a matter of winding a coil of copper wire around the material they suspected of being magnetic, and seeing if it attracted another piece of the black rock to itself when energized.

The test coil was wound, with a little difficulty, it had to be admitted, and the cells connected up ready for the great moment.

A small piece of the heavy black rock was placed close to the end of the coil which was wound around a larger piece of the same rock, and Kal brushed the connecting wire against the home made battery.

A tiny bright blue spark flashed at the connecting point, and the little piece of black rock leapt towards the coil, and stuck to the larger piece of rock. As he disconnected the battery, the small piece of rock fell from the coil, and the case was proven.

The black rock was electromagnetic and what they needed for their generator.

They now had the knowledge and materials to build a simple electric generator, and could power it from the water wheel. But there remained one more problem, and that was how to shape the electromagnetic rock into a suitable form for the coils to be wound on.

Kal suggested that they crush it in the ore mill and mix it with a little of the low melting glass powder, and then refuse it all together in the kiln. This was done, and they later found that the magnetic properties of the material were not diminished by the process, as they feared it might be.

It now remained for Kal to outline the basic principles of the generator to the 'engineers', and leave them to it.

The casting and firing of the great magnetic cores for the electric machine got under way, and the wire manufacturing was soon much improved, as were most things done by the little people, and the machine began to take shape.

On Kal's instruction, they wound an extra coil on the generator to act as an 'exciter', through which a small electric current would be passed from their batteries to initiate the generation. Once current was being generated, some of it could be used to sustain the magnetic field.

Kal thought it was time that he showed some interest in his offspring, not just because he was curious, but it may act as a delaying tactic with regard to the fathering of any more, as he was still not happy about the elder's proposals.

He enquired as to where the child might be, and was at once taken to see it. In all fairness, it was a handsome child, although a little alien when compared to himself.

The little people seemed to grow at a prodigious rate, and the child was no exception to that rule.

It was already taller than its mother and of a more slender build when compared to its height.

The body hair or fluff, of the little people was hardly visible, but it had a light covering of hair on its head, as did Kal, although not quite so thick as yet.

The features were different also, the lips being more pronounced and the nose a little longer. There was no doubt about it; the blending of the two races could produce a being with the attributes of both, and none, as yet, of the disadvantages.

Kal had noticed that the vocal cords and possibly the hearing of the child were registering somewhere between the two races, as it seemed to have little difficulty in understanding it's mothers squeaks and whistles, and replied in a lower frequency, which she in turn was not finding too easy to interpret.

Now was the time to see if he could teach the child his language, as there was no way he could ever understand the squeaks and whistles of the others.

If it worked, then maybe the child could act as a go between for them, and so a greater understanding between races could come about.

Using the sketch board he explained to the mother what he proposed to do, and she understood and agreed.

It was mid afternoon before Kal had got the little one to say his name, albeit in a very high voice, but it was clearly spoken along with a few other words. Kal was being very careful to clear the meaning of each word thoroughly.

It looked as though at long last one of the barriers between them was about to come down, and he felt very satisfied with the day's work.

The mother must have explained to the child that Kal was its father, as the little one soon developed an attachment for Kal, and seemed to enjoy being in his company.

He didn't feel quite so uneasy about this as he would have expected, and to some extent found it an enjoyable experience; he also looked forward to their next meeting.

The days went by, and Kal thought it was about time to pay the engineers a visit to see how they had progressed with the generator. He could hardly believe his eyes.

They had made very good progress indeed, and were assembling the main generator coils on the outer section, or stator. It was the size of the thing that shocked him.

They had scaled it up by about four fold, and had reached a point where they were having difficulty in lifting the sections of the machine into place.

If this thing worked it would be very powerful indeed, but he doubted if they would have enough water to power the water wheel sufficiently to drive the generator to full capacity.

The machine was housed in its own building, and this was the first sign of the little people having any interest in building construction, as opposed to hollowing out rooms in the soft rock of the cliff.

They had constructed it from blocks of the sandstone-like rock cut from within the cliff, making new rooms and housing the electric generator in its own building at the same time, so wasting little material or effort.

'A nice touch of efficiency' thought Kal. He left them to it, as there was little that he could do to help, and made his way over to the glass blowers.

Earlier he had explained the basic theory of fluorescent or discharge lamps to them, and they indicated that they would try and make some glass globes and tubes for him to experiment with.

He needed some rare gasses for the lamps to work properly, and was at a loss as to where he could get them.

The blowers were as good as their word, producing a selection of shapes of different sizes with fine tube like outlets at each end for the electrodes to be inserted.

He had better come up with something or lose face over this one, as the blowers had obviously put a lot of effort into their work, and would be watching with interest to see how well they functioned.

A workshop had been hollowed out next-door to Kal's room, and he had a selection of basic tools supplied to his specification, manufactured by the forgers and engineers.

Some of the tools were improved upon from their basic design and this indicated to Kal that their purpose had been fully understood by the makers.

What still amazed him was the ability of one group of workers to understand basic principles so easily, modify them to improve them wherever possible, and then transfer that data to other groups of workers who were probably working in a different material.

What came to mind were the smelters and casters, who later linked up with the forgers, all making one great team and able to do each other's jobs when necessary.

These later joined forces with the potters, who also made the firebricks for the furnaces and kilns, and the metal engineers, who made the tools for everyone else.

So far, no doctors had shown up, probably because no one seemed to suffer from any illnesses. Even he had not noticed a sniffle or sore throat since he had been here.

Everybody carried bacteria on their bodies, and he was no exception, but the little people had not suffered from anything he had introduced into their group, and he certainly hadn't picked up anything from them. 'Odd that', was the best he could come up with.

There were one or two broken bones, but no one made a fuss about it, as usually a splint was applied by someone, and the whole thing forgotten.

There was no sign of religion in any form that he could detect, and to be honest, he had not given it much thought himself. When he came to think about it, there were a lot of things which were so different to what he would have expected, and yet it all seemed to be acceptable to him now.

What was it about this strange planet, with its bizarre life forms, and the little people which didn't seem to fit in anywhere, or even belong here, that somehow made him feel that it was all quite acceptable?

Looked at in the cold light of day, he should have been scared out of his wits and sitting in some dark corner hoping not to be found. And yet he took it all in his stride, and was even thriving on it.

There was some strange mystery here somewhere, and he was determined to solve it.

Kal had spent several afternoons with the child, teaching it to speak his language, and thought he should give it a name, but what? And what should it call him?

Dad seemed strange somehow, as if it belonged to a long time ago and far away, which in a sense, it did.

He had never married, the exploration of space being his only interest, so the problem hadn't occurred before.

A smile started to curl up one side of his mouth. Tibs, that's what he would call him. Taken from the initial letters of Trial Insemination By Subterfuge. Not exactly earth shaking, but it would do.

He mustn't tell the child how his name was derived, in case he got a complex, and then he remembered these people didn't suffer from the same frailties as his race.

That settled, he decided to name the child next day, and explain to the mother what it was all about, not that it really mattered, as he was the only one who would use the name.

'Time to go and check on the generator again' he thought, and headed for the workshops.

There was a steady hum coming from the generator building, and Kal was surprised that they hadn't called him before they started up the huge machine.

He was in for another surprise when he got inside, as the generator was powered not by a takeoff from the water wheel, as he had suggested, but by the biggest Pelton wheel he had ever seen.

The housing for the wheel was a good three metres high, which meant that the wheel inside it was not a lot smaller.

There must have been hundreds of cups on the periphery of the spinning disk, and the power it could deliver would be enormous.

Next to the wheel housing was a gear box to reduce the speed a little before it was feed to the generator proper.

How they had cut the gears or even realized the necessity for them had him stumped.

This would normally have been a major work of engineering, using very complex and expensive cutting machinery, and here they were, spinning around as if they had been made by the best engineering company in the galaxy.

What amazed Kal most, was the fact that the whole machine was perfectly balanced and vibration free.

That alone was an engineering feat which would have put his engineers to a good deal of trouble considering the size of the project, and these little people had done it in their stride, and not bothered him once about it. They were getting too clever by far.

As yet, there was no electrical take off from the generator, and finding something for it to supply current to was going to be the next job.

The voltage was not controlled in any way, except by the speed of the Pelton wheel, and that was only a crude method.

This would limit the kind of things which they could use the machine for, as most things that Kal knew about relied on a constant voltage, and there was no way in which they could achieve that without some complicated electronics.

Kal was very impressed with the whole set-up, and conveyed his thoughts on it to the team. They seemed pleased that he approved, but it was hard to tell what they really thought, as usual.

Back in his workshop, Kal got down to some serious thinking about a discharge lamp, as the filament type was out of the question, needing tungsten for the filament, and that was something that they hadn't got, yet.

After several hours, he was still stumped, and thought the best solution was to give the problem to the engineers, and see what they came up with.

He described the function of the gasses in the tube of glass, and how they were excited to a point where they gave off light in the ultra violet range, and the phosphor coating inside the tube changed that to visible light.

They didn't have a chemical with which to coat the inside of the glass tube, so he supposed they would find a way around it, one way or another.

When Kal and the crew returned from the expedition, he noticed that as well as the oil lamps, there was also what seemed to be some other form of lighting, and in the excitement of the home coming and then the generator, it had completely slipped his mind to find out what it was.

With sketch pad at the ready, he set off to find whoever was responsible for the lighting. In one of the workshop caves he was to find yet another example of the ingenuity of these people. Two of them had been experimenting with a lichen that had been discovered in one of the deep caves.

It would seem that if the growth was fed a nutrient solution, it glowed quite brightly with a pale blue-white light. In so doing the lichen grew in volume, and could then be divided up into several batches, and more lamps were made.

The life span of the strange growth when forced to grow at this increased rate was only a few days, so the glass containers had to be flushed out every so often, and a new stock of lichen put in.

A team had been looking for new materials in the cave system, when they came across the lichen on the walls of one of the caverns. It was very thinly spread on the rock, and the glow from it was only noticeable from a distance, as the light from the oil lamps swamped its meagre light output when close up to it.

One of the party thought it interesting, and scraped some off the rock, bringing it back. They had reasoned that it either used the light to attract whatever it fed on, or the light was an accidental by product of its growing cycle.

Either way, they tried feeding it a range of compounds from ground up rock to liquids extracted from plants, and found that a finely ground mixture of a chalk-like rock, added to the juice from one of the acid fruits was what the lichen needed to accelerate its growth and light output.

The only problem was, that to generate enough light to be useful, the life cycle had to be speeded up with the nutrient solution, which meant they had a permanent job refilling the light globes every few days.

The light globes were a very good demonstration of the kind of basic research which these people were capable of, using only the simplest of tools, a lot of patience and an ingenuity that put Kal to shame.

He wondered again what they would have come up with if they had been put into a fully equipped laboratory.

Kal had asked for two insulated copper wires to be fed from the electric generator to his workshop. These were to be put on poles, and china insulators would stop the current leaking to the ground or to anything else, if it rained.

As he had no idea what voltage the generator would produce, he was going to be very careful when handling it.

The electric supply was duly put in, and he devised a simple fuse system using a thin wire which would burn out if he drew too much current in error, and so save the winding of the generator from overheating.

The light tube experiments could now begin, and a little team of engineers looked on in fascination as sparks flew every now and then, but no light as such was produced.

Kal had explained in as much detail as possible the danger of electricity, as it was invisible and gave little warning of its presence, allowing them to experience a mild electric shock to drive the point home.

They were even more respectful of the new energy source than they were of him, and for that he was pleased.

A small hand operated vacuum pump had been made to his specification, with of course, the usual modifications which the engineers had anticipated, and generously added.

It worked far better than he had expected, and he was now able to lower the pressure in the glass tubes enough to see if he could get an arc to strike. A couple of days later saw the first flash of light from the new fluorescent light tube.

It was just a flash, as the tube blew apart with the force of the arc, but they had proved the point that it could work.

Over the next few days, many tubes were brought to him; all coated with different substances on the inside, and were put on the vacuum pump, and tried.

Kal had long ago explained the basic principles of the fluorescent tube light, and some bright spark had noticed that when certain minerals were heated in the smelting process, gases were given off.

He had collected some of them in glass globes, and now offered them to Kal to see if they would be of any use in the light tube experiments.

Having evacuated the tube of air, it was not too difficult to introduce the gases one by one, to see if they had any effect on the electric discharge. One did.

Although an arc could be struck, most tubes didn't produce any useful amount of light output, and Kal was on the point of giving up the quest. He thought that a higher voltage might be needed, and had wound a small transformer, using the black rock to make the core piece.

It worked quite well, and had stepped the voltage up considerably. He was now able to control the current flow and the increased voltage enabled the arc to be struck more easily.

Eleven days after the tube experiments had begun, they had their first success. The tube lit up and gave out a bright white light which illuminated the cave to a level that almost hurt their eyes.

They had done it. The only thing that now remained to be done was to find a means of controlling the energy flow to the tubes, so that they wouldn't burn out, as the first one did after a few hours.

Kal handed the whole project over to the engineers; or rather he liked to think he had done so. A new team was put together, and light tubes began to appear in the caves, one after the other.

Sometime later, unknown to Kal, the engineers had constructed a new generator with more windings on it, so that it would provide a higher voltage just for the lighting system.

Lights were everywhere, and when they showed a slight dimming due to there being too many on the system, another small generator was added for that sector.

Sooner or later Kal knew it had to happen. A meeting was called with the elders, and the proposition was put to him again about the breeding program.

He could see the sense of it, and could not fault their logic, but somehow didn't like the idea. The arguments went back and forth, except that he was hard pressed to offer a good reason for not embracing the idea wholeheartedly.

Once again he implied that he would give it some more thought, and that was the end of the matter, although he suspected it was not really so.

The lighting system was now almost complete, insofar that every cave had its own lights, complete with switch, and flood lights were fixed all around the inner compound so that life could go on after the sun had gone down.

The waste water from the generators was fed to a huge pool at the bottom of the main compound, and from there it went into channels to water the fields below.

The increase in water produced a corresponding increase in crops, so nothing was wasted, and everyone gained.

The heavy load on the water supply worried him, but although it didn't seem to alter the flow, Kal was concerned that one day their demand could exceed the supply.

To this end he suggested that they explore the source of the water if they could find it, and make sure that it could replenish itself adequately.

A team assembled, and they entered the tunnel system which led to the water supply. Kal had not realized that the new supply was piped from deep within the cliffs, and came from a level high above them.

This explained the force behind the water, and the small amount that was needed to drive the generators. Massive bronze pipes, with flanged connections, led them deep into the system to a point where they went vertically up a natural channel which disappeared into the darkness above them.

A series of ladders led them up beside the pipe to a dizzying height and eventually led out to a gigantic underground lake.

The light from their lamps could only light up a very small portion of the area, but it was obvious to Kal that this was very big indeed.

They could not see where the water came into the lake, or where it left when it was full, but then they could only see a little of the whole cavern.

The end of the pipe dipped below the surface and Kal bent down to see how far it went under the water.

He was immediately pulled back from the edge, and only just in time, as a pair of jaws large enough to have sliced him in two broke the surface of the dark waters.

Kal wondered how many of the little people had met their fate setting up the pipe system, especially the section that went under the surface of the lake. There must be other life forms in the water to sustain a creature as big as the pair of jaws which tried to get him, also there had to be a constant supply of food coming into the lake to keep the whole ecosystem going. Interesting things to find out, some day.

Kal was a little disappointed to find that the little people had done so much work unbeknown to him, and they hadn't even bothered to mention it.

Was it that he didn't matter to them anymore? Or did they think it was not important to tell him, as they just seemed to get on with any project which they were interested in and made very little fuss about it. He felt left out somehow, and didn't like it.

They made their way back down to the base of the tunnel system, and Kal suggested that they go a little deeper into the caves to see if there was anything else of interest. They agreed, and set off at a brisk pace, which suggested to him that they had been this way before.

They had been travelling for some time when they came across some more of the glowing lichen, but this time it was of a different colour, and further on yet another colour change. This excited the group, and Kal couldn't see why it should do so. It was, after all, just a lichen growth on the wall of a cave.

'What's the big deal' he asked himself, and as usual, got no answer. Samples were taken of each colour, and then they all proceeded on down the tunnel, twittering away among themselves as if they had just discovered the meaning of the universe.

A deep thump, thump became apparent after a while, and the pace slowed down to take into account anything which might contain a surprise.

'At least they haven't been this far before' he thought.

The further they went, the more pronounced the noise was, not louder so much as clearer. And then they were into another huge cavern. Before them was a construction that beggared belief.

A vast shaft rose up above them to disappear into the darkness, and it continued on down below the level of the ledge they were on.

Set in the middle of the shaft were massive blocks of black stone which rocked back and forth, one above the other, until they went out of sight above.

They could only look down on a few of the blocks before the light from their lamps faded into the darkness below, but what they could see was enough. Each block had been hollowed out into three sections with two of the sections seemingly joined somehow.

Water flowed into one section and out again into the other, forcing the massive block to rock about its middle for about two metres, with a deep rhythmic thump.

As it did this, water in the other section was somehow forced up and into a channel in the shaft wall where it swirled around and into the block above.

The water was going uphill in effect, driven by the force with which it was expelled from the chamber below.

The seemingly impossible was happening, and they all stood transfixed to the spot, watching it happen before their eyes. The rocking blocks cascaded down, one below the other for as far as they could see, and carried on above them into the blackness of the shaft.

This was most likely the pumping system for the lake above, but who had constructed it, and why expend so much effort just to fill a lake in the middle of a mountain, albeit a very big one.

Kal couldn't quite understand how the whole system worked, although somehow he felt he knew, but the bits didn't quite add up to the whole. Was there something else powering the monster pump which he couldn't see?

Or was it just water power. He knew that two litres of water falling a certain height would push one litre of water up higher than the original two litres were to start with, but the power loss was quite heavy, and he couldn't see how such a loss could be sustained in a huge system like this, and still deliver water at the top. No, there had to be something else in the equation, but he just couldn't see it.

They had at least solved the problem, if one had existed, of the water supply. He didn't think they needed to worry about that again, or at least not until the colony had at least quadrupled in size, and that wouldn't be for quite a while.

As there was nothing else to do other than marvel at the giant water pump, they decided to return to base, and look out for anything else of value on the way.

They hadn't gone far, when a side tunnel which had been missed on their way in because of its oblique angle to the main passage, came to light. It just had to be explored, there was something inviting about it, and then Kal felt something trigger in his memory.

He shouted a warning to the others, making his voice as high and squeaky as possible, and they all halted, looking a bit surprised. He tried to explain that there was danger here, but didn't know what it was.

They proceeded slowly for about fifty metres, but nothing untoward happened, and the pace quickened. Kal still felt that they were being lulled into a false sense of security, but could not justify his feelings.

The tunnel opened out a little, and ahead of them they could see a dim light.

'It couldn't be an exit, as we are too far within the cave complex, so it must be a luminescence of some kind' he thought.

As they approached the glow they could see that the light came from what could only be described as a profusion of flowers, cascading down the walls in glowing colours, and such pretty ones too, he was almost sure that he could smell the scent of them, yes he could, it was lovely ..... and then the alarm bells rang loud and clear.

'Get back' he cried instinctively, but it was too late for one of their number. Whip like tentacles lashed out from holes in the walls which they hadn't noticed, and the poor unfortunate was lashed up like a parcel.

Several of the party ran forward with knives at the ready but were in turn attacked by flying tentacles, and so had to retreat. The captive was drawn into a large hole in the wall and disappeared inside within seconds, the tentacles then retracting to their former positions.

It was all over so quickly and Kal felt sick at not being able to prevent it from happening. Now he knew what the warning feeling was all about, as he remembered the hypnotic effect of the creatures in the first sand lake they had found.

This was something similar, but the effect was the same, they were dazed for a while and felt that to go to the flowers was the right thing to do.

The flowers no longer looked like flowers, just ugly lumps of a lichen-like material on the wall of the tunnel. Surprisingly the little people didn't show any sign of anger at the loss of their companion, just a sadness.

Kal wanted to rush in and slash the tentacles to pieces, the chances of him getting away with it were small, but the feeling was there. In some ways, they were much more mature than he was, or was it that they had a different outlook on life.

One thought did strike Kal. If the thing in the walls of the tunnel was used to catching prey of this size, and it certainly seemed to be, where were the creatures which it would normally have caught?

Apart from the giant maggots, and they couldn't have got up these small tunnels, there must be something else providing food for the creature, and they hadn't seen it yet.

And that was a worrying thought. Kal got his idea across to the rest of them, and they were extra vigilant on their return journey.

They had reached the point where they had left the main tunnel to go exploring, and one of the party drew a series of symbols on the wall as a warning to others, or so Kal assumed.

At least no one else would be tempted to look at the flowers, he hoped. The rest of the journey back was uneventful.

When they finally reached the compound the team related their story to the others, and Kal could sense the sadness they felt. Emotions were developing fast in the little people, or maybe he was more in tune with them and so was able to pick up their feeling more easily.

Tibs came to see him that evening, and surprised him by his mastery of the words Kal had taught him earlier. The boy showed no sign of wanting to leave after their somewhat stilted chat, so Kal set about teaching the lad some more words to add to his vocabulary.

The rate of learning was not the sole province of the little people, as Tibs soon picked up the more subtle meanings of words, and it would not be long before he would be able to ask some embarrassing questions.

Kal enjoyed the evening, and in a way was sorry when the little one left to return to his mother.

Paper making was now in a state of full production, and much improved, clay being added to the sheets before the final rolling, giving a much better surface to write on.

The days of the old sketch slates were numbered, and a lot of space would be released when all the old records were transferred to the new medium.

A few days later, Kal was asked if he would like to open the new engineering workshop. Where they had got the idea of a ceremony for such an occasion was a mystery, but ceremony it was.

The leader of the elders made a speech, everyone clapped, and the leader of the engineers was given a medallion to hang around his neck. Kal was asked to open the great doors into the cave workshop, with the usual clapping, and the whole thing passed off in a very civilized manner indeed. A feast was the culminating point of the event, and Kal enjoyed it all immensely.

One evening while eating his meal, he noticed his 'cave person' seemed to be hanging around more than usual, doing little things which were not really necessary.

Tidying up, rearranging some of his things, and just generally being there. He should have spotted it coming a kilometre away, but was too relaxed.

The second part of his meal was served and he was just thinking of how enjoyable life was now, with all his needs taken care of, and this lovely food, and his smiling friend always to hand when needed, and how tired he felt after such a hard day's work, which of course, he had enjoyed so much, and those kindly helping hands which led to his bed. His eyes felt so heavy, so why bother to keep them open....

They must have used a more refined drug this time, as when he awoke he didn't feel groggy or tired, just furious at having been caught again.

The anger soon passed when he looked at it from their point of view. They knew what was best for the survival of their race, although it would be changed in the process.

They had asked for his co-operation twice, and found him unwilling to meet their request for no reason which they could understand. And so they did what they saw as the best thing possible for all, they helped themselves, again.

It was some time later when Kal managed to get the whole story of the cheeky event, as he now looked upon it. They had drugged his meal, and at the right moment had laid him down to rest.

One of the females had removed from him that which was necessary for the project, shared it out among the others chosen for the mothering of the new race, and all had gone to bed that night having felt they had done a good job of work. Which of course, they had.

He could smile at the event now, but he was hopping mad at the time. Being caught once was bad enough, but twice?

In time, if the new ones didn't already know, he would tell them how they got started, as a sense of humour was showing itself these days, and he could afford a laugh at his own expense now.

Kal was kept busy thinking up new projects for the various teams to work on. At one time he felt they only came to him for advice or help to humour him, as a kindness in some way, but he was not so sure now.

They never indulged in lies or deceit that he was aware of, and nothing was done without a reason, although the reason was sometimes a little hard for him to understand.

The little people's rate of development seemed to be slowing down a little, or so he thought. They were still making good progress in all the things which they did, and engineering had taken off to an amazing degree, but they came to him more and more for advice, which was good for him, but he wondered what was going on.

Kal felt that he should have kept a date system from the start, so that he would have a gauge of how long things took to happen, but he didn't bother in the beginning as there was too much going on, and now it seemed too late to make any difference really.

He had no idea of how long a year was, and only reckoned things as 'so many days', if at all. It didn't matter much as far as he was concerned as the others had no meaningful sense of time either, and so the time element was disregarded.

Life was good, interesting, pleasurable and he wanted for nothing, except for when he thought of the life he used to lead, and the people he had left behind, but that was long ago, and paling into insignificance, almost.

One thing which would make a great deal of difference to life would be the development of iron, and steel if they could get the temperature of the furnace high enough.

So far the only ore which contained iron was the black crystalline material, which was used for the generator magnets, and that was only obtainable in limited quantities.

Kal got the smelters, forgers and 'new material seekers' together, and explained the problem. He did his best to describe all the ores of iron that he could remember, as the ship's detectors did most of the hard work of locating minerals and classifying them. The teams soon realized the potential of steel, and set about organizing an expedition to find the necessary iron ore for its manufacture.

If they could find a wood which was dense enough, they could carbonize it to make the necessary carbon rods for an arc furnace, as that would be needed to make good hard steel. The rods would not last very long, but he thought the engineers would soon come up with an alternative.

Many days later the first of the teams came back, not with the iron ore which he had hoped for, but a more plentiful supply of the black crystals.

This was good news, as they could now begin to experiment with it to find out if it had any other uses, apart from making magnets.

Tibs came to see him most evenings now, and their conversation was reaching a point where it could be enjoyed by both, as the vocabulary they shared had increased to the stage where Kal was having to explain the finer points of grammar and the more subtle use of some words.

The child was hardly a child now, more of a young man, and getting more like his father every day. When fully grown he would not be as tall as Kal, but his build was strong and stocky, which gave him a neat and compact look.

Kal was at first a little uneasy as the bond between them grew, but he was now used to it, and was looking forward to the arrival of the next batch of offspring, which should be due any time now.

On rare occasions Tib's mother came also, and the lad translated for her so that she could join in the conversation.

One evening much to Kal's surprise, the mother through Tibs, apologized to him for the 'help yourself' incident which had led to the arrival of Tibs.

She explained that to her it was a great honour and privilege to be the one chosen to start the new race, and hoped that Kal would understand the reason for so doing.

He put her mind to rest by telling her that he did understand the main purpose behind the experiment, and was in favour of it, but a little shy. She gave her version of a smile and lowered her head a little, but whether she believed him or not was another matter.

More of the ore hunters returned, but with little ore. Small deposits had been found, but not enough to make it worthwhile mining.

It was looking as though they would have to make do without steel, which was a pity, as Kal had in mind so many things he would have liked to try out. The one place which they hadn't checked out was the further end of the black mountain range, and Kal thought it may well be worth a try, and when the last of the search teams returned. He would organize it.

Distant communications was one thing which was still missing, and Kal remembered the piezoelectric crystals which they had retrieved from the old mine workings in the black mountains.

His understanding of electronics was limited to the modern usage, with plug in units and a very rudimentary knowledge of the individual components, as most of it now consisted of subassemblies which were usually non repairable, and were discarded when defunct.

The very basic data was omitted in the early days of the academy, which only goes to illustrate the fact that if only the top end of a subject is fully understood, the ability to improvise at the lower end becomes somewhat limited.

They had very little chance of making anything too sophisticated, as their efforts would be limited by the components which they could manufacture with the restricted materials and tools to hand.

But if the crystals could make a spark, he didn't see why they couldn't make something which would pick up the radiation generated, and so be able to make a crude form of radio link.

A new team was brought together, and the basic principles of electromagnetic radiation were explained, along with the details of how a resistor, a capacitor and a few other components worked, and were usually made. Kal thought it wouldn't be too long before they came up with something.

He was not too surprised to get a visit from one of the team a couple of days later, who was trying his hardest not to show his excitement. Kal was presented with a box with a rod sticking out of the top, and a hole alongside it.

Next to the hole was a switch. The little chap leaned forward and tap tapped the switch, a few seconds later a series of tap tap taps came out of the hole in the top of the box, and Kal saw the first real grin from the little people.

It looked as if his mouth would split open, so pleased was he. Kal took him by the hand and shook it vigorously, and that started another fashionable thing to do.

It was not long before the 'radio' was working over a good distance, and simple messages could be sent and received by using an agreed upon series of 'taps'.

The electronics team intimated that they were working on something else, but would not say what it was. He could wait, and it would be worth waiting for, he felt sure.

The final team returned from the iron ore hunt, and brought back samples of many things, but not iron ore. They showed their disappointment, but cheered up when Kal told them of the black mountain quest he had planned.

They would use the new super steam wagon which Kal had been waiting to put to use ever since it had been built.

Two days later they were off on the ore quest at the far end of the black mountain range. The new wagon made good speed and was much more comfortable to ride in than its original model.

Maps which had been made on the early sketch slates, and later on boards of crude paper, had all to be transferred to the new paper sheets and were backed with a fine cloth, which made life a little easier, as the whole journey could be seen on one sheet.

They bypassed all the more unpleasant places they had visited on the first journey and it was only a few days before they reached their destination, and stopped at the foot of the mountain range just before it sloped down to the plains.

The team equipped themselves with a good selection of weapons and mining tools, and set off for the rift in the rock face which led to the summit of the lower section of the range.

The glaze makers back at the pottery had come to the aid of the metal makers in an unusual way. Metal oxides added to glazes often give a colour to the glaze, as copper will give green through to a blue, depending on the type of glaze. Iron will colour a pale yellow through to brown and almost red, and cobalt gives a brilliant blue, like no other metal.

This helped the metal makers identify which ores were which, as they had no other method of doing so at the moment.

As well as looking for the main ore, iron, the team would also be collecting anything else which looked of value, as this was the only way they had of obtaining new materials that could be identified, and added to their stocks.

There was very little evidence of ores on the surface of the rocks they passed on their way up to the plateau.

Either the ores had been collected already, or were only to be found deep within the mountain, as weathering of the outer rocks had not been sufficient to expose them.

This meant going into caves and tunnels, or making their own, and they were not equipped for tunnelling, so the former option was the only one they had.

On the way up the slope, several small caves were explored, but produced nothing of value. Near the top they had better luck, as a square hole had been cut into the wall of rock, and they stopped to survey it.

It was not a natural opening, and had been cut into the solid rock with a precision which made them wonder what kind of machinery or cutting tools had been used.

It looked safe enough, and the lamps were lit to see what lay inside the tunnel. Who, or whatever had made this opening, had gone in dead straight and level for nearly half a kilometre, and had left no debris on the outside.

'And that must have taken some doing', thought Kal.

There were no signs of tool marks on the walls or floor of the tunnel, except at the end, which they had now reached.

It was blocked off with huge blocks of stone which looked as if their edges had been fused together.

There was no way past this barrier that they could see, and certainly no way of moving it. It looked like a dead end, and a lot of travelling for nothing, but Kal was not one to give up easily.

He asked for some of the spears to be lashed together, forming a crude climbing frame, and sent one of the smallest members of the team up to see if there was a gap at the top, which he thought there might be, but which they couldn't see from ground level because of the low light level from their lamps.

He had been right, there was a block of stone that was not fused into the rest of the mass, and with a bit of effort, it could be moved.

It took a long time to lever the stone out of its hole, but they did it, and one of them crawled through to see what was on the other side. A lamp was lowered on a rope, and the tunnel seemed to carry on as before.

One by one, the team climbed the poles, went through the hole and down the other side on ropes. Kal found it a bit of a struggle to get through the hole, and had to be pulled through in the end.

There were only two good reasons to have made such a good job of sealing the tunnel up, and that was to keep something in, or others out. As nobody could make up their mind as to which it was, they were all very careful as they went along.

Another half kilometre brought them to a large cavern, in the middle of which was a machine, or so they supposed, as it looked as though it had been made rather than grown.

It was only when they got enough light on it that they realized it was the tunnel maker itself, as it was about the same size in width as the passage they had just come down.

The worrying question was, why had it been abandoned instead of being removed for future use, as it must have been an expensive machine to make, also why block up the tunnel so firmly, and part way in?

Something had caused whoever it was that had been here, to be somewhere else a bit sharpish, and that didn't look good for the team.

The machine was just a huge block of some metallic material sitting on the ground, with a square frame-like device at what they assumed to be the front end.

There was a control panel mounted in a recess at the top of the box like section, and Kal climbed into it. No sooner had he done so, when a soft humming noise filled the air, and he felt the machine move slightly. It had risen a few millimetres above the ground, and was now floating free.

Kal told the others to stay well behind the machine, as he was going to try the controls to see if he could make it work.

In front of him there was a panel of shiny metal plates set in a black frame, but there were no directions or symbols as to what did what.

He touched the top most plate very lightly and the gentle hum increased in volume, while the machine slowly slid forward. Pressing the plate a little harder and the speed increased a little, but no more than a good fast walking pace.

The plates just below and to either side caused the device to turn left or right, and the one below that pair put it into reverse, as he soon found out.

'So far, so good.' thought Kal, 'That was straight forward enough.'

Besides the main touch plates, there several others, but a little smaller, and he assumed that they would control the cutting action of the machine, or whatever else it did.

Telling the others what he was about to do, he edged the tunnelling machine up to the wall of the cavern, and tried the smaller touch plates in turn, but nothing happened.

He continued to fiddle with the plates, frustration mounting by the minute, and then a small panel slid to one side at the top of the control unit. Beneath it there was another set of plates, and he began to touch these in turn.

All of a sudden the whole place was bathed in a pale red tinged glow. He had found the light switch! He touched the plate again, and the light went out, leaving everyone in the dull glow of their oil lamps.

With the lights back on, Kal tried to see where the light was coming from, but there was no specific place, it just flowed out from all surfaces of the machine, and bathed the cavern in its pale glow.

Kal tried touching two plates at a time, systematically perming one against the others, and that did the trick.

The gentle hum had changed. A deep whine was now coming from the tunneller, and a touch plate at the top of the new panel lit up with a dull red light.

Kal then moved the machine up to the cavern wall such that the square frame in the front was just touching the rock, and then put one finger onto the glowing plate.

A section of the wall just disappeared, no dust, no falling rocks, it just wasn't there anymore. He edged the machine forward slightly while touching the glowing plate and the tunneller ate its way into the rock.

He stopped just as he was about to draw level with the new tunnel he had created, and backed the machine out again.

Kal had had enough of the alien technology for the time being, and trembling slightly, got down to confer with the others as to what they should now do.

So far there didn't seem to be any dangers in the cavern, and the tunneller worked. They could escape from the cavern if anything threatened them, as long as it didn't move too fast, although the last in line through the hole in the barrier wall would be at a disadvantage.

The options were, to try making some new tunnels of their own to see what they could find, leave everything as it was, and return to the outside world, or they could use the machine to remove the barrier they had crawled through, but that would leave the cavern open to whatever the previous users of the machine had tried to close it from.

It was finally decided to go around the sides of the cavern and see if any tunnels had been made by the previous operators of the machine, and if none were found, then it was unlikely that anything too unpleasant was going to come out of the stonework and attack them.

If all was well, they could experiment with the tunneller and make some more openings in the cavern wall to see what the mountain might contain.

After a close search around the cavern, no openings were found, except the shallow one which Kal had made. So, the machine had made its way in here, had been abandoned, and the entrance tunnel sealed up.

But why? It didn't make sense to any of them, and they felt that there was something else which they had missed.

The only place that they could not explore was the roof of the cavern, as it was too high for their oil lights to reveal. Maybe if there was a threat, it was up there.

In the end, after much discussion via the sketch blocks and copious arm waving, they decided to make a few exploratory tunnels, and if nothing was found, then they would exit the cavern the way they had come in, block up the hole temporarily, and one day come back to retrieve the machine when they could rebuild the barrier wall properly.

Kal mounted the machine once more, and drove it towards the cavern wall. He had penetrated the rock for only fifty metres or so when the tunneller broke into another cavern, but this one was very different.

The walls glowed with a pale yellow green light which was somehow different to that given off from the lichens, and then he knew why the whole project had been abandoned. It was radioactive, and the glow on the cavern walls was probably due to a radioactive isotope.

Kal yelled a warning to the rest of the team who were following up behind the machine, and backed it out of the tunnel he had made as fast as he could.

They had no means of telling if he or the others had received a lethal dose of radiation, but it was a very unhealthy place to be in, even for a few seconds.

What he couldn't understand was the fact that the original tunnellers could build a machine like this, and yet could not protect themselves from radiation.

That didn't make sense to him, and he tried to explain it to the others. There was no need to discuss what to do next, Kal put the machine back in the main cavern, and they all ran for the exit as fast as they could.

They would return one day and retrieve the tunneller, but would be protected by lead shielding.

Once out in the open air, the dangers of the cavern seemed a little less somehow to Kal, but he did understand the silent dangers of radiation, and would be on the lookout for signs of damage to himself and the others.

It had been interesting and informative, but disappointing with regard to the iron ore which they were seeking. They carried on up to the top of the incline to find that it levelled out into a small plateau.

In the distance, the rocks continued on up to form the next stage of the mountain range, and it was thought that it might be worth a visit as they were up here, to check out the next level of the mountain for the iron ore they wanted so badly.

The next two days were spent searching for the elusive ore in among the gullies and small natural caves which formed this part of the range, but none was found. They did have a very nice collection of coloured crystals, and some samples of what might be metal ores, and had to settle for that.

As they couldn't get the steam wagon any higher up the mountain, the only thing to do was to go down again and try somewhere else. The journey down was uneventful, except for the occasional steep section, and that was more of a thrill than anything else, as the wagon picked up speed and the steering had to be very accurate to avoid a crash into the rocks lining the track.

Having reached the plains, they travelled north again along the mountain chain, looking for caves to explore in the hope that they would find the elusive iron ore. Several stops and searches later produced nothing of any significance, except a few lumps of ore which Kal couldn't identify, but hoped the metal workers could.

They hadn't realized just how far north they had travelled, until the lonely mass of the Clump Trees hove into sight.

Kal suggested they pay the trees another visit, and gently overrode the reluctance of the crew, who were not too keen on the idea, remembering the last time they were here.

There seemed to be a change in the trunks since their last visit, several of the outer ones had died, or looked dead, as far as they could tell.

Having parked the wagon a safe distance away from the clump, Kal went over to the nearest trunk and found that the outer skin had shrivelled and split, and on hitting the column, produced a dull ringing note.

If it really was wood, and it looked as if it was, then it would make a very dense charcoal indeed, and they could use it for their iron smelting, that's if they could find the iron ore in large enough quantities in the first place.

It was worth a try, anyway, and a long rope was attached to the dead trunk. After hitching the other end to the wagon, Kal gave the signal to pull, and the wagon inched forward.

There was a series of loud snapping noises as the roots gave way, and the huge trunk tottered, and then fell to the ground with an earth shattering crash. Again, there was that strange dull ringing note, which confirmed Kal's idea that it was not only hard but very dense.

It wasn't until it was lying on the ground, that they realized just how large the trunk was. Kal thought the wagon could pull it home, but they would need to find some extra fuel due to the increased resistance the huge bulk would put on the wagon's pulling power.

It was with difficulty that they pulled the giant tree well clear of the main clump, and Kal realized that they would have to attach more than one rope to drag their prize home.

Also, the end of the trunk was tending to dig into the ground as they pulled it along, and as it was too heavy to lift the end up onto the back of the wagon, they would have to try and shape the end a little so that it behaved like the bow of a ship, and didn't try to bury itself.

The wood proved to be a lot harder than expected, and by the time the crew had sawn and axed the end to shape, blunting the tools, they were ready for a rest.

Some of the wood they had removed from the end of the tree was fed into the firebox, and it burned brightly, sending a shower of fine sparks up into the air from the smoke funnel.

After another short pull, to see if they had got the bow shape correct, they checked the firebox, and the new fuel was glowing a clear bright yellow, confirming Kal's thoughts about its quality for iron smelting.

Five more dead trunks were pulled out from the clump, and dragged well clear in case the living clump wanted to ingest them before the crew could return to collect their new material.

The first trunk was hitched up to the wagon again, and they began the long journey home.

Kal rarely sat around letting his mind drift pointlessly on without purpose, so most of the uneventful part of the journey back was taken up with an idea he had to harvest the dead trees from the 'clump', and put a little back into the system. He reasoned that the dead trunks were probably due to the lack of nutriment in the surrounding area, and also perhaps a lack of water.

Back at the compound they had plenty of waste organic matter, most of which contained nitrogen. The tree clump, like most plants here, were short of fixed nitrogen, hence the catching of animals instead of getting it from the ground.

He thought that if they were to tank some of their waste over to the tree clump and pipe it into the middle and then fill the tank up again from the not too far distant lake and add that to the clump, it should promote healthy growth.

If they then left the tree clump to fend for itself for a while, the outer trunks would die off again, and they could harvest them, and then give the clump another dose of that which it so badly needed, and so on, ad infinitum.

If his theory worked, and they could possibly find another clump of trees, then their high density fuel problem would be solved for some time to come.

As they wended their way back home, Kal put his idea to the crew, who after considerable thought and discussion on the matter, agreed it could be a good idea, if the trunk they were towing proved to be really useful.

He hoped his theory of what the wood could be used for would turn out to be right, as he still didn't like the idea of losing face with the little people, although he felt sure it didn't matter one jot to them.

They passed the dead sand lake shortly after the discussion about the tree trunks, and Kal thought while things were going his way, a slight diversion to the lake would provide them with a quartz and bone mix which might be useful for the ceramic engineers.

The crew agreed, and they collected as large a sample as the wagon would take, leaving little room for anything else, should they find something of value.

Somehow, the journey back to the compound didn't seem to take as long as the outward trip, and Kal put this down to the time taken up with the business about the dead tree trunks and the scheme for harvesting them, plus a few other little ideas he had tried to convince the crew were vital to their existence.

He had noticed that they were getting a little more self determined as time went by, but were usually right in their judgement, all the same. Perhaps he was not so important to them now, although they did go to great lengths to protect him unthinkingly when danger threatened.

As they approached the compound, an excited little group came out to meet the wagon, which had slowed down a little to enable them to climb aboard. A sample of black shiny rock was presented to Kal by a beaming Tibs.

Somehow he had joined the mining and mineral team, or they had thought it a nice gesture for him to take their find to Kal, reinforcing the bond between them.

'They don't miss a trick' thought Kal, but maybe he was wrong.

It certainly looked like iron ore, and had about the right weight for its size. But the surprise was where they had found it. After the wagon had been parked, and the firebox let out, an eager little team led Kal up into the pool rocks.

Just above the place where he had built his shelter, there was a sign of rock breaking, and a pile of the dark ore. It transpired that a group of the little people had been tidying up Kal's old shelter, almost as if it were a shrine, and the lookout had been positioned high above the site.

He had found nothing to do really, as there was no likelihood of a large predator creeping up on them during daylight, so he had gone on an exploration tour of his own.

Finding a small piece of the black ore, he remembered the description Kal had given the search team, and hurried back to the compound with it. One of the metalwork team confirmed his discovery, and a group went up into the rocks to see if there was any more to be found. And there was, lots.

Kal suggested that the smelters try to extract the iron from the ore, but they were already ahead of him, and produced a sample of crude cast iron. It was not of very good quality, but if it was refined, it could produce quite good steel.

They needed to cut up the dead tree they had brought back with them, and convert it to charcoal, as Kal was sure the extremely high density of the wood should produce the extra heat required to smelt the iron ore properly, and then refine the resulting pig iron to good quality steel.

Evening was drawing in, and a small feast for the returned crew of the steam wagon was under way. Kal, as usual had the position of honour at the head of the table.

The first surprise after the actual eating was that Tibs got up and told Kal he would do the interpreting for the little people, so enabling Kal to tell his own story of the journey to the assembly for the first time.

The evening was a roaring success, and Kal felt part of the group again. Perhaps they did appreciate him a little more than he thought.

They all slept very well that night, and first thing next morning Kal was up bright and early, eager to try cutting up the tree trunk they had brought back with them.

The bronze saw wasn't going to do the job by the look of things, and he conveyed this to the charcoal team, who promptly produced a large collection of the blade like teeth from the type of jaw bone he had found way back when he had first arrived, so long ago.

By mid day, a new type of saw had been produced, consisting of a long thin bronze bar with the jaw teeth set in one edge, each alternate tooth slightly angled outwards, so cutting a narrow groove for the bar to follow in as it cut through the trunk. And it worked.

Kal never ceased to be surprised by the understanding the little people had of engineering principles, and the setting of the saw teeth was no exception. The cutting up of the trunk into lengths which could be handled, was a tough job, but there were many willing hands to help, and relay teams of 'trunk cutters' were soon organized.

Once the tree had been cut into suitable lengths, it proved relatively easy to split length wise with bronze wedges, and so the charcoal making could begin.

It was while Kal was waiting for the charcoal stocks to build up, that one of the radio group came to him in a state of great excitement, and requested his presence in the workshop.

He wasn't quite ready for one of the biggest surprises so far, with regard to the little people. Upon entering the work shop, he was directed to the window which gave a good view of the distant pool rocks, and perched high up near the top was a little figure, desperately waving its arms to attract his attention.

On the bench below the window was a small box with a hole in the front, and a thin metal rod sticking up from the top. One of the team squeaked into the box, and a second later, a reply of squeaks came back out.

Kal assumed the facial expressions now exhibited by all present were grins of satisfaction, but he was never quite sure. The radio team had constructed a radio transmitter and receiver system which actually conveyed the spoken, or in this case, squeaked, voice.

This was no mean achievement, considering the very basic equipment they had to work with, and he asked to see inside the incredible contraption.

The box was opened, and inside were two basic circuits which Kal was able to recognize quite easily. The hole had a sprung diaphragm behind it, and stuck to the centre of the diaphragm was a small metal bead which impinged onto the end of one of the cylindrical crystals they had obtained for the giant maggot in the caves.

Speaking into the diaphragm caused the little metal bead to tap in harmony on the end of the crystal, so producing an electrical signal from it, as in the earlier radio.

Another crystal was made to vibrate at a high frequency, and some of the signal produced was taken off and amplified before being fed to the metal rod on top of the box, creating a carrier wave which radiated out into the atmosphere.

The clever bit was that the speech signal was superimposed onto the carrier wave, and so a voice pattern was being broadcast for anyone with a suitable receiver to pick up.

The receiver section was just the reverse of the transmission action. The transmitter on the pool rocks, when spoken into, sent the signal out, and the box in the workshop picked it up with its rod aerial.

The speech signal was then stripped off the carrier wave, amplified a little and fed to a crystal which responded by vibrating and moving an attached diaphragm, so creating sound waves which could be clearly heard.

Kal wondered how long his race would have taken to develop an efficient transceiver unit like this, with so little help, and paled at the thought. These were very bright people, and getting brighter all the time.

The new radio units would certainly be very useful on future expeditions, that's for sure, but he wouldn't be able to use them, as there wasn't another 'him' to receive the low frequencies his voice used, or was there? Tibs could possibly be the go between. He wondered how long it would be before they had vision transmission.

The new extra hard charcoal stocks were inspected a few days later, and were nearly enough to start smelting the iron ore, but it would take a little extra skill to turn the iron so formed into really hard steel. Kal thought they would find a way, once they understood the principles behind it.

SIX:
Flight

THE NEXT GENERATION of crossbreeds began appearing shortly after the iron smelting began, and Kal was astonished at the number of the females who had opted for the program.

Very soon, it would seem, Tibs would have his very own little clan, albeit a bit younger, but the same as himself, if nature ran true to form.

Kal was sunning himself up on the pool rocks, which he did when he wanted to be alone with his thoughts, when something which had been hovering at the back of his mind, came to the fore. He had seen no flying creatures of any kind. No birds or flying insects, nothing with wings. A grin spread across his face as a new project sprang to life in his mind.

Flying. What would they make of that?

They had seen nothing to stimulate them into developing the idea, so why not raise their interest? A kite would be the simplest form of demonstrating the 'lift' principle, and that should be easy to do.

The weavers had in the past produced some very fine fabrics, and he went to them to ask for the very finest and thinnest they could produce, with a very close weave. It was promised for next day.

A small group had developed a form of paint from the juices of certain plants, adding ground up minerals to them to achieve a coloured finish. All he needed now was to be able to split the bamboo like poles into thin strips, get some glue, and he was ready for his kite making.

There were no doors on the openings to the internal caves, so he dragged a table over to block the entry, and hung a piece of cloth above it to keep prying eyes out until he had finished his project. He wanted this to be a real surprise.

Next day the kite was finished, the fabric having been given a thin coating of coloured varnish, and a tail added for stability. It turned out to be a little bigger than he had intended, and only just passed through the cave opening and along the passage to the open compound.

It wasn't long before a large crowd of onlookers were assembled, and were obviously trying to make out what the strange contraption was all about.

A couple of the elders joined the group, and he was then ready for the demonstration. Instructing two of the little people to hold the kite, he payed out the line and waited for a steady increase in the gentle breeze which was blowing.

At the right moment, he called for release and ran a few metres forward, the kite soaring up like a bird and pulling on the line like a live entity.

Paying out more line, the kite went higher and higher, to the astonished gasps of all assembled. As he had attached two lines to the kite, he was able to make it swoop and turn, bringing it low over the crowd who scattered in all directions like frightened rabbits.

The fear was soon replaced with awe, and then understanding began to form in some little minds. He had planted a seed, and would now wait patiently for it to grow, but into what he had no idea. It should be worth waiting for.

The next few days brought forth the first of the steel makers' samples. Using the new hard charcoal and forced air from a simple compressor powered from the water wheel, they had achieved the necessary high temperature in the smelter.

It wasn't long before they had found a way to burn out the impurities in the crude steel, and control the amount of carbon present. Kal knew that tools of much improved quality would soon follow, and he was right.

The days rolled on as they do, and the first of the man carrying kites appeared. It was a box like construction with a sling to hold the passenger, the whole thing being winched up by a steam engine at the end of the compound.

The volunteer flyer, at a given signal, ran along the ground as the winch powered up, and was soon airborne, climbing higher and higher as the winch pulled in the line.

There was soon a little queue of people waiting to have their turn at the new contraption, and Kal knew that air travel would follow before very long.

These were indeed exciting times, but Kal was hard put to think of anything new to add to the growing number of skills these people had achieved. A boat for the ocean perhaps?

But first he would have to find out what else the sea held before venturing out on that idea.

Tibs's siblings were growing on apace, and he had already begun to teach them the 'human' speech. Kal wondered if the elders would let the original little people die out, replacing them with the new crossbred.

If they did, he thought it would be a shame somehow, as they were unique as far as he knew. That however, was something for them to decide, and he had no doubt they would get it right, come what may.

The smelting had been so successful that the charcoal burners had almost run out of the new fuel, despite the size of the giant trunk they had brought back, and asked if they could have some more.

A meeting was held at which Kal's idea of harvesting the clump trees was discussed. They had a job to fault his reasoning, although there was a hesitancy to have anything to do with the 'clumps'. He couldn't find out what it was that made them so wary, doubting if they even knew. It seemed to be a 'hunch' thing somehow.

A large tank was to be built on a trailer, so that it could be towed behind the steam wagon. It would leave the compound filled with liquid waste from the drainage sump which served the whole community.

Being rich in nitrogen and other compounds, he thought it should produce a rapid growth of the 'clump', and then the tank could be refilled with water from the lake, and that could be pumped into the middle as well.

They would continue doing this until there was a substantial increase of growth, stop the feeding and then let the outer trees die off, harvest them, and then begin the cycle all over again. Someone suggested growing a clump nearby, so saving the long journey, but this was adamantly thrown out, which illustrated the deep fear most had for the 'clumps'.

There was something about the 'clumps' which struck deep into the subconscious minds of the little people, and Kal was more than a little intrigued about it. No amount of questioning brought any more light on the matter, and he thought either they didn't want to tell him, or they genuinely didn't know themselves.

It looked as if Tibs had stopped growing, and the second batch was fast catching up. Kal wondered if they had all been told he was, in effect, their father, but when he approached the elders about this, they were very evasive on the matter and even with Tibs doing the interpreting, he gleaned little information that was conclusive.

At last the great tanker trailer was ready, and they set off early in the morning to cover as much ground as possible in the first day. Also there had been a few modifications to the steam wagon since the last long journey.

A power winch had been fitted, safety screens were on all sides, and cross bows, capable of delivering a bronze tipped bolt were installed for the crew members to use, should the need arise. Also a giant cross bow, of huge proportions was mounted on gimbals just above the drivers head.

This was a weapon of considerable destruction, if ever there was one. The bolt alone weighed in at ten kilos, while a small hand winch was used to load the very powerful bow. It looked as if the little people were expecting trouble, or were they just being careful?

They made camp the first evening near an outcrop of rocks which, although they had been added to their maps, had not been explored, as they were just off the main course taken on the last visit to the region. As there was still a good amount of light left, two of the crew, heavily armed, decided to take a look at the outcrop for anything of interest.

By early dusk they hadn't returned, and a search party set out to find them. And didn't. There was no sign of the two, or their weapons, not even a footprint. Lamps were fetched, but it was deemed too dangerous to proceed any further in the now approaching dark.

The crew reasoned that their companions had met their end, and nothing more could be done until there was adequate light. The evening meal was a sombre affair, and no one slept very well by the bleary eyes next day.

A quick meal was taken early next morning, and the rescue party, heavily armed, set off headed by Kal.

They skirted the rock pile, just to make sure they wouldn't be surprised by anything lurking around the corner, but it was just a jumble of black rocks, somewhat out of place in the middle of the flat sandy plane.

Nothing grew here, and there were no footprints in the sand which would have indicated something hungry and on the prowl for a meal. There weren't even any prints of the two explorers, and that caused a bit of concern.

Kal was all for climbing up the pile to see what lay in the middle, but was forbidden to do so in no uncertain terms.

The rock was a dark grey brown, and lay in a series of jumbled levels, as if it had been stripped from the centre core, stage by stage, by some giant cutting tool.

Two of the crew went up first, stage by stage, and Kal was only allowed to follow when they thought it was safe.

Near the top of the rocks, the advance guard suddenly disappeared from sight, and two more rushed up with cross bows at the ready to see what had happened.

Squeaks and whistles indicated something was amiss, and the rest of the party quickly climbed up, Kal ignoring the 'stay back' orders, and leading the pack.

The second two were in a small hollow, and looking down a hole in a block of rock which must have formed the central core of the pile, making the sort of face one does when confronted by a very unpleasant smell.

Kal reached the two, and recognizing the odour at once, waved them back out of the hollow around the hole, and up onto a nearby ledge.

The hollow was filled with the heavy vapours of petroleum oil, and must have displaced the air, so that anyone entering the hollow would be overcome by the fumes and would have fallen down the hole, and so out of sight.

They all withdrew to a higher ledge, while Kal tried to explain what must have happened to the first two explorers, and the invisible dangers to anyone else trying to go down into the hollow.

Kal sent one of the party back to the wagon to bring back a flaming fire brand, explaining that the vapours were inflammable, and he hoped to burn them off. Then it would be safe for them to go down for a few minutes to see if they could locate their unfortunate companions.

The fire brand was brought up to him, and he made them all stand well back while he crawled as close as possible to the hollow, and lobbed the flaming bundle of sticks in.

There wasn't an explosion as such, more of a dull thump as the gasses caught fire, and leapt skywards in a plume of livid red and yellow flame.

Black oily smoke curled up every now and then as the flaming gases used up all the oxygen, and more air rushed in to replace the rising hot fumes.

Eventually the flames died down, with the odd puff of black smoke, and then all was still, any remaining flames being below the edge of the hollow, and out of sight.

Kal thought it safe now to go down into the hollow, and he explained that as the heat from the burning gases would have risen and taken any fumes with them, they had hopefully been replaced with breathable air.

The rest of the group were a bit hesitant at first, but followed Kal into the hollow, gazing down into a black hole in the rock. He tried to explain what he thought must have happened to the first two the night before.

They had climbed up, gone into the hollow to see what the hole was all about, been overcome by the fumes without realizing what was happening, and fallen down the hole, and would now almost certainly be dead.

Kal asked for a long rope with a hook to be brought up, along with a metal container to take a sample of the oil. The rest of the little group sat around the edge of the hollow while they waited for the rope to arrive, a sad looking lot, although there was no specific expression on their faces.

Kal thought he might be able to hook the bodies up on the end of the rope, but then thought better of it, their friends were gone, and the sight of two oil soaked bodies would do little to put things right.

The rope and hook arrived, along with a big beaten bronze tank and a smaller pot with a handle on it. The hook wouldn't now be used, but he saw no reason not to take a sample of oil back with them. They lowered the rope with the pot on the end to its fullest length, and brought it up again. No sign of oil or anything else. More rope was sent for and joined to the first piece.

This time they brought up a pot full of thin black oil, and the rest of the crew recoiled from the smell of it. Kal explained that it could be a very useful commodity, and they should fill the big tank and take it back with them.

They were a little reluctant, but did as he asked, but the tank could only be half filled because of the weight and getting it down through the rock pile again.

They said their farewells to the two lost ones in their own way, Kal supposed. The wagon was made ready, and they were off towards the clump trees. There was little chat among the crew for some time, but then things got a little more relaxed, and more interest was taken of the passing countryside as they came across different growths.

On the third day, the clump hove into sight, and they parked the wagon some fifty metres away from the nearest tree.

Many more trees had died since their last visit, and Kal went around the clump to see how many they could harvest.

A total of forty three trunks had died, but this was only a very small proportion of the whole mass, so the loss to the main clump wasn't too serious. It was decided to pull all the dead trunks out of the main group, and take them over to where the wagon was parked, for later collection, as they couldn't take the whole lot back in one go.

By the time they had worked out all the little details of what they would do, and how they would do it, it was time for the evening meal, and a good sleep. After they had eaten, Kal explained what mineral oil was all about, and how it could be refined and used as a burning fuel, much in the same way that the nut oil was used, but with more uses.

The steam engine was very similar in a way to one powered by gas or vaporized oil, and a keen interest was taken by a few of the more engineering inclined members of the crew.

A lookout was posted, working in shifts throughout the night, just in case the tree clump got any ideas of an easy meal, but the general conclusion was that it was too tired or weak to do much about it now.

An early morning meal was enjoyed all the more as the sun rose, painting the sky in strips of coloured bands of light, shifting and changing all the time, until the sun itself rose into sight, and the day proper began.

The wagon was fired up, and the tree pulling out began. It didn't take as long as they had thought, and the collection of dead trunks was parked well away from the living clump, just in case it tried to retrieve its missing members.

The bronze pipes, which had been specially made for the job, were joined together and fed as far into the main clump of the tree group as they could get it. As the trees moved so slowly, one of the braver members of the crew, much to the astonishment of the others, went in among them, guiding the pipe in between as many trunks as possible, and using the wagon to push the last few lengths in until they hit an obstruction which could not be bypassed.

The sludge pump was started up, being run from a takeoff point on the steam wagon, and the waste from the compound was squirted into the middle of the clump.

When the sludge tank was empty, they left the pipes in place among the tree trunks, and headed off for the lake to fill the tank with water to complete the tree feeding.

The journey was uneventful, except for what looked like a large plume of smoke moving along the horizon. It was dark grey, almost black in places, and although it was difficult to tell because the distance was unknown, seemed to be moving a lot faster than they were. The crew exchanged worried glances, and using sketch pads asked Kal what he thought it was, but he was no wiser than they were.

They reached the lake, and another set of smaller pipes were connected up and very carefully pushed into the water, no one getting any closer to the edge of the lake than they absolutely had to.

With the tank now full of water, and no attack from any water monsters, they set off for the tree clump. Late afternoon saw the water being pumped into the tree mass, the pipes withdrawn and stowed away ready for the return journey to the compound, and a happy crew.

There had been no further sightings of the mysterious dark cloud, so they were in a relatively cheerful mood that night as they settled down for a well earned rest.

During the night, despite the lookout, something big had been prowling around the wagon, and left a very large set of footprints behind it.

Next morning saw the smiles disappear as the footprints were discovered, and a lot of 'looking over the shoulder' was going on. Four of the dead tree trunks were power winched up to the back end of the tank trailer, and the ends positioned and made fast on a ledge at the rear.

Kal had estimated that dragging four trunks would be just about all the wagon could cope with, even with the latest modifications they had just done, but a fully wheeled trailer could move many more. But then they would have to lift them onto it, which meant making a special crane.

On the way back on the second day, they saw the dark cloud again, but going the other way. By the time they had made it home, the theories of what the cloud could be would have filled a couple of books, and the crew had worked themselves up into a right old state, which surprised Kal as he always thought of them as being so stable.

And then it dawned on him. They were very stable normally, and accepted the inevitable very well; it was the unknown which left them in a nervous state.

The design for a special log trailer was soon drawn up, and manufacture began at once.

A few days later a logging team was assembled, and set off to retrieve a full load of the tree trunks, just in case something else found a use for them in the meantime.

Feeling in a particularly mischievous frame of mind one day, Kal called for Tibs, and when he arrived, asked him to bring around ten or so of the younger siblings who were interested in any form of engineering.

A few minutes later an eager looking little crowd stood before Kal, and he motioned them to assemble around the other side of the table at which he sat. On the middle of the table he placed a ten centimetre long model of the cat creature which had begun the whole relationship with the little people in the first place.

The youngsters looked a little apprehensive, despite the fact they probably had never seen a real one, but no doubt had heard tales of the creature from their elders.

Using Tibs as translator, for he wasn't sure how much the little ones knew of his language, he said he would make the model do his bidding, without touching it.

There were what he took to be one or two giggles, and general looks of disbelief. Placing one hand on the table, he beckoned the cat model towards him, and after several attempts it moved in a series of little jerks towards his hand.

At this point the little crowd backed off a little, as if the model had acquired a life of its own, and they couldn't understand how. When they had recovered from the shock, and gathered around again, he motioned it to move across the table, and it did so.

As they seemed no longer frightened of the model, he turned it to face them, and advanced it towards the group in a series of little jumps.

At this, they all jumped back, completely taken by surprise.

Through Tibs, he explained the main point of the exercise.

'That which you see is not always what it appears to be' and with that he brought from under the table a little stick with a coil magnet on the end, powered by a small battery.

He then showed how a piece of the electromagnetic material had been placed in the base of the model, so that when he moved the magnet under the table, the model followed.

Smiles and hand clapping indicated that the tension had gone, to be replaced by understanding, and a general request for samples of the trick.

This was to be the first of many scientific lessons he was to give to the youngsters, awakening their curiosity and giving them a good grounding in physics.

The next time they took sperm from Kal, he was totally unaware of it, except for a very strange dream, and he gave little thought to that. They had used a more subtle drug, so he just slept a little deeper than usual, and felt none the worse for the unconscious donation.

Kites had developed into fabric covered flying wings, and on a day when there was a steady breeze, they could be seen soaring above the compound and out across the plains.

The oil they had brought back from the black rock pile still remained in its container. Kal thought they either didn't like the smell of it, or associated it with the death of their two friends, although he doubted the latter, as they were a fairly pragmatic lot, given time to let things settle.

He asked for a small group to develop the oil into useful products, explaining all he knew on the subject to give them a head start, and soon had another branch of chemistry on the go. A distillation tower was built, and modified a few times before they got it right, and oil for lamps, lubricating and waterproofing were not long in following.

Kal's main interest was in making a high grade light fuel, so that an internal combustion engine could be developed, and when he gave them the known facts on the subject, that too, was produced, in time.

The first engine was a little crude, but it worked. Fired by a spark crystal, as they called it, the main problem was getting the timing right. Once that had been fathomed out, large and small units were produced in fair numbers, and a multi-cylinder engine was incorporated into a new exploration wagon.

One rather disturbing offshoot from the understanding of the firing cycle, was the development of a gun like device, which, using the explosive force of combustion, propelled a quite heavy projectile a very considerable distance.

Kal didn't like the idea of such weapons, but accepted the fact that they were just improving their chances of survival against any unknown adversary which may show up in the future. He could have done well selling them insurance.

The second generation of Kal's offspring were growing up at an alarming rate, or was time passing by very quickly?

A new section had been added to the main compound, and was partly roofed over. Inside this new building they were assembling a giant flying wing.

Kal was surprised at its size, and realized that it would carry at least twenty people and himself, with ease.

The smelters had come up with a new light weight alloy, which Kal was unable to identify at first, and from this, the air wing was constructed. Below the huge wing, there was slung a cabin to hold the crew and whatever they needed for their flights. A three wheeled undercarriage completed the colossal machine, which was powered by two of the new multi-cylindered petrol engines.

It would be a while before it was finished, and Kal was looking forward greatly to a trial flight in it. There had been a few mishaps with the flying machines, not to mention an untold number of broken bones, but nothing stopped these people once they had a goal in sight, and Kal admired their unswerving tenacity.

Several of the second generation crossbreeds (Tibs was considered to be the first) had paired up, and were about to produce offspring of their own. Kal wondered if they would breed true to the new type, and was later pleased to see that as they grew up, they did.

The numbers of the original little people were now beginning to dwindle as they were replaced with the new type, and in a way, Kal was saddened by this. He mentioned it to the Council of Elders, as he liked to think of them, but they were not in the least bit perturbed, and he got the impression from them that a better thing couldn't have happened.

The bond between Kal and Tibs continued to grow, and they spent many hours together, Tibs' favourite subject being when Kal told him of the old days, when he was one of a team of mineral hunters flying around the galaxy and exploring new planets.

The language barrier had all but ceased to exist between Kal and the new ones, although he found it a little difficult to understand them when they got very excited, and the pitch of their voices rose, which was quite often as new discoveries were made, and equipment developed from them.

At last, the day of the trial flight of the giant wing came, but Kal wasn't allowed to go on it. He argued long and hard, but to no avail, and just to make sure he didn't sneak aboard, he was accompanied by what amounted to a four person body guard, just to make sure he didn't.

The first few trial flights proved successful beyond their wildest dreams, with no mishaps whatsoever. On the fifth flight, Kal was ushered aboard and given a front seat with a panoramic view of all before him, but not the controls.

The wing lumbered along the ground with its engines roaring flat out, and was suddenly airborne in a remarkably short distance. The pilots had quickly learned the art of looking for hot air thermals, so gaining altitude without using so much fuel, and thereby extending the distance they could cover on a given quantity.

Once a reasonable height had been achieved, the engines were throttled back, and they cruised along in a world of their own, with just the rush of the wind.

A feast was held that night to honour the accomplishment of the designers and builders, and the pilots too were lauded for their ability, but to a lesser degree.

Kal was later asked where he thought they should fly on their first real airborne expedition, and he suggested that they go north along the mountain range, and possibly out over the desert to see where it ended, and what took its place if and when it did terminate.

Next day they were off to an early start, and were equipped with the new radios so that a communication link could be kept open, should a problem arise. In very little time they had reached the point where the mountains finished and they turned east, passing over the large block-like building where they had so long ago sent a load of sand to someone, somewhere, who didn't really want it.

When Kal retold the story of the sand, he became aware that they had developed a sense of humour after all, as the crew doubled up with laughter, suggesting that one day, they might do it again. But he wasn't sure that was such a good idea.

The wing droned on, and they began to wonder if the desert went all the way around the planet, when a high flat plateau came into sight. They had to climb a little higher to clear the huge cliffs, and looked around for a suitable landing site.

This decision was chosen for them, as they saw in the distance a large collection of what might be buildings, and the temptation to investigate was too much to pass up.

The wing flew over the site several times to make sure there wouldn't be a reception committee waiting for them when they landed, and eventually touched down half a kilometre away from the nearest construction, just to be on the safe side. Armed to the teeth, and checking every little detail ahead of them, the party advanced towards the very businesslike structures.

They needn't have worried, it had been abandoned long ago, and only the buildings of a great complex remained.

It took them the rest of the day to get only the basic outline of what the huge site had been used for, and as they ate their evening meal in the eerie silence of the vast construction, they tried to put together the pieces of information they had gathered, to make a coherent whole.

It would seem that it had been a mining and refining complex, as vast smelters lay alongside huge storage bays and crushing plants. A few billets of an unknown metal lay scattered about near what looked like a ground to space vehicle, and it looked as if everyone had left in a bit of a hurry. There were several shuttle like craft, similar in a way to the one Kal had landed in, but of a different origin, and of a totally alien construction to his eyes.

What they assumed to be several bulk ore carriers were grouped off to one side, badly battered as if some giant hand had dealt them a series of blows in extreme anger.

It was evident from the way things had been left about that this hadn't been a gradual run down, or an orderly exit from the site. Someone or something and descended on the place, and everyone had abandoned what they were doing, and hightailed it out at maximum velocity.

Suddenly, the inky blackness of the night took on a more sinister nature, as all agreed that something out there was watching them. It was too late to try and fly out, as they would have to make sure the wing had a clear runway from which to take off, and it was too dark for that.

It was finally decided to try and get into one of the abandoned buildings, and by posting a few guards, at least get some sleep to be refreshed for the morrow. Not that anyone really expected to sleep much.

It was a bleary eyed bunch who staggered out of the building at the crack of dawn, and finding nothing threatening in the vicinity, cheered up a little while they prepared breakfast. By the end of the meal they thought it might have been an over active imagination which had deprived them of their beauty sleep, but the wrecked bulk carriers and the remains of the three shuttles, albeit one of which had obviously been cannibalized for spares, took some explaining.

Looking around the site and putting two and two together still added up to something causing a lot of damage in a very short space of time, and a hurried general exodus of the operators of the equipment.

Kal went over to one of the battered shuttles, and found that it had been rendered inoperable by a series of heavy blows on one side, cracking the seams of the outer hull plates and probably destroying the integrity of the inner chamber where the crew would be. Even so, he couldn't gain entry to the vehicle, try as he might.

He thought that the metal ingots could be explained by the threat of something causing the personnel on the site to have thrown the ingots out of a working shuttle to make enough room for themselves, and then hitting the lift off button.

There were no bones or signs of bodies having been left lying about, in fact there was no trace of the race who had been here. No pictures of anything which would give a clue as to their likeness, no clothing, in fact no sign of there every having been anyone here at all, except the equipment.

Kal wasn't happy about this, there was something he was not seeing or understanding, and it worried him.

One of the crew came hurrying up to say he had found some tracks which might have been made by one of the ore carriers. If they followed them, it might lead to where the ore was coming from, and they could retrieve some.

As there was no sign of the terror which had caused the general exodus, in fact, no sign of any life form at all, it was decided to follow the tracks to see where they led, and then reconsider the situation again.

Arming themselves with everything they could carry, which unfortunately excluded the heavy weapons which wouldn't go in the wing, they set off.

The vegetation on this part of the plateau was sparse and of a different type to that of the lower lands on which they lived. Here it consisted of low tough rubbery growths with no sign of the usual fruits or berries, and Kal wondered how such plants, if plants they were, propagated themselves.

The well worn track made by the ore carriers was still visible as compacted ground on which nothing grew, and so was easy to follow. In the distance they could see what might be a building of some sort, and fortunately the track led in its general direction.

The flying wing had been turned around and lined up ready for takeoff, should anything unpleasant turn up, and with which they couldn't cope. The four crew manning it being instructed to take to the air if threatened, circle around, and return to pick up the exploration party when conditions were more favourable.

The little group plodded on towards the block-like building, keeping an eye out for anything which moved. The plateau was flat, featureless and almost barren, the ground consisting of a mixture of sand and gravel, with the occasional stone breaking the surface, and the odd plant.

There was a constant gentle breeze blowing, which had a dry and dusty smell about it, reminiscent of something long since dead and decayed.

As the building loomed up, it was apparent that it was a lot larger than they had thought, consisting of a main block with several smaller units surrounding it on three sides.

The track led right up to the main block, being replaced with an apron of some very hard material as it reached the face of the building. On the wall they could see what they assumed to be the outline of a door or opening, big enough to have taken one of the ore carriers they had seen earlier.

There were no controls, knobs, levers, or switches visible to operate the door, so they thought it likely that the controls were inside the block, or one of the other buildings.

There appeared to be no damage to the site that was obvious to Kal, so they were in high hopes of finding a way in, and then working out what it all represented.

It was some time later that one of the crew found what they thought might be a ventilation shaft high up on one of the side units. They lowered a very brave volunteer down it on a rope. Kal wasn't allowed to go.

Kal was about to send someone else down, when there was a slight hiss and a doorway opened up before them with the volunteer standing framed in the opening, and a large grin on his face. They had gained access, but to what?

It was decided to try the opening and shutting procedure of the door first, so that if inside the building, they could at least get out again. Inside the portal there were three silver plates set in the wall, two of which opened and shut the door, but no one wanted to try the third one as they couldn't reason out what it was supposed to do.

The crew plus Kal went in, and shut the door behind them just in case anything else should turn up, and want access.

The room was almost featureless, except for what looked like a control unit on one wall, and a passage leading in the general direction of the main block.

There was little point in fiddling with the control unit until they had worked out what it did, so they went down the passage, hoping to get into the main block.

The walls of the tunnel were made of a very hard shiny material, as were all the constructions on the site, but there were no signs of it being assembled from single blocks, as there wasn't a joint in sight.

They reached the end of the passage, and were confronted by a solid wall, and there were three silver plates set in the side of it. Remembering which one opened and shut the first doorway they had come through, they hoped the sequence was the same for this one, and the top plate was touched by Kal. The passageway opened up with the same gentle hiss as the first door, and they were in the main hall.

Kal noticed that there were no separate light sources, just a gentle glow which somehow seemed to pervade everything around them.

To their right was the archway housing the big door which led to the outside world, but no sign of the necessary controls for it. Ahead was just a big empty space, and as they began to walk across it, Kal urgently called them back, as he thought it must be a lift platform.

Closer inspection did reveal the outline of something on the floor, and it had to be the lifting gear for the ore carriers as it was about the same size, and he couldn't see what else it could be.

Naturally, they wanted to go down on the lifting platform to see what was below, but it took them some time to find the controls for it. It was while they were exploring one of the side rooms that they found the necessary silver plates, and this time there were only two of them.

When in the main chamber, all the walls seemed to be solid, with no window or opening out to anywhere else, yet in the side room there was a square transparent section which looked straight down, giving a good view onto the lift platform in the main chamber.

The only reason they could think of for this was that the lift might have someone or something on it that the operators didn't want to know about the controls, hence the one way window. So was there something not so nice down there still? The only way to find out was to go down.

Kal suggested that after sending the lift down on its own and returning it successfully, one person should go down first to check it out, and then the rest would follow, leaving two of the crew above to work the lift, in case there were no controls below.

They tried the silver plates, the bottom one sending the lift down, and after waiting a while, the upper one returned it, level with the surrounding floor of the main chamber.

So, they had control of the platform. He was surprised there were so many volunteers for the solo journey into the unknown. One of the portable two way radios was handed over to the traveller, and he would signal when he wanted to come up again, that's if the radios worked in the depth of the shaft, if not, they would bring the lift up after what they thought was a suitable time.

One lone crew member stood on the centre of the platform as Kal touched the lower plate, and then disappeared from view. From where they were in the side room, there was no sound from the lift, and they wondered what motive force was employed to drive it.

Time dragged, as it always does in circumstances like this, but after a while, the radio requested 'up', and the upper plate was pressed.

The platform returned after what seemed an eternity, and was complete with passenger, to the relief of all.

According to the returnee, the bottom of the shaft ended in a chamber with one exit which was closed by a massive set of metal bars. It had looked as if these should be movable, but there was no sign of controls for this, so they assumed that they must be here, in the upper level.

This meant there must be some form of visual link from the controls in the side room to the chamber below, or the operator wouldn't know when to bring the lift up.

There were no screens or other means of relaying a picture as far as Kal could tell, so they either had to be powered up somehow, or didn't exist, and some other means of communication was used.

Leaving two of the crew behind in the side room to work the controls, the rest of them and Kal stepped onto the platform, and signalled to go down.

The platform seemed to accelerate as they went deeper and deeper into the heart of the planet, and then stopped as suddenly as it had begun, but without the expected lurch from such a quick stop.

Facing them were the metal bars, as described, and a passage leading off into the distance, lit with the same strange glow as the main lift chamber above.

The distance between the bars enabled them to squeeze through without any trouble, although a tight fit for Kal.

As they only had the crossbows, and a tube like device which gave an electric shock when the handle was pulled, they couldn't hope to overcome a large adversary should one be met. Every centimetre of the tunnel wall was checked as they went along, but it was just a smooth glassy rock, very hard and without even a tool mark on it.

A split in the tunnel, with one branch going off at right angles to the main run, meant a decision had to be made as to which one to go down, and the 'branch off' won on a show of hands. They had been going for a couple of minutes when the first of the side chambers came into view.

Massive metal bars formed a door to each cavern, but there was no light in them to show what they contained, if anything. Squeezing past the bars, Kal called for a light, and then he saw why the bars were so massive.

A huge pile of bones lay scattered about on the floor of the chamber, more or less where the 'whatever it was' had fallen, but there wasn't a trace of skin or flesh, or even the powdery remains he would have expected. And then it dawned on him, something had eaten the softer parts of the creature, and left the bones. So, what did the carcass cleaners eat when there were no more carcasses? And how big and hungry were they?

By now several of the crew had joined him, and were standing in awe at the size of the remains. Kal tried to lift one of the larger bones, and couldn't.

It must have weighed close on seventy five kilograms, and was very hard and dense. The creature itself must have been a real monster, and their weapons would have had no effect on it whatever, except as an annoyance maybe.

How long ago it had died, or the tunnels abandoned, they had no way of knowing, but hoped it was a long time, as they didn't want to meet a living version of the creature.

The walls of its cavern were made of the same shiny glass like rock as the tunnels, and they supposed it had starved to death when the operators had left.

Other caverns, containing similar remains were spaced all along both sides of the side tunnel for a considerable distance, and they gave up counting them when they reached fifty or so. Whatever else it was, this was a big operation.

A return to the main tunnel seemed the sensible thing to do, and they retraced their steps to the junction. Speculation as to what the creatures were kept for was batted back and forth as they went along, the main conclusion being that they were used for something to do with the mining operation.

It couldn't have been as beasts of burden, as the operators of the complex seemed to have powerful machines to do that kind of work for them.

The main tunnel having been reached, they went along it for nearly a kilometre before coming to another side passage.

This didn't contain any caverns, and had been machined out of the living rock by the same means as the main tunnel, and about the same size. They were about to give up any further exploration and return, when the passage opened out into a vast cavern, lit by the same strange light.

They could have put most of their home compound in this cave, and the roof was well out of sight.

Going around the wall of the cavern, they saw huge grooves in the rock, and as the tunnel borers didn't leave any marks, and they supposed their mining machinery didn't either, they put the marks down to something which had literally gnawed away at the surface.

Perhaps it was the work of the creatures in the caverns, as they were certainly big enough to have made the huge curved grooves, but what kind of teeth did they have to cut rock?

And then Kal remembered that the giant maggots had done so. Perhaps the rock wasn't quite as hard as it looked, and the reason they couldn't get out of their cages was that the tunnel and cage rock had been that much harder, as were the metal bars holding them in.

When he tried chipping at the rock face it confirmed his theory, it was hard, but nowhere near as hard as the material the tunnels were made of.

Kal suggested that the creatures had been used to process the ore bearing rock in a similar way as the crystal maggots had been, and then began to worry again about what had caused the whole operation to be abandoned in such a hurry.

As there was little more to be gained here, and a sample of the rock face had been taken, Kal thought it best to return to the lift, and get back to familiar ground.

There was little need to take a vote on the matter, as they had all turned as one, and headed back towards the main tunnel with a degree of eagerness which denoted that their decision contained an element of fear.

They were about half way back to the lift shaft when a deep rumbling noise brought the party to a halt. Something large and heavy sounded as if it was on the move.

Deciding where the rumbling sound came from was difficult, as it echoed back and forth in the tunnels and Kal's guess was as good as anyone's.

He felt real naked fear for the first time that he could remember since landing on the planet, and the look on the faces of the crew didn't do much to help the situation.

They all took off for the lift shaft at a very fast pace, their only fear being that whatever it was could be in the tunnel going off from the junction they were approaching, and they would have to pass that.

Their pounding feet drowned out the sound which had caused the panic in the first place, and it wasn't until they slowed down at the divergence of the tunnels, that they heard the rumbling again, this time it was louder and nearer.

A quick glance around the corner of the cell chamber tunnel eased their fears a little as there was nothing moving in sight, so they sped on towards the lift.

Somehow the tunnel seemed longer on the way back, and the noise was getting louder, as were their heart beats.

The little troupe raced into the lift and with their backs to the far wall of the shaft, loaded their six cross bows with bronze tipped bolts, not that they would have much effect, but the action was automatic.

Frantically the radio carrier called for the lift to be taken up, but there was no reply from those above, and the lift didn't move. There was nowhere else to run, they were trapped. The rumbling had now taken on a distinct foot fall quality, and it sounded very heavy.

The radio operator's voice had gone up several octaves, and if he could have managed a few more decibels, the two in the control room above wouldn't have needed the radio link at all.

The light at the far end of the tunnel dimmed as something very large lumbered towards them, the radio emitted a squawk of static, and then fell silent.

Only the foot falls of the approaching hulk in the tunnel and their own heart beats could be heard, and the lift platform remained rock steady.

By now the radio operator had lost his voice and passed the box over to the next in line, not that that did any good as far as moving the lift was concerned.

The creature was now plainly in view, and they could see the massive armoured head with two huge protruding blades like teeth advancing towards them.

It seemed to fill the whole width of the tunnel, cutting off any chance of some of the crew running past it. A few metres from the opening into the lift shaft the monster slowed down, coming to a halt with its head just outside the chamber, and up against the bars.

A gush of hot metallic smelling breath enveloped the crew as the creature tried to manoeuvre itself to get a foreleg through the protecting bars, and into the chamber.

Six cross bows released their bolts as one, the bolts bouncing harmlessly off the tough armoured head. A great taloned limb swept into the lift chamber at the same moment as the platform began its ascent, severing off a good three metres of death and destruction.

The roar of pain would remain with the crew to haunt their most feared nightmares for a long time to come, along with pictures of the massive limb writhing about on the lift floor with a seeming life of its own, the steel grey claw sliding in and out of its sheath, trying to get a grip on the smooth platform. By doing what amounted to an aerial ballet, the crew managed to dodge its contortions.

As the lift slowed down at the top of its travel, they all leapt for the relative safety of the chamber floor, the creature's forelimb still twitching in its death throes, and the claw moving in and out of its housing with a metallic clicking sound.

They raced for the control room, and cannoned into the couple they had left to operate the lift. When the tangle of bodies had been sorted out, it transpired that when the panic laden radio signal to 'come up' had been received, they had both made a dash for the control pads, tripping over each other in the rush, and the radio flying across the room to smash itself to pieces on the far wall.

When everyone had calmed down a little, it was decided to explore the site for any useful information which could be gleaned from the alien installation, collect the metal ingots which they had left behind, and head for home.

It was decided that sometime in the future they would send another team out to gather any valuable materials or data which they had missed.

The severed foreleg was still moving as they left the main hall and entered the maze of passageways which connected the outbuildings together.

More could be learnt, but first they would have to work out how the different units went together, and what they did.

The next two days were spent going through every part of the mining plant which they could get access to, although some of the rooms seemed to be locked, or they hadn't used the correct method to gain entry.

It would seem from their exploration of the plant, that the aliens had found some mineral deep in the rocks below, and for some reason couldn't or wouldn't just go and dig it up.

Instead, they used the strange creatures found in the caverns.

Having somehow persuaded the creature with chisel like teeth to do the work for them, they then sent the ore up the lift shaft to the processing plant on the surface.

How the smelter worked they were unable to determine, but no doubt a future team would solve the mystery, and the knowledge could then be added to their already vast data banks of 'how to do things.'

Some of the units contained equipment which made little sense to Kal or the other members of the team, and they didn't see how those items fitted in with the general mining operation, so perhaps they didn't. But what did they do?

Maybe something else was going on here, but they doubted if they would be able to fathom it out unless they could get into some more of the buildings. The plant turned out the ingots which they had seen at the main site where they had landed, so maybe that was the collecting point, and there were other mining plants dotted about on the plateau, but out of sight. An aerial survey would soon find them.

There had been no sign of animate life, apart from themselves and the creature in the mine, so where was the 'whatever' which had sent the others scurrying off? Or was it so long ago that it had died of old age or boredom.

The team headed off for the landing site and were relieved to see the wing was still there. The pilots had picked up the frantic radio message from the lift, and feared the worst until a subsequent message had been sent to say all was well.

They were able to load two of the metal ingots into the wing without overloading it, they hoped. A quick look around the main collecting point confirmed Kal's thoughts on the matter. It was just that, a place where all the metal blocks were assembled together ready for transporting up to the alien mother ship.

Sadly, the shuttles had been damaged far beyond use for space flight, but they might well be intact enough for the engineers to figure out how they worked, and so advance their knowledge several generations in one go.

Although there had been no sign of the thing or things which had caused the hurried exodus of the operators, Kal still had an uneasy feeling nagging away at the back of his mind, and was continuously on the lookout for a reappearance of it.

They made camp for the night in the same building they had used on their arrival, posting guards on Kal's insistence, one of which was to observe the wing at all times.

Tomorrow they would fly home, and organize a team to return and scour the place for information. Kal wondered if it would be worthwhile building an even bigger flying wing to salvage as much of the heavy alien equipment as possible, as an overland journey seemed almost impossible due to the distance and the terrain.

During the night, something rather large inspected the wing and the building housing the exploration team, and thought it best to leave them alone for now, as more of these delectable morsels might well come back in the future.

Sunrise from the high plateau was a sight not to be missed, and the whole team marvelled at the brilliant colours displayed before them. A meal was taken, the wing checked out, and the huge footprints of something possibly unpleasant discovered for the first time. The guard had seen nothing.

They followed the tracks for a short while until they faded out on harder ground, and were unable to pick up the trail again, which was just as well, in the long run.

Everyone climbed aboard, the engines started up, and the huge wing began to taxi across the plain towards the cliff.

As the wing gathered speed with its heavy load, something was in two minds as to whether it should rush out and smite the wing, and sample its contents, or wait for an even bigger arrival of the tasty little creatures, as the second visit usually provided more of them.

The wing lumbered up into the air just before it ran out of plateau, slowly gaining height with its extra load as it headed out across the dry and barren desert, and home.

The team were pleased with what they had found out, and the new metal sample, but all agreed they could have done without the incident in the lift.

The speculation as to whether the creature in the mining tunnels had been brought in from another world, or was a native of this one, occupied the main part of the conversation for most of the way back.

Kal was surprised that the little people accepted the fact that other life existed in the universe, taking the knowledge in their stride, as they always did. He wondered just what would have to be presented to them to cause a ripple in their calm acceptance of things.

At long last the wing swept in towards the compound, side slipping to lose the extra height they had maintained as a safety measure because of the extra load, lined up with the landing strip, and touched down smoothly as if the pilot had done it all his life.

'They certainly are a competent lot' Kal thought, as he climbed down the short ladder to the ground. Of course there was the usual late night party to welcome the exploration team back, and it was a late one, by the time everyone had told their individual tale.

Early next morning, the metallurgists eagerly got to work on the metal ingots the crew had brought back.

By the time the third batch of crossbreeds arrived, the new race outnumbered the original little people, and Kal was still a little saddened by this, but they seemed to know what they were doing, and he had no right to interfere anyway.

He still gave his science lessons, except that now the class had grown to almost unmanageable proportions and had to be held out in the open to accommodate them all.

Tibs had taken up the unofficial position as Kal's second in command for most things, and everyone accepted it quite happily. There were now no restrictions on their conversational ability, and they often talked on late into the night.

Kal had many times tried to get Tibs to outline the Elder's general strategy with regard to the advancement of the mixed race, but he either didn't know, which Kal doubted, or he wasn't telling due to some greater loyalty, but to what, Kal was at a loss to know.

The metallurgists were really excited over the new metal the team had brought back, and the engineers having spotted its extreme hardness when the surface had been worked, were now able to develop their rotary engine, which they had had on the drawing boards for so long.

The prototype certainly proved to be more efficient than the piston type, and gave virtually no vibration. This meant smaller engines with more power, and using less fuel.

'Where will it all end' Kal thought.

As there were now so many new materials to use, Kal brought up the ship building idea again at one of the Elder's meetings. They showed polite interest, but that was all. Did they know something which he didn't?

But then how could they, bearing in mind how they were when he had first found them. Somehow, he didn't feel quite fully in the picture, again.

Kal thought the flying wing which took them to the plateau was big, but it was dwarfed by the new one with the four rotary engines. This was an efficient machine which his people would have been proud to have made.

Aerodynamics was certainly their strong point, it was small wonder they weren't interested in ships.

The rest of the metal ingots had been recovered, and more were found at other mining sites they had located during their aerial survey. Volunteers were a bit thin on the ground when it was proposed that they should do their own mining.

The threat of what they could find which might not have a kindly nature towards them promoted the development of some more powerful weapons, including a missile firing device with a high explosive head.

Kal was a little disappointed that things should have had to take a turn in this direction; as such things in the past had led to trouble, on a big scale.

Once they knew they could defend themselves against just about anything, the mining team was cheerfully assembled and sent on its way. Several large batches of different types of ore were sent back before trouble hit. A small exploration team had left the main base on the plateau for a 'bump' on the horizon, when a terrified radio message indicated that something had gone horribly wrong. The voice was cut off in mid speech, and no trace of the team was ever found.

Kal was invited to join the 'trouble shooting' team, and he accepted without question. The new wing took off next day, with the new missile launcher and an assortment of smaller projectile firing devices. Kal marvelled at the fire power they could produce, and didn't envy anything which got in its way, especially if it made unpleasant overtures towards them.

The new wing was a lot faster and smoother in flight than its predecessor, and they landed on the plateau only a few short hours after leaving the compound.

The armourments team debarked, and marched off in orderly fashion towards the main building, which had been made into the mining team's headquarters.

A short briefing, detailing what had happened to the missing team didn't throw much more light on the matter, so the 'hunters', backed up by a supply team, set off in the general direction of the incident.

There was little to show what had happened, apart from a few scuffle marks on the ground. There was no vestige of clothing, tools, or even bones in the area, nothing.

The missing expedition team had arrived at this spot, gyrated around a bit, and then disappeared.

Kal would not accept this, and retold of his feelings when he had been here on an earlier visit.

There was something here, and Kal was sure it had a degree of intelligence, which was going to complicate matters more than somewhat, he felt.

There was nothing here now, just empty space in all directions, and no bright ideas from anyone. Kal called a meeting of the heads of each of the teams, and laid out his reasoning as best he could.

Whatever had taken the first team must have been in the vicinity, or they would have seen it coming and given more of a warning. Ergo, it was here already, and the team must have stumbled upon it quite suddenly.

As there was nothing in sight for a considerable distance all around, it must be heavily disguised as a piece of the plateau, thin air, or it must be hiding under the ground. That reasoning brought a few startled looks from the team.

The armourment team stood their ground with weapons primed and ready, while the others spread out in a series of fan like sweeps, thumping the ground as they went, listening for a hollow sound or a difference in ground texture.

During the third fan like sweep, one of the team stopped, and raised both arms into the air, the agreed upon signal that he had noticed something different.

Everyone froze, and looked expectantly at Kal, who went over to the one who had signalled. The ground seemed to be the same here, just sand, gravel and a few small stones, but the little one was pointing to his feet, while trying to move one of the stones.

Kal bent down to inspect the surface, and found that it was different. The stones looked and felt like stones, but were stuck firmly to the surface, as was the gravel and sand.

This wasn't the normal ground surface, but something imitating it, as a form of camouflage. He walked back the way he had come, checking the surface as he went, and when he came to loose surface material, he beckoned one of the little people over to make a small pile of the loose stones at that point, to act as a marker.

Carefully he moved along the edge of the change in terrain, leaving small stone piles as indicators of the change in surface, until he had marked out a roughly circular area, some fifteen metres in diameter.

Everyone was signalled back to what was considered to be a safe distance from the marked circle, and the missile launcher was pointed towards it's centre, the operator being instructed to fire at anything which might appear from below and looked the least bit aggressive. Kal could hear his heart beating, and hoped the others couldn't. It looked as if they had found what they had been looking for.

Kal considered that the circle was the top or lid to a shaft or hole in the ground, and might be something the mining operators had left behind, although he could see no reason why they should go to this much subterfuge to hide anything, or it was the home of whatever it was they were seeking?

Going to the edge of the circle, Kal began digging away at the real ground to see how deep the camouflaged section went down. Two of the little people courteously but firmly requested that he go back and join the others, while they did the digging themselves.

When they had gone down about half a metre, the ground gave a slight twitch, and they dropped their tools and ran back to the rest of the group.

Kal asked for some fuel to be brought from the wing, as he thought that if the marked circle was what he thought it was, a little heat should provoke some action.

They anxiously waited for what seemed like an eternity while the fuel was fetched, and then Kal instructed that half of it be poured on the centre of the circle, and the rest into the hole they had dug at the edge of it, and a trail of fuel be run back to where they were standing. This was done, and everyone retired a little further, just in case.

The fuel was lit, and the flame snaked along the trail they had made like a living entity, flashed across the circle to the centre, and with a huge whoosh, roared up into the sky.

They all backed away from the heat, which even at this distance was quite considerable. The ground beneath their feet shuddered, and the camouflaged circle rose up into the air. At twenty metres it stopped, and beneath the flattened top there was the most hideous creation any of them had ever seen. A cylindrical wrinkled column, the full diameter of the hole, had exuded itself from the cavity below.

Near the top there was a cavernous mouth part, gaping wide and dripping a thick yellow slimy substance. Just below this, four tentacle like arms writhed about in a random fashion, thrashing the air in a desperate bid to avoid the searing heat of the burning fuel, which must have seeped deep down into the hole from the excavation they had made at the edge of the circle.

Kal stared paralysed in disbelief at the nightmarish sight before him. His vision blurred for a moment, and then he saw his old crew from the Star Search, just in front of him.

They were waving and smiling and beckoned him forwards, and besides them were two of his class mates from the academy, and his mother... Mother? She had died in an accident before he went to the academy. The vision faded, and he was back in present time, but several metres nearer the writhing monstrosity from the hole.

Several of the little people were staggering about as if they were drugged, one of which had wandered too near the grotesque creature and had been grabbed by one of the flailing tentacles. It had curled around him, lifting him high into the air and then flung him many metres higher.

The crushed and distorted body fell to earth with a sickening thump, whilst another wave of disorientation hit Kal, and he was back in his childhood, playing with friends at home. The scene faded as quickly as it had come, and he was plunged back into the same terrifying situation again.

Another member of the team had been caught by the creature, and after being crushed by the entwining whip like tentacle, was flung towards the missile launcher.

The operator instinctively ducked, unfortunately jamming his nose straight into the shielded recess of the firing button, with a sickening crunch.

Fortuitously for the rest of them, his nose was a perfect fit for the recess, and the firing button was depressed, the missile streaking out from the launcher tube and heading straight for the writhing creature before him. The missile entered about half way up the column, and disappeared inside with a dull plop.

A split second later there was a deep muffled cough, and the column ballooned out in the middle, to then slowly collapse in on itself, the monstrosity falling over on its side.

The rest of the creature heaved itself out of the hole, and around the now exposed base there were what amounted to several stumpy appendages, which it used to move around on, and probably dig its hiding hole with in the first place.

The team had gathered together around the missile launcher, which had been reloaded, and most of them had sat down, mentally and physically shattered at the unbelievable series of events which they had just experienced.

The creature was obviously near death, having sustained such colossal internal damage, and was now relatively still, except for a series of strange undulations which seemed to be going on under the wrinkled hide near the base end.

No one wanted to go any closer to it at the moment, so they didn't see a small number of slits appearing at the base.

The alarm was raised when one of the more adventurous members of the team had strolled over to take a better look at the dying remains of the hideous creature, and came streaking back with a look of horror on his face, and his voice several octaves higher than normal.

Led by a very worried Kal, the armourments team grabbed their weapons and rushed over to the base of the hulk, where they were confronted by several four metre long replicas of the original, but thankfully not yet fully formed.

The creature, in its death throes, must have triggered off the birthing process in a desperate attempt to propagate itself into the next generation.

The stun tube was used to incapacitate the duplicates, and this was followed by a ferocious attack with bronze tipped spears. The team were still remembering their two lost companions, and Kal was glad he wasn't on the receiving end of it.

When the monster was finally still, and all the offspring had been rendered lifeless, they went over to the hole from which the creature had come. It was a massive excavation, and went down some twenty metres.

At the base they could just see several smaller cavities going into the side of the hole, and wondered if these were where the base appendages went, or were they tunnels which were used to attract an underground food supply.

No one was going down to find out, so they were left to speculate on the matter for now.

They checked once more to make sure that all was lifeless, and decided to return to the base camp to rest. They had achieved what they had set out to do, but were totally overwhelmed by the events which had ensued.

At Kal's suggestion, they all spread out in a single line about ten metres apart, the idea being that as they made their way back, they could check the ground for any more of the creatures which lived in holes, and if they found none, then this strip of the plateau could be declared safe to travel on.

The testing of the ground was quite easy, and involved little effort on the part of the searchers. All they had to do was walk twenty paces and kick a stone. If it moved, then they were on solid ground, but if it was stuck down or part of the surface, then they could have a problem.

They made it back to the main building without mishap, and all breathed a sigh of relief at not having to fight another hole dweller, just yet.

Later that evening, they had recovered enough to eat a meal, but without the usual enthusiasm, and began to discuss the horrendous happenings of the day.

Combining their observations and knowledge, they were able to work out what had happened to the earlier exploration team which had disappeared, and probably the original miners who had fled the area so inexplicably.

They reasoned that the creature dug itself a hole in which it lived for most of its life, creating on its head a flattened area, duplicating the surrounding terrain.

Here it lay in wait for a suitable meal to approach, whereupon it raised itself from its layer, radiating some kind of mental energy wave which caused its intended victims to hallucinate scenes from their earlier memories, so causing a paralytic confusion.

The creature was then able to scoop them up at will with its long tentacle like arms, and eat.

What they couldn't understand was how such an enormous creature could sustain itself on the meagre picking of the almost barren plateau, for they had seen no other life forms above ground at all. The only explanation Kal could come up with was that it either had a very efficient metabolism, or there was another food source, probably underground.

Either way, it wasn't the sort of thing one would want to come up against on a dark night, and it wouldn't have to be very dark.

Sleep that night was fitful for all, judging by the bleary eyes next morning, and no doubt a few nightmares were experienced as a bonus. Kal still wasn't happy that the creature was the sole reason the others had left.

He thought it was unlikely that the creature was just a solo experiment of nature, and there were likely to be more of them around. If they were to operate in this area, and they needed to for the extraction of the new minerals, then they would have to find some way of detecting the creatures, before they were detected and converted into nourishment for the next generation of horrors.

This problem would have to be given some thought when they got back home, and perhaps some more efficient weapons developed, specifically for this kind of creature.

They had got over their initial shock of meeting the hole creature, and as far as they could tell, there were no more dangers at the hole site, so Kal asked for a few volunteers to accompany him to gather a little more information from the tattered remains of the monster.

Arriving at the hole, the first thing he wanted to do was determine the structure of the 'lid' or top of its head. It was now canted over at an angle, and easily accessible to them, so he began by trying to ascertain the thickness of the hard outer layer, which would then give them an indication of how to penetrate the top layer, and do some damage below.

It had to be organic, as it was part of the creature, but the hardness of the surface and the accurate duplication of the detail of the surrounding ground, was quite amazing.

Kal found that the tough outer surface was nearly a metre thick, and below this there was a honeycombed section of bone-like material which supported the top layer, and gave it its rigidity. Many metres below this was the mouth of the creature, now clamped shut, and just as well, he thought.

The missile had ruptured a large internal section of the middle of the creature into a pulp, and from this area they were unable to gain much information.

Below the damaged section, there was one more surprise. The carcass had split open near its base where the young had been expelled, and some of the internal working could be seen. A little cutting here and there with a long knife revealed a little more detail, and it was from this that they were able to understand how the creature was able to rise so quickly from its hole.

Near the base, there were a series of large bag like structures, very thick and tough, and even a knife couldn't cut through the outer layer. These seemed to be connected to tubes of the same material, which went up the trunk and into another series of bags, one above the other.

Somehow or other, the creature either gulped air or generated a gas from some sort of chemical reaction, which was stored under pressure in the lower chambers.

When it wanted to rise quickly from its hole, it released the compressed gases from below, inflating the upper bags, and the whole main column then expanded, pushing the top portion up out of the hole like a rocket.

They were in for an even bigger surprise when the research team they later sent, returned with details of how the creature really achieved its amazing feat.

As there was little more they could do at the hole or the mining site, it was decided to return home and devise some easy means of detecting the creatures, and dispatching them with the least amount of danger to themselves.

Kal already had a few ideas on the subject, and these no doubt, would soon be improved upon somewhat by the engineers, and the problem would be solved.

The flight back was uneventful and quick, as was to be expected, and a group of engineers was hurriedly put together to solve the problem of the menace at the mining site.

The device for dispatching the creatures was simple enough, and was comprised of a framework holding a self propelled missile, which would blast downwards and into the head section.

Just below the main missile, there was to be a group of three smaller ones, which would be fired off a split second before, ripping out the tough upper top surface, and exposing the honeycomb section below, so that the main projectile could then penetrate on down through the layer, and into the internal working of the creature.

'A thoroughly nasty device for a thoroughly nasty creature', Kal thought, hiding his grin, lest he had to explain it.

Finding the actual hiding place of the creature was another matter, and this proved to be a little more difficult, unless large numbers of volunteers were willing to march across vast areas of the high plateau in lines, putting themselves at constant risk. This was not a very popular option, and was shelved as a last resort.

The smelters had managed to extract metal from an ore found in one of the plateau mines which Kal hadn't seen before. It seemed to be very much like steel but didn't rust, and was extremely tough.

Metal turning lathes of quite a sophisticated nature were now to be found in the metal workshops, and he wondered how they had been developed in such a short time, with no basic suggestions from him.

The discovery and learning curve of the little people was on the up again, or maybe it always was, and it was Kal who thought it had slowed down somewhat.

The engineers came to him a few days later, bringing two electronics experts with them. They thought they had solved the problem of locating the 'creature in the hole'.

The idea was to build a machine which would rake the surface of the ground with sprung tines, such that as it progressed along, the large gravel and smaller stones, and there were few bigger that Kal's fist, would be pushed into lines about five metres apart.

Having traversed back and forth across a selected portion of the plateau, a small wing could then over fly the raked ground, and any circular areas without lines of stones on them would denote stones which couldn't be moved, and a possible 'hole creature' beneath.

Kal was most impressed with the design, but wondered who was going to ride the machine. The little team looked at each other, grinning, and said 'No one'.

When Kal looked blankly at them, they hastily tried to explain that they had worked out a way whereby they could control the machine remotely.

The machine would go forward a certain distance, say one kilometre, turn back on itself, and return, having moved over to run parallel to its first track by its own width. This way a large area of the plateau could be checked for anything under the ground without putting anyone in danger.

The electronics team were quite happy that they could build a simple memory unit, so that the machine would know where it had been, and where it should then go.

Now Kal was now not only impressed, but quite staggered by the resourcefulness and skill of the two teams. He agreed this was the best way to rid themselves of the creatures, and he wanted to go on the first trial run.

The team members suddenly looked very serious, and muttered among themselves for a few moments, until one of them burst out laughing, and, joined by the others, said they had guessed he would want to go.

They had agreed among themselves to look a bit doubtful about his request, for a bit of fun. This was the first time a straight forward example of a sense of humour in the little people had manifested itself to Kal, and in a way, despite having been taken for a bit of a ride, he was very pleased, as it made them a little bit more like him, and gave them a bit more common ground to express themselves.

The hole hunting machine was ready before the missile set up had been completed, which surprised Kal somewhat, so he went along to see how they were doing with the project.

The main difficulty seemed to be that they couldn't be sure of getting the projectile to explode at the correct depth within the creature. They had decided that they didn't want to blow it to pieces, but just to kill it, leaving it as intact as possible so that they could take it apart themselves to see how it worked.

'These people are full of surprises' Kal said to himself. They had worked out where they thought the missile should explode in order to kill the creature outright, using a small charge, but if they didn't get the depth of penetration right, it would only be injured, and could possibly still be a danger, as they had no defence against the 'mind wave'.

Kal suggested that they have a coil of very strong wire attached to the projectile, and the other end of it fixed to the launch frame. When all the wire, which would have to be of the correct length, had been pulled in behind the projectile, it could trigger the firing mechanism when fully stretched.

The idea was taken up immediately, and he was thanked profusely for his contribution to the project. It was a little while later when Kal began to wonder if he had been taken for another ride perhaps. Why hadn't they come up with the wire idea, as they were quite capable of it?

Had they set it up to allow him to add his ideas to the project, and if so why? The solution to the problem had been too easy, so it looked as if something was going on, but Kal could make no sense of it.

The wire firing system was tried and proved most successful, the wire singing out to its predetermined length, and a small charge exploding to signal the fact. A short while later the launcher had been completed. Kal watched a demonstration of the remote control searcher machine, and although it didn't find any 'holes', it did leave a very even series of lines, and seemed quite happy to trundle up and down the test area without any supervision apart from being told when to start and stop.

The whole system was loaded up on the wing, and would fly out next day for an actual trial on the high plateau.

That evening, Kal was requested to attend a meeting of the Council of Elders, and found that their numbers had decreased somewhat since his last meeting with them.

There was the general discussion of how all the different projects were going, with the heads of departments being called in when necessary to give any extra information the Elders needed, and then when he thought the meeting was about over, they turned to him and asked how he felt about being the leader of the whole community by taking their place at all meetings, and virtually having full control of all that went on.

Kal was surprised and honoured at the request and wanted to know why he had been asked at this particular time.

The reason given was that the numbers of the original little people had been dwindling since the crossbreeding program had begun, and no more of the original little people had been born since that day.

The Elders knew that their days were now numbered, and although they were very clever, the new breed hadn't reached the degree of maturity they had expected, and so were concerned for the level of stability and guidance of the future Councils, and hence the race as a whole.

Kal understood their concern, but felt it was not right to take up the post offered, but agreed to act as a moderator on the Council, having a veto vote until he felt they were fully capable of running things themselves.

This was finally agreed upon, and just before the meeting broke up, Kal expressed his sorrow that the original little people would soon be no more.

'You have not fully understood our motives for the breeding program, or you would not feel sorrow for us'.

'Some of us realized long ago that we did not belong here, we have no racial memory of arriving, and no history which makes any sense. Very long ago we realized that we could not survive here for more than a few generations more, and your coming was the saviour of our people'.

'Through you, we shall live on, a little of you mixed with a little of us, generating a new race with the best of both our peoples, will subdue this world.'

Kal felt a moistness in his eyes, and tried to hide the lump in his throat which he felt sure was visible to all, despite the soft light of the evening.

'It is we who should thank you for your contribution to the project, although we had to use a little subterfuge in the early days. Without you, we wouldn't be here now.'

'We had sensed rather than knew that there was something dormant in us which you somehow released when you showed us how to defend ourselves, and later began the various research projects'.

'So you see, we owe you far more than we can ever repay, as you would see it.'

It was a somewhat contrite and humbled Kal who went to his bed that night, thinking of these people's selflessness to the common good of their race, willing to give up their own identity for a greater purpose.

He had seen no sign of crime in any form, so real anger, only frustration when understanding failed them. No one had to be ordered to do anything, it was just done by the most able to do it, because it was necessary to be done.

All worked for the greater good of the whole group, and seemed to consider it was the correct thing to do, and he doubted if they even considered that! They just did it.

Only recently had an overt sense of humour surfaced, although he had noticed little events which he suspected were humour, but peculiar to their way of thinking.

Next morning they flew off for the high plateau, the big wing being accompanied by a smaller version, which would stay there to view the areas which had been tested by the searcher machine.

They were greeted like long lost brothers by a group from the mining team, who reported that they had had no further trouble from the hole creatures, but would be very glad when they knew the whole area was safe.

The equipment was unloaded, and the searcher was sent about its business, causing a great sensation among the miners, who had to have the theory of the machine explained to them before they would get on with their own work.

The searcher moved out across the plains until it was just a little dot on the horizon, and then it was out of sight, only coming back into distant view some while later, the sunlight glinting on its tall aerial.

Kal was impressed with the accuracy of its controls, as it ran exactly parallel to its outgoing course, and was only a few centimetres adrift from the outgoing raked track by the time it had returned to its starting point.

The machine came right up to the little group of watchers, turned about, and went off again towards the horizon, causing great beams of satisfaction among the engineers.

Mining had carried on while they were waiting for the creature deholing equipment to arrive, but had been reduced a little because of the extra precautions taken for the safety of the operators.

It would be some time before the machine had traversed enough of the plateau to make it worthwhile doing an aerial survey, so Kal said he would like to go down one of the mines again, to see how things were going on.

Seven mine heads had been located altogether, but only three had working lift platforms, the others had either been shut down during the general exodus, or the machinery had failed somehow.

The mine they had first visited where the creature's foreleg had been chopped off by the lift, had not been visited again, as they had discovered another one, which, as far as they could tell, had no living creatures in it, and was assumed to be safe to work in.

Although the engineers had spent some considerable time trying to find the power source and the method of driving the lift platforms, they had been unsuccessful to date, and had to be content with just using the equipment.

It was causing a fair degree of frustration among them, as they wanted to incorporate the principles into their own field of knowledge, and so far had been unable to do so.

Kal joined the next shift of miners, and as the platform was dropping down the shaft, he got to thinking about the original builders of the complex.

They were certainly a bit austere in their buildings, not a picture or chart in sight, no furniture or loose equipment laying about, just the bare walls and control panels.

He didn't think there had been time to remove what he thought were the normal artefacts of industry from the site before they left, so perhaps they didn't have so much junk and clutter as he was used to. It still seemed a little strange though; he had expected to see something left behind.

There was a slight lurch, as the platform reached the bottom of its shaft. The mining teams had certainly been very busy, as he could see boxes of ore lined up all along the tunnel into the far distance. And they had found out how to open the barrier bars. They proceeded along the tunnel for about half a kilometre before they came to one of the side passages, which led into a huge cavern where the main work was going on.

The minerals seemed to be in veins, about half to one metre wide, and the method of extraction he thought was novel, and certainly different to anything he had ever seen before.

A hand operated hydraulic ram forced the mining tool against the sides of the cavity, and then another ram, with a long claw like arm, was driven into the ore, cutting in deeply and then scooping out a great chunk. As long as the width of the cavity was enough for one of the little miners to follow the device into the cleft, there was no limit in theory as to how far they could go up the vein.

There were several teams working away around the periphery of the cavern, and they all seemed to be extracting a different coloured ore.

Some of the extracted minerals he recognized, but others were completely new to him, and he was surprised at the brilliant colours they displayed. Kal visited several other caverns before returning to the surface, and was amazed at the scale of the whole operation, and the way it was organized.

He couldn't help but wonder if the original operators of the mining complex might return one day, and be not a little miffed at what had been going on during their absence.

Once more on the high plateau, Kal went to inspect the small spotter wing which had flown out with them.

As the little wing had kept up with them on their long journey to the plateau, he wondered how they could slow it down sufficiently to use it as an aerial observation device, and was eagerly shown something which caused him to rethink his assessment of these people.

They had anticipated the problem, and had solved it in the most ingenious way. The pilot climbed into the control pod on the front, and the engine hummed into life.

The big surprise was when wing suddenly split and grew to twice its normal width, and then moved forward, the surface area being increased two fold. It was easy to see that the lifting effect of the wing had now been increased considerably, and it would fly at a much lower speed.

The other big surprise was when Kal asked what the odd looking box slung under the belly of the wing was for. He remembered telling the engineers a long time ago when they had first discovered silver the basics of photography, and had thought no more about it. This box like device was a camera, but unlike any camera he had ever seen before.

There appeared to be no lens that he could see, or any other recognizable controls, and he looked forward to viewing the resulting pictures which he thought would probably be in colour, and they were.

Some three days after the team had arrived on the plateau, the roving rake device had done its job, and they were ready to fly the wing to locate the areas which hadn't responded to the raking action of the hole searcher.

The little wing took off and climbed into the sky, circling to gain height, and then set off to fly up and down the area where the ground based searcher had travelled. By mid afternoon the wing had returned, and the pictures processed in one of the buildings alongside the main depot.

A series of pictures had been taken, most of which overlapped each other, and the team began cutting the edges off them so that they could be assembled into one big picture of the high plains area which had been under the search pattern of the hole locator.

It was plain to see nine circular areas which hadn't responded to the raking action of the machine, and these were noted down in some sort of code which Kal didn't understand, but the missile team certainly did.

A motor powered truck rolled onto the scene, loaded with the missile firing platform and a quantity of other odds and ends. Kal asked if he could go along with the team, and after some hesitation on the part of the team leader, he was allowed to do so.

Using the co-ordinates obtained from the aerial map, they drove straight to the first of the hidden hole creatures, and Kal couldn't help feeling a bit sorry for them in a way, as they didn't stand a chance against the little people and their newly acquired skills.

The truck stopped short of the circular area by fifty metres or so, and the team leader firmly instructed Kal to stay with the truck, while the missile launcher was carried by the rest of the crew to the centre of the circle.

They had figured out that the creature wouldn't show itself unless there was enough bait waiting above the hole to make its appearance worthwhile, and they had deemed that three was a safe number. He hoped they were right.

The tripod was set up, and the controls fiddled about with for some time before they all ran back to the truck.

A few seconds later there was a bright flash followed by a sharp concussion, as the peripheral charges blasted their way into what amounted to the top of the creature's head.

Almost instantly, the creature reared up into the evening sky, and then there was a deep cough as the second missile which had penetrated deep down into the main body, was triggered by the wire.

The whole hideous thing toppled over to lay flat on the surface of the plain, as the momentum of its springing up from the hole carried it upwards far further than it would normally have intended.

Feeling quite satisfied with their work, the whole team retired to the main base for the evening meal, and to plan the rest of the extermination program which they would begin next day. Kal was impressed by the cold efficiency of these people, and was thankful they hadn't appeared at an earlier time in the history of the universe, coupled with an aggressive attitude.

As there was little more Kal could do on the plateau at the moment, for everything seemed to be under the able control of the little people, he decided to return to the compound at the earliest opportunity.

The following day, the big wing was due to return home, and he boarded it knowing that the mining operation could well carry on without his help, although there were a few questions he would have liked answered with regard to the original operators.

The flight back was diverted from its normal course home so that they could take a look at the sea, which seemed to go on without interruption to the horizon.

The pilot was very skilful at using the upward drifting thermals to save fuel, so extending the range of the wing, and even after a long flight towards the horizon, they hadn't found another shoreline.

There was something in the far distance, which looked like a haze, but it would take too long to reach, and so, a little disappointed, they turned for home.

They had just about reached the midway point on their return journey, when one of the crew called out to look below. A gigantic dull brown shape, fully eighty metres long, was ploughing its way through the sea.

A huge bow wave curled away from each side of it as it cleft the waters, and Kal marvelled at the size and power of the creature. If there was anything like it on land, they wouldn't have stood a chance if it had been aggressive.

It was just as well they hadn't taken to the sea in ships, as something this big would have posed a threat they couldn't have hoped to cope with.

On the long journey back, Kal got to thinking about the three diverse races which had been on this planet. There were the little people, who for all intents and purposes, had no racial knowledge beyond just being there, and had then developed at such an astonishing rate, triggered by his intervention in their way of life.

And then there were the people who had built the water condensing cave with its little stream, which then evaporated back into the condensing cave again, for no purpose that he could see, and of course, the huge stone water pump they had found in their own caves in the cliffs.

It pumped the water up into a large lake, high in the cave complex, but why? It didn't go anywhere.

The third, and he assumed, the most recent, were the people who had built the mining complex, and who, despite their advanced technology, were unable to combat the hole creatures. That was more than a little odd.

The mining set up must have been very expensive in time, labour and materials, and yet they had given it up so easily.

It didn't make sense. Who the big block building in the desert belonged to may have been yet another group of people, but he didn't think so somehow.

It seemed to have been built by the mining type people, but why was it so far away from the mining area, and no sign of anything else. And then there was the tunnelling machine they had found in the mountain. It seemed odd that there were no remains of bones or tools at any site.

The big wing circled around the compound, and swept in for a smooth landing, as always. They had a lot to talk about that night, one of the crossbreeds doing the interpreting for the now diminishing numbers of the original little people.

Kal still felt sad that they would soon be extinct, despite their acceptance of the event. Things had come a long way since their first meeting, so very long ago, but how long that was, measured in his years, he had no way on knowing.

And then he had the idea of giving a talk to the new generations of their history, how they had met, and the progress they had made together.

He mentioned this to the Council of Elders when they next met, and the idea was given a warm welcome. They would organize it, a feast to celebrate the changing point in their lives, and a history of their combined progress to date.

It was several days later when one of the Elders came up to Kal with an interpreter, and asked him to attend the big meeting that evening.

There would be a feast, and then Kal could tell the story of their lives since they had first met, from his view point. Others would fill in some of the story from how they saw it, and someone would take notes so that a complete history could be recorded for the future.

Measurements somehow had been taken from his old clothes and a new set made for him, more like a military uniform than anything else, but very smart.

After the main meal was taken, the story telling began. Kal recounting his exploits from the moment of departure from the mining ship to the present day. After several other additions, Tibs arose and addressed the whole crowd 'Let us always remember those who went before, they made us what we are today, and we are part of them as they are part of us. Let us honour them and hold them in high esteem, for they unselfishly gave their all, so that we could have that which we now have, and without their efforts we would be as nothing. Let not the passing of the old race ever be forgotten, for from it have come great things, and from them, through us, shall come even greater things'.

Kal's eyes passed from moist to a full flow of tears as Tibs summation of their history hit home. He would miss the old race; they had a certain something about them that was special. For once, Kal didn't mind his true feelings being seen by all and sundry, and he proudly held his head high as the tears coursed down his cheeks.

SEVEN:
The Deep

SO FAR, THERE hadn't been any sign of the alien miners coming back to see how their mines were doing, so the operations continued as before, but as discretely as possible.

At one of the meetings, it was put forward that the control of the population should now be considered, as the amount of land to support them was finite, as far as they knew.

A subcommittee was appointed to look into the matter, and work out a suitable way of achieving a sensible balance between the available resources and the number of people which could be supported.

Kal's hair was now reduced to a small fringe around his head, and this caused some amusement among some of the younger members of the science classes which he still held.

There had been no sign of baldness among any of the new race, and Tibs was now nearing the relative age when Kal began losing his hair, but so far there was no sign that he was going to follow suit, although he was now a grandfather.

The track way had been driven north, with respect to the original compound, and as the two new compounds had been well established and populated; it was decided to go south, towards the area where Kal had landed, so very long ago.

The big ridge barrier, which Kal had so much trouble getting through, was bypassed by driving twin tunnels through the massive cliffs after recovering the tunnelling machine they had found in the cave at the far end of the mountain chain. A small team had decked themselves out in thin lead suits for protection against the radiation which was coming from the tunnel Kal had made when experimenting with the machine.

Although they could use the machine, the technology was beyond their grasp as there was no way they could get at the working parts of it. It seemed to be made all in one piece, and the controls were just small metal plates which only needed the touch of a finger to activate them.

There were no wires, knobs, wheels or other moving parts to be seen anywhere. When the frustration of not being able to acquire the knowledge of how the alien device worked had died down, they just got on and used it, knowing full well that one day they would gain access to its internal workings.

A flying wing had been sent eastwards, over the rolling deserts, over the plateau where the mines were, and out to the far edge of the land mass, which terminated in a sheer drop to the sea.

They had flown out over the sea for some distance, but no other land mass was found, so the general conclusion was that the land they were on was possibly the only land mass on the planet, and the careful husbanding of it was now of paramount importance.

The population level was now stabilized, recycling of most materials encouraged, and although there were some unpleasant plants and creatures to be found, they were given their own sanctuary as it was considered they too had a right to existence, especially as they were here first.

The only exception to this rule was when there was a genuine threat to life, but that wasn't very often.

There were several more abortive attempts to get at the internal working of the alien tunnelling machine, but to no avail. A clue as to how it made the tunnels came to light when someone tried to cut the actual tunnel wall, and found they couldn't even scratch it, no matter what they used.

The general conclusion arrived at was that it somehow altered the atomic structure of the rock, collapsing the space between the actual electron rings of the atoms, so creating a very hard and dense material, but it was only a theory.

Tibs was now the Chief Elder, and had been for some time, guiding the development of their world with a firm and steady hand. Kal still attended their meetings, but had very little to offer in the way of technical advice, as their sciences had far outstripped his knowledge.

The smelters and metal workers had devised a method of cold casting of whatever metal they chose. They had patiently tried to explain to Kal how it worked, but all he could grasp was that they had found a method of using an energy field to loosen the atomic bonding between atoms without generating heat, so the material flowed and set when the field was removed.

This of course meant that very accurate castings could be made quite simply, as there wasn't the usual shrinkage involved due to the cooling process.

Sadly, Kal was torn between his genuine desire to understand their technology, and not wanting to show his ignorance and inability to comprehend it. As time went by, he became less and less involved with scientific decisions, and concentrated on the more philosophical aspect of life.

Occasionally he thought about the Star Search and the old crew, and wondered what they were doing now. Had there been an attempt to find him? He didn't think so, and if there had been their chances of finding him were so remote as to be negligible.

But that was so very long ago, and so much had happened since then that it was almost unreal to him now, only the haziest of memories persisting to haunt his dreams.

At long last, Kal's eyesight began to fail him, and despite the fact that he wouldn't face up to it, he knew deep down he needed help. They examined his eyes and told him that the muscles which controlled the shape of the eyeball had degenerated, so allowing the eyeball to deform and thereby distorting his vision.

They would apply microsurgery to correct the muscles, but there was little they could do for the failing rods and cones within the eye, which actually transmitted the photons of light into pictures of what he saw.

He didn't remember losing consciousness, but when he came round, his vision was a little sharper, but the bright colours seemed to have faded a little from his early days.

He had been dimly aware for some time that a close eye had been kept on him, his diet had been altered occasionally, and there had been periods of time which had gone missing.

When he approached the medics on the matter, they were very tight lipped about it, and tried to evade the subject, distracting his attention onto other matters.

In the end, he went to Tibs, and told him of his suspicions. Tibs must have given the medics the go ahead to release the whole story, for a short while later he was invited to the main medical research centre. There they told him what they had been doing for a long time.

'Because we thought what you referred to as 'pride' would preclude any help we could give you to sustain your body, it was decided to help you without your knowledge. When you were naturally asleep, your level of unconsciousness was deepened, and we could then examine your body, and do any little corrections we thought necessary. You will have noticed that your teeth have survived without cavities, and are all still in place.'

Kal didn't say anything, in case it stopped the flow of information.

'We're not sure, but we think you have lived for about three of your natural life spans based upon your type of body tissue and the slowdown of cell regeneration.'

'As your body ages, the cellular regenerative process is less able to operate because of what are called free radicals, which occur naturally in your body. By adding anti oxidizing agents to your diet, we have been able to help the cells to replace those which die naturally, so prolonging your life.'

'There is a limit to what we can do, as you have found out with your failing eyesight, but we hope to keep you in general good health for some time yet, if that is you wish.'

Although he had suspected something of this nature had been going on, he was shocked to learn of the extent to which they had gone.

'The combining of your genes with those of our original ancestors, have given us bodies with the best of both types, and few of the faults. We are more grateful for this than we can ever convey to you, and keeping you in the best of health is the only way we can repay a little of the debt.'

'We do this mainly because we want to, not really as a means of repayment for your contribution to our race'. Kal sat back to absorb the significance of all this, and was surprised to find the old fear of being controlled by others, was absent. They were doing this out of pure affinity, or as he would put it, love.

No, that wasn't right. Love contained emotional feeling, affinity was just a pure liking for something, and that was what they had for him. Kal felt that warm prickling feeling behind his rheumy old eyes, and hoped he wasn't going to shed tears in front of them.

'We realize that you have different feelings to us, which you call emotions, and it was because of this that we did what we did, using a fair amount of subterfuge so that your feelings wouldn't be compromised. We all have to give up our bodies in the end, but it is our wish to keep you with us for as long as possible'.

The meeting went on for some time, and Kal learnt much about the philosophy of this new race, and realized that his people could have benefited greatly from studying their attitude to life.

The twin tracks had now been extended to the furthest point south of the land mass, and two more compounds had been established. Compound was the old word Kal used for the cities which had sprung up, the original old compound was now a museum piece, visited by the young as part of their learning process.

Life these days was very good, and he wanted for nothing, except youth. How he envied the young, and their enthusiasm for life and adventure. It was the unpredictability which had gone out of life, and he missed it.

The old excitement was no more, and he longed for the days when they were out looking for new things to discover, and dodging the various creatures which wanted to turn them into something on the menu. There must be something which was driving the new race onwards, but he didn't have it, or know what it was.

Still, there hadn't been a visit from the original miners who had built the complex on the high plateau, but a sharp lookout had been instituted. A strange looking device, which he assumed to be a kind of telescope, scanned the heavens for anything which moved faster than the freewheeling stars and their accompanying planets which reflected light.

What they would do if a visit had occurred, he wasn't too sure, until he inquired about the subject. Completely unknown to him, they had built a weapon based on the old laser principle, except this one packed a punch that was almost unbelievable, and he felt sorry for anyone who might cause them any hassle in the future.

An extension of the track way had been run up to the cliffs of the plateau, and a series of tunnels driven into them. These connected up with the mines, and so transportation of the minerals was made that much easier, with no need to use the mine heads on the plateau, or the lift platforms.

The whole of the plateau area had been returned to its original state, so if anyone came nosing around, they wouldn't know what was going on beneath their feet. But this had been done before the cities had grown to their present size, and these alone would indicate that life was going on at full tilt.

Using a rocky promontory as a way of circumnavigating the dreaded sands, they had built a harbour complex just south of the main city in which Kal now lived. He had been invited down one day to perform an opening ceremony of a new unit, and after that had been accomplished, was taken underground to see their latest invention.

Deep below the main structure, there was a vast pen in which lay, for want of a better word, a metallic replica of the huge sea monster they had seen from the flying wing a long time ago. They wanted to explore the oceans, and preferred to have a vessel which could go under the water if the need arose, rather than a surface ship.

Concerned that the huge creature they had seen so long ago might still be around and was capable of a fair turn of speed, Kal inquired what speed the vessel could achieve.

He was answered with a grin 'Quite adequate for the foreseen circumstances it might encounter', and it was left at that. He was told they intended to try the vessel out in a few days time, and he would be most welcome aboard.

This was the first bit of real excitement Kal had felt for some time, and he was looking forward to the adventure like a small child would.

The next few days dragged for Kal, and his heart wasn't really in the lectures he was still giving to the youngsters.

Word must have spread around about the expedition, for he was bombarded with questions about it from the class, but having little data on the new ship, he talked about the vessels he had known long ago, and this seemed to satisfy the eager young minds, at least for the time being.

The great day came, and the transport was waiting outside his door early that morning. The underwater ship was huge by any standards, and if he didn't know better, he felt he could be forgiven for thinking it was an extension of the science complex on land.

There were viewing screens showing every possible detail outside the ship, and from every angle, but what was more disconcerting was the fact that they appeared to be three dimensional, giving the impression that they were just holes leading to the outside.

Once everyone was aboard, the giant torpedo shape silently glided forward, and the lock doors behind it closed. Looking at one of the screens, Kal fully expected the water to rush in and drown them all, so real was the illusion of depth in the picture. He wasn't aware of motion, but it was clear that the ship was moving forward at quite a speed, and was soon out into open water, but at a depth.

The continental shelf sloped down at quite a steep angle, and there were many strange growths waving about in the turbulence caused by the passing of the great vessel.

A few swimming creatures were to be seen, but nothing which could threaten the massive ship. The edge of the shelf was passed, and they began dropping down to the dark unseen depths below.

As the natural light began to fade, the area around the ship was floodlit from above, showing a vast multitude of plant like fronds which seemed to reach toward the vessel, but Kal put this down to the swirl of the water as the ship passed.

He still couldn't get used to the realism of the screens, as the ship levelled out at the ocean bed, and continued to cruise along slowly.

Ahead he could see vast columns of mineral deposits, glistening multi-coloured in the wash of light given out by the powerful lamps above, and tried to guess at what wonders they might hold in the way of new minerals.

The vessel rose slightly to avoid breaking the scintillating fingers of inorganic growth which reached up to it, and cruised onwards. The mineral columns passed below them, and then there was nothing for several minutes, except a few fish-like creatures which swam off at high speed, probably thinking the ship was a predator of some kind.

Up ahead there was something. The water seemed to be clouded by a mist of some sort, and as they approached it, the mist cleaved apart to let them enter. The outside sensors reported in, and it was discovered that the mist was a vast cloud of a jelly like substance.

Whether it was one creature or a colony of many thousands, they didn't know, but it had a slowing down effect on the ship, and power had to be increased to continue forwards.

One of the crew estimated the thick jelly cloud was at least a kilometre across according to the instruments readings, unless it was moving and following them, but that didn't seem likely. Soon they were free of it, and on their way again at reduced speed, so as not to miss anything.

Another forest of mineral columns came into view, and a remote controlled sub, which Kal hadn't noticed before, glided off to take samples from one of the strange pillar like growths.

The ocean floor dropped away again, and the ship followed to the new depth. It was now quite dark, the only light being from the floodlights on top of the ship, which lit everything up very well without blinding the viewers.

Several large worm shaped creatures swam into view, but quickly turned and fled when they recognized the familiar shape of the giant predator, except the original wasn't as big as the ship, Kal hoped.

He asked one of the crew just how deep they now were, and was shocked to learn that they were nearly a kilometre beneath the surface, and could well go deeper if the sea floor fell away again, which it did shortly afterwards.

The water ahead had acquired that misty look again, but as they approached it became clear that it was just disturbed sediment, but on a grand scale.

Something was moving away from them, and the turbulence it

caused could just be felt acting on the huge bulk of the ship. Up ahead there loomed a giant dark brown shape.

They had found the sea monster of long ago or at least a relative possibly. The ship was slowed down and then halted, so that observations could be made, when the thing suddenly moved forward, opening a pair of jaws big enough to have swallowed a lesser vessel.

There was a shudder as the huge jaws tried to bite a chunk off the bow section, but it was made of sterner stuff than the attacker, and all they had to contend with was a very noisy scraping sound and the odd jerk.

Not knowing what else it might do, it was quickly decided to discourage any further attacks, and a harpoon like missile left the bow section, trailing a wire behind it.

As it struck the creature, someone threw a switch, and a massive electric shock hit the creature, causing it to recoil in a dazed state. It paused for a moment, and resumed its advance towards the ship, but very slowly this time.

The switch was thrown again, probably with more power behind it, and the monster jerked backwards, causing the ship to lurch to one side as the surrounding water swirled about. It didn't much like the second belting, and moved away slowly to disappear into the gloom.

Kal asked how the weapon worked, and was told that when the harpoon embedded itself into the creature, an electric charge of several thousand volts was sent up the insulated wire. As the ship was one terminal, the current then flowed out to the creature, through it and out to the sea water, which conducts electricity very well.

The current then flowed back to the ship, so completing the circuit. As muscles work by electricity, the creature's muscles got a very big 'move' message, and not a little pain along with it, as the surge of current completed the round circuit.

'Simple, but very effective' though Kal.

As they cleared the murky waters caused by the turbulent thrashing about of the monster, the external sensors picked up a slight temperature rise and a more gentle and even disturbance in the waters ahead.

There was nothing to be seen causing this effect, so the lights were doused, and everyone scanned the screens for anything which might be moving. As their eyes got used to the blackness surrounding them, they could just make out small periodic flashes of light below.

The ship slowly went down to investigate, and as they neared the flashing lights, it became apparent what was happening. There must have been a split in the ocean floor, and molten lava was welling up in huge billowing lumps, bursting asunder as the outer skin hardened, and the internal pressure forced more lava to be revealed.

The flashes of light were being caused as the white hot lava was exposed momentarily to the water before chilling into a hard crust. This was the first true volcanism Kal had witnessed on the planet, and was surprised that it hadn't shown up anywhere on the surface.

The pressure down here must have been tremendous; hence the water didn't boil as it would have done at sea level, and so the molten core of the lava was visible. There was nothing further to be gained from the spectacle, so they moved on to seek out any other anomalies the ocean had to offer.

They cruised on for a while with nothing out of the ordinary happening, except for an area of the sea floor which seemed to be covered in large lumps of knobbly rock.

Somehow it didn't look like normal rock should, so the small sub was sent down to obtain a sample for future analysis. Where the knobbly rocks ended, there was a giant forest of plants growing. In height, they must have been many times the ship's length, and looked tough and fibrous in nature. Undaunted, the crew stepped up the power, and the ship ploughed her way through the forest of tangled strands, as if they weren't there.

As they broke out of the strange growths, the area ahead seemed empty of life forms. Not even a plant decorated the ocean floor, and when they had travelled for some distance with no change in the surroundings and were about to turn onto a new course, there loomed up an underwater cliff of such magnitude that even the crew gasped.

It was very solid looking, black and menacing, but as they drew nearer, an opening showed up before them. It was big enough for the ship to have gone into, but the crew didn't like the look of it, and so the samples were transferred from the small sub, and that was sent into the jet black cavernous hole in the cliff's face.

They were able to watch on the screen what the small sub saw as it slowly entered the gaping hole ahead, the picture being relayed back to the main ship. The crew didn't seem to be effected by the realism of the screens, but Kal, despite knowing it was only a picture, still felt uneasy as the little vessel edged its way into the yawning cavern.

Powerful lights on the front of the little sub swung back and forth as it proceeded forward, sending back pictures of the cavity's side walls, which were just dark grey and black rock. There was no sign of vegetable or animal life to be seen, and the water was crystal clear, much more so than the open ocean they had just been through.

About two kilometres into the vast tunnel, the little sub came to a halt. Ahead was a solid wall of rock, the tunnel had ended. The light was swung around and when it was directed downwards, they could plainly see an enormous black hole beneath it. The lights were swung up, and the hole seemed to continue upwards for as far as the light could penetrate. It was like a giant 'T' junction, with the leg of the 'T' being the passageway the sub had come in by.

While the crew were deciding what to do next, things were taken out of their hands as the small sub began to surge upwards. The main ship also indicated via its instruments that it was moving forwards, as if being drawn into the hole in the cliff face due to water flowing strongly towards the hole in the cliff.

Reverse thrust was immediately applied, and their position stabilized, but not so for the sub, which was being speedily whisked upwards, out of their control. As the sub rose upwards, ledges came into sight around the walls of the vertical tunnel, and from one of these a long tentacle could be seen waving about as if seeking something.

The upwards surge of water lessened a little, and they were able to gain control of the sub to some degree by using maximum downwards thrust. As the sub drew level with the ledge from which the tentacle was hanging down, they saw a large round construction, and it was from this that the tentacle reached out into the inky waters below.

Kal and the crew recognized the sphere and the tentacle for what it was at the same time, with a combined gasp of disbelief. It was a spherical deep water pressure vessel, with the remains of its lowering hawser still attached, and not the fearsome submarine creature they had at first thought it to be. The sigh of relief was quickly extinguished by the implication of what they had found.

The little sub edged closer to the ledge, and that was when they saw the pseudopodia like extrusions which appeared to have grown out of the rock, and were holding the sphere in place on the ledge. The surface of the sphere was heavily corroded, and must have been down here for a long time, but who had it belonged to? The original miners? The other people who had built the giant water pump?

They let the sub rise up a little, until it was level with the next ledge, and there for all to see was another large device shaped not unlike their own sub, but bigger and similarly locked in place by a tangle of rope like growths.

Some of the ledges were empty, but every now and again they saw the remains of other attempts made by someone, to fathom out the secrets of the hole in the ocean floor. Just above the sub, they could see another large ledge jutting out into the water, and let the sub drift up and over the lip.

The sub was slowly edged in towards the surface of the rocky wall at the back of the ledge, to see if there were any signs of the rope like things which had anchored the other artefacts to the rocky shelves.

It was at this point that the surface of the ledge disgorged a vast mist like curtain of bubbles which surrounded the sub, and it began to sink towards the surface of the rock.

Maximum horizontal thrust was applied, and the little sub picked up speed, clearing the ledge and shooting out into clear water just in time.

The curtain of micro fine bubbles died away, and they could see a series of pod like growths which had begun to extrude themselves from the back wall of the ledge.

Kal tried to explain that the bubbles would have lowered the buoyancy of the water, so causing the sub to drop, but obviously the crew had already worked that one out, but patiently listened to Kal's explanation just the same.

They sent the sub up higher in the vast column of water, keeping it in the centre as much as possible to see what else had been caught in the bubble curtains.

There were several other alien attempts at plumbing the depths of the under sea cliff, but all had succumbed to the bubble taps which had been set on the ledges.

Whether any had escaped to return to the surface they had no way of knowing, but it seemed strange that there were no other people extracting the rich resources of this planet, apart from themselves. Was there something else which they hadn't noticed, that kept the others at bay?

They were just about to recall the little sub, when looking at one of the screens they saw an eye looking back at them.

It looked like an eye, round and with an iris in the middle, and as they watched, it moved slightly. They panned the remote camera back a little and saw several other eyes, all looking directly at the sub.

Kal couldn't help a cold shiver going down his back, as the realism of the scene overcame his knowledge that it was only a picture. The crew estimated the eyes must be about two metres across, so how big was the creature which owned them? Or was it one giant organism which lived within the rock, and had many extension eyes dotted about the walls so as not to miss anything edible.

Kal suggested that they could bring the sub back, collect a large bundle of the towering sea growths, and release it on one of the ledges to see what would happen, but the crew didn't seem too interested in that experiment, as they had probably already assumed what would become of the bait.

The sub was sent up a little higher, but the ledges seemed to be empty of any artefacts, alien or otherwise, except one which had a huge collection of very large white stick like objects on it protruding from a mass of entangling growths, and they assumed that might be the remains of one of the giant sea creatures which they had encountered earlier.

Slowly and carefully they withdrew the sub, returning it to its cradle on the main ship, and then backed away from the opening in the underwater cliffs.

No sooner had they begun to move back, when there was a huge surge in the surrounding water, and they had to use full power to resist being sucked into the opening. Something within the cliffs didn't want to lose a potential meal, and was making a Herculean effort to prevent their escape.

Slowly they gained distance from the cliffs, and the pulling power of the hole lessened, enabling them to turn away and cruise along beside the towering mass of rock, keeping a careful lookout for any more openings.

After about half a kilometre, the frond like growths of the sea plants appeared again, and a few large and peculiarly ugly swimming creatures came to see what the intruder in their midst was all about.

Another bald patch of the seabed was coming up ahead, and they swung away from the cliffs as another large threatening hole came into view.

Gradually the sea plants began to populate the undulating sands beneath them again, but as they went further into the prolific growing masses of waving fronds, the size and luxuriousness of the plants increased until the ship had to increase power considerably to force its way through.

A break in the densely growing mass came into view, and they halted the forward movement of the ship until they had ascertained what had caused the lack of the foliage.

Ahead was a hole in the seabed, nearly three times the length of the ship across. A murky turbulence in the water indicated that there was a rising current from below, and the cloudiness was probably due to dispersed minerals and other fine matter being swept up, and dispersed into the surrounding sea. The rising water was probably loaded with nutrients, which would account for the extra growth of the plants near the hole.

If water was being forced up from the hole, it must be sucked down somewhere else, and that was something they would have to look out for. There were a multitude of creatures living in among the towering plant life around them, but nothing large enough to threaten the ship.

Gently the ship was edged forward so that the forward sensors could measure the velocity of the water flow, and they were surprised to find that it was a lot faster than they had expected it to be, and too dangerous for them to enter.

A vast amount of water was on the move, bringing up with it a copious quantity of material from beneath the seabed.

Somewhere down there, huge tunnels must exist, and they must be expanding all the time as material was being scoured from their sides.

The big ship carefully skirted around the gaping hole in the seabed, and then forced its way out through the swirling fronds and back into relatively clear water. So far, they had been lucky, and not fallen prey to any of the horrors of the deep, but now they would have to be even more vigilant because of the down draft holes.

The turbulence detectors, which worked on the principle that a beam of light would be distorted by water moving in a direction other than that of the ship, were turned up to maximum sensitivity, in the hope that they would give adequate warning of any down flow into the holes in the ocean floor which fed the massive up surge. The ship had now moved in towards the cliffs again, but kept a respectable distance from them just in case there were any more caverns.

The undersea plants littered the floor of the ocean for as far as they could see, but then they came across what appeared to be a track made through the plant growth on the ocean bottom.

It was as if something had killed or removed all the plants, both large and small, for a width of about twenty metres.

The bare sea floor track began at a cavity in the cliff face, and led out across the undersea plain.

The crew moved the big ship in towards the cavity, and then sent the little sub in for a closer look. The forward light beam lit up the hole in the cliff face to reveal a round chamber some fifteen metres in diameter, the inner surface of which was pock marked with thousands of small holes, which in turn went back into the rock much further than the sub's light could reach.

At the entrance of the cave, there was an amount of broken rock, which looked as if it had been forced out from the face of the cliff by some internal force. The track began right outside the cavern, with a cleared semicircular apron of seabed, and then continued off into the distance.

The crew decided to follow the bare sand to see what had removed all the growth, and to make the whole operation a little safer, they sent the little sub on ahead by several hundred metres.

Some six kilometres into their journey, a large area of the seabed had been disturbed, great gouges in the normally smooth surface indicated that a struggle of some sort had taken place, and possibly led to the demise of whatever had made the tracks.

As the main ship came alongside the disturbed sandy bottom, they could see a faint track going off at an angle, and decided to follow that. Before long, the track was back to its normal width, and they assumed that whatever had made it, had now fully recovered from whatever mishap it had experienced earlier on, and had resumed its normal feeding pattern.

In the distance, the detectors picked up some movement in the water, and speed was reduced, while the little sub was sent on ahead. As it sped along following the bare sand trail, they could see from the main ship a large hemispherical gelatinous mass where the track ended.

They had found the trail maker. Slowly they edged the big ship up towards the mountain of jelly-like substance, but there was no reaction from it as the sub approached.

The little sub was sent in and halted a few metres from the surface, and through the optical relay system, they could see quite a lot of detail of the translucent jelly mound.

The outer skin was a little more opaque than the internal workings, which could be seen clearly enough by increasing the light output of the high powered beam lamps.

The increase in light seemed to worry the creature somewhat, who responded by darkening it's skin in the area of high light intensity, so the power was turned down until they could see the inside while the outer layer cleared to its normal level of opacity.

The sub was moved around to the leading edge of the creature, to see how it removed the marine growths from the sea bottom. Although the detail was not as clear as it would have been in ideal conditions, it seemed that there were several long lines of rippling lips right across the front width of the creature.

These worked synchronously to roll and fold anything it came across, passing it from one line of lips to the next, the plants being gradually ripped out of the sand and passed back to a bag like structure within, where they faded from sight as they were dissolved in some form of digestive juice.

The creature was certainly efficient, as it left nothing behind it as it scoured the ocean sands.

The little sub was brought right up to the surface of the creature, and gave it a gently nudge. As there was no reaction, they increased the power, and the sub bumped into the jelly like mass with considerable force.

Still no response, except that the sub sank into the surface for half a metre or so, and was then pushed out again.

Another ramming produced a better result. The surface of the blob darkened, and a pod like lump formed. Beneath the pod shaped extension, there could be seen fine veins or tubes, which seemed to materialize out of nowhere.

The pod extended itself until it was nearly touching the sub, and then the end exploded in a silent burst, a black liquid jetted towards the sub, causing the water to boil and froth as it passed through it.

The expulsion of the liquid must have been quite forceful, as the sub was pushed back a few metres before it was brought under control by its driver.

It wasn't until much later that they found the front end of the sub had been seriously corroded, and put it down to the encounter with the jelly creature. As there was little point in annoying the creature any more than was necessary to provoke a reaction to see what it was capable of, the ship was swung back towards the undersea cliffs, the little sub going on before as a precaution against unpleasant surprises, of which they were sure there were more.

There were several other fields of knobbly metallic lumps encountered on the way back to the cliffs, and a few samples were gathered from each by the sub, for later analysis.

Kal thought they may be pure metal, as he had heard of this

phenomenon before on other worlds, and it had proved a very efficient way of mining, if what you were mining was what you wanted in the first place.

The cliffs loomed in the distance, and the big ship turned to run parallel with them, keeping a safe distance as before.

At one point on the cliff face, they could see what appeared to be a jet of air or gas escaping. It blasted out horizontally to then curve upwards, the bubbles expanding a little as they rose and the pressure of the water above dropped.

Kal's first thought was oil, this being the gaseous portion which was escaping through a fault in the strata. The sub was sent to collect a sample of the gas, as this could be a source of fuel if they could tap into it easily.

And then he remembered just how deep they were, but when he mentioned this to the crew, they didn't seem put off the idea by the depth so much as locating it again.

It was decided to surface the big ship, find the point where the gas reached the surface, and try and get a fix on their actual geographical position.

The big surprise was when they neared the surface, and found the top of the cliff was only a few hundred metres below the surface of the sea. A fix was taken, although Kal didn't understand how they did it, but they seemed to be satisfied with the result.

The long journey home began, the ship travelling on the surface of the ocean so that they could all get a good breath of fresh air. They had gone about halfway according to the navigator, when rolling towards them was a vast bank of mist or cloud. Warning bells rang in Kal's head.

It seemed harmless enough, and they knew they could always submerge if anything threatened the ship, so they just ploughed on into it. The first unwelcome effect was a deep wailing noise which came from nowhere in particular, but was all pervading, setting Kal's teeth on edge, and causing not a little discomfort to the crew.

As they penetrated deeper into the cloud, the temperature dropped considerably, and most of the crew, including Kal retired below. This left only four of the team on the upper deck, whose curiosity had got the better of them, and were determined to find out what was causing the strange noise and the coldness.

The forward view screen then relayed to those safely inside that curiosity can carry a very heavy price, especially when not augmented with sensible caution.

What could well be mistaken for enormous sheets of dirty grey green coloured leather, but about half a metre thick, lay floating on the surface of the water.

From each crinkled surface there arose a thin cord for about five metres, and attached to the top of each cord, a three metre balloon-like object bobbed and wobbled with a life of its own, although there was little breeze.

Dangling down from the balloon, several thin whip-like tendrils writhed about, sometimes intertwining among themselves, but generally giving the impression that they were feeling the air around them.

As the ship moved forward, the bows ploughed into the leathery mass, and the keening noise grew in intensity to the point that the four crew remaining on deck clapped their hands over their ears, and bowed their heads in agony.

The nearest balloon ejected a stream of vapour from its side and swung over the deck, the tendrils twisting around the unfortunate crewman for a split second, before retracting back up to the balloon.

The crewman crumpled to the deck, senses stunned, and in a writhing heap, and then slid sideways on the curved surface of the vessel to land on the leather pad to which the balloon was attached.

The surface instantly erupted into a series of flaps and engulfed him. It was all over in a second or so, and the second crewman followed suit a split second later. The other two were a little further back than the first two victims, and made a mad dash for the hatch shielding, cowering behind it as the balloons moved by on either side of them.

Several balloons jetted in their direction, but missed the target as the crewmen were detected too late, being protected by the shielding and the ships movement carrying them forward and so out of the balloon's reach.

As they cleared the cloud, the hatch was opened and a trembling couple of crewmen descended into the ship, badly shaken and looking quite stunned.

It later transpired that the numbing material in the tendrils had spattered onto them, but as they had only been exposed to a small dose of the liquid, they were only partly non compos mentis.

The crew were clearly saddened at the loss of their friends, but to their credit they didn't go berserk and take it out on the leather pads, as they were only doing what they did to survive, probably under difficult conditions.

But then the new race didn't have the same sort of reaction to things which Kal was used to, and he had to admit, it was a better attitude to life really.

They continued on their way home, with little else to cause any excitement, except for another cloud on the horizon, and they quickly side-stepped that one.

The big ship docked, the samples were unloaded and sent to the metallurgists, and life got back to normal, after the usual evening feast and storytelling. Kal had been right insofar that the nodules found on the ocean floor were indeed metal, and almost pure.

Lumps of manganese had been found before on an expedition way back in the days of the Star Search, but it was the ship's locators which had found them, not a bunch of adventurers in a metal fish, scuttling about on the floor of an alien ocean.

More expeditions were planned to take place after a few modifications to the ship had been completed, and Kal was looking forward to this. Although life was comfortable and he lacked for nothing, he needed that little edge to things to really come alive.

EIGHT:
Beyond

MICRO ELECTRONICS WERE developing at a rate which Kal couldn't keep up with. They got smaller, more powerful and more diverse in their functions. Just what had he released on an unsuspecting universe?

The passing of Tibs hit him far more than he had expected. One day Tibs was discussing with him a new education system for the youngsters, which would filter out the brightest for intensive learning, and the next day someone came to him and said that Tibs was no more.

He had slipped from his body during sleep, the project completed and written up beside him, the writing stick lying on top of the documents, like a full stop. When working directly with Kal, he still used the old fashion method he and Kal had developed, more as an acknowledgement to Kal, than as a means of efficient data handling.

Kal tried to show as little emotion as possible under the circumstances, and it wasn't until he was alone, sitting on the edge of his bed that the full loss of his one and only true friend caught up with him.

Calic, Tibs's eldest son came and sat beside him, and with an arm around his shoulder, they shed their tears together, letting the grief charge run its full course.

Looking back on the incident, Kal realized that this was the first time he had seen real raw emotion from one of the new race, and he began to wonder if it was truly genuine, or had Calic dramatized that which he thought necessary for Kal to release his own pent-up feelings.

Kal sometimes wondered just how old he really was. They had patched up his body to a remarkable degree, replacing old joints where necessary, and goodness knows what else while they were at it.

His skin had gone very brown and considerably more wrinkled than it used to be, but he still felt quite bright, but not as quick in the mental department as he thought he should be. Thinking back to his first days here, he asked if he could once again walk up the old track leading from the landing beach, and into the forest.

A little party set off a few days later, and he was amazed to see that the area hadn't changed very much in the intervening years, that's if his memory could be relied upon. The Whip Trees still flourished, as did the bamboo clumps which had supplied his first drinking water, but of 'Big Head' there was no trace.

A small group of Finger Nut trees brought a smile to his face, and he asked for one of the nuts. Between them, they managed to scrape a few flakes from the hard kernel, and a roar of laughter broke the stillness of the grove as Kal's face screwed up in disgust at the flavour.

'How the hell did I ever think this was edible' he asked no one in particular.

The 'Leather Flaps' were still up in their trees, waiting to drop on anything unfortunate enough to wander beneath them, and the occasional 'Water Trap' plant glistened in the sunlight, with its false promise of a drink.

It was some time later he found out that this area had been declared a 'Nature Reserve of First Contact', whatever that meant. But he took it as a sort of compliment to his arrival here, and left it at that.

Several more undersea expeditions had gone out, but he had been gently discouraged from going, as his body wasn't really up to it now.

They did, however, show him pictures and samples of the wonders they had discovered, and explained everything in great detail. It was almost like being there, but without the blazing excitement of the actual discovery.

He had broken several bones of late, through tripping over things which he should have seen. They opened him up, and stuck the bones back together with some goo they had compounded for the purpose, but there was going to be a limit to what they could do with his old and failing body.

Kal spent more and more time in his room, thinking back over the old days, and recording his adventures from the beginning, just in case anyone might be interested.

His memory was still intact, and as he went through the early stages of his time here, he could almost smell the smells, and hear the sounds of his battle for existence.

They were good days, and he wouldn't change them if he could. The excitement of his first meeting with the little people still sent a thrill through his rickety old body, and he could still hear the squeaks and whistles of joy which greeted him when they returned from their first expedition along the edge of the mountain chain. And then there was the first steam wagon, rattling and clanking its triumphant way along the old track on their first expedition.

As time went on, he wasn't too sure what was present time, and what was memory, but it was all fun, just the same.

Kal wasn't one to give up easily, but when his time came, he did. Lying on his bed one evening, he wanted to get up to urinate, but couldn't raise himself.

He just couldn't move any more, and he wet himself.

'Oh no, this is too much', and with that he slipped quietly from his body.

They held a national day of mourning. All work was stopped, and everyone stayed at home to think about the one who had given so much, and asked so little in return.

The governing body of the Scientific Research and Development Facility decreed that a museum of scientific development should be built to house samples of their progress from the very beginning. And so it was done.

Upon entering the main hall, the first thing one saw was a ten metre high holographic three dimensional projection of Kal in his middle years.

It was almost as if he was standing there, the eyes followed you where ever you went, and it was especially enjoyed by the younger ones. Below this, mounted on a plinth, was a solid block of a transparent crystalline material, in which the perfectly preserved body of Kal lay.

They had cleverly swept away the ageing of the last few years of his life, so that he looked not too unlike his projected image above.

Leading on from the plinth were replicas of the first bronze tipped spears, bronze pipes and simple pumps, a replica of the bronze steam wagon which had enabled their long expeditions to take place, and the lovingly restored first electrical generator, which on special occasions was run up to power a bank of the first florescent tube lights, to the amazement of the onlookers.

Bronze replicas of the original little people, Tibs of the new race, and a model of Kal stood in a little group, illustrating the main turning point in their history and progress.

Progressing on down the hall, were all the inventions which had made their life so very full and interesting.

Nearly a kilometre from the main entrance, they had just finished building the new extension, and were assembling a replica of the first space vehicle to orbit the planet and return safely.

Somewhere, deep in the Research Facility, there was a large blue white flash and an almighty thump. Some clever person had just

discovered the basic principles of the Warp Drive......
The star drive wouldn't follow until sometime later.

* THE END *